Praise for the ⸺ T. C. LoTempio

"Nick and Nora are a winning team!"

—Rebecca Hale, *New York Times* Bestselling author

"A fast-paced cozy mystery spiced with a dash of romance and topped with a big slice of 'cat-titude.'"

—Ali Brandon, *New York Times* Bestselling author

"Nick and Nora are the purr-fect sleuth duo!"

—Victoria Laurie, *New York Times* Bestselling author

"A page-turner with an endearing heroine."

—*Richmond Times Dispatch*

"Excellently plotted and executed—five paws and a tail up for this tale."

—*Open Book Society*

"Nick brims with street smarts and feline charisma, you'd think he was human . . . an exciting new series."

—Carole Nelson Douglas, *New York Times* notable author of the Midnight Louie mysteries

"I love this series and each new story quickly becomes my favorite. Cannot wait for the next!"

—*Escape With Dollycas Into a Good Book*

"I totally loved this lighthearted and engagingly entertaining whodunit featuring new amateur sleuth Nora Charles and Nick, her feline companion."

—*Dru's Cozy Report*

Books by T. C. LoTempio

Nick and Nora Mysteries

Meow If It's Murder
Claws for Alarm
Crime and Catnip
Hiss H for Homicide
Murder Faux Paws
A Purr Before Dying

Urban Tails Pet Shop Mysteries

The Time for Murder Is Meow
Killers of a Feather
Death Steals the Spotlight
Cats, Carats and Killers

Cat Rescue Mysteries

Purr M for Murder
Death by a Whisker

Cats, Carats
and
Killers

Urban Tails Pet Shop Mysteries

T. C. LoTempio

BEYOND THE PAGE
PUBLISHING

Cats, Carats and Killers
T. C. LoTempio
Copyright © 2024 by T. C. LoTempio.
Cover design and illustration by Dar Albert, Wicked Smart Designs

Beyond the Page Books
are published by
Beyond the Page Publishing
www.beyondthepagepub.com

ISBN: 978-1-960511-55-3

Prologue

Fox Hollow, September 2013

"Uh-oh. Here comes trouble."

Nola Conroy glanced up from the ledger she'd been writing in and looked at the thin gray-haired woman beside her. Velma McAllister had been a staple at Van Nuys Jewelers ever since their doors opened in 1982, and she could smell a deadbeat from ten yards away. In the six months that Nola had been employed, she'd learned to trust the older woman's instincts and now, as she stole a quick glance at the couple, she figured Velma was right once again. The man was tall and rugged-looking—outdoorsy, her mother would have said. His close-cropped hair suggested a military background. The woman had a pretty face, but she was painfully thin, anorexic almost. Nola had seen girls like that in high school, the ones who starved themselves to fit into a size zero dress, and she ran her hand rather self-consciously over her own ample hips. They both had on long-sleeved T-shirts; his was gray, hers a burgundy color, almost the same as her hair, and baggy jeans. Nola's nose wrinkled, an involuntary gesture. She'd seen better outfits on some homeless people.

"Just what we don't need," Velma hissed, with a brisk shake of her head. "Window shoppers, no doubt. Mr. Van Nuys will have a fit if he should come in and see them. Find some way to get rid of them. I'm going to see what's keeping Olivia. She should have been back by now." With that, the older woman turned on her heel and glided past Nola and into the stockroom without a backward glance.

Figures I'd get to do the dirty work, Nola thought. *That's what I get for being the newbie.* Forcing a pleasant expression onto her face, Nola stepped resolutely forward. She cleared her throat loudly. "May I help you?"

The man glanced up, and his lips split in a wide smile, revealing gleaming teeth so perfect and so white that for an instant she was almost blinded. "I certainly hope so. I'm looking for an engagement ring for my girl, here. Only the best will do."

"As you can see, we have a lovely assortment of engagement rings." She nodded toward the large display case off to her left. "Beautiful stones, fine quality, very few inclusions." She paused. Just how do you tactfully tell people the cheapest ring in your stock is ten thousand dollars, surely way more than they could afford. *They don't teach you this in business school,* Nola thought ruefully. She cleared her throat and continued, "Our jewelry is of the finest quality, a fact that is reflected in our prices."

"Are they now?" The man's eyes narrowed into thin blue slits. He reached into his pants pocket and withdrew a bulging wallet. He opened it and whipped out a thick wad of bills and laid them on the counter. Nola saw a hundred-dollar bill on the very top. The man leaned over and fanned out the bills, and Nola gasped as she saw all of them were hundreds. "Your reputation is the reason we came here in the first place," he said, and there was no mistaking the note of irritation in his tone. "I assure you, I can afford your prices."

Nola swallowed. "Of course, sir. I didn't mean to imply . . ."

He brushed away the rest of her comment with a brisk wave of his hand. "Of course you did, but it's okay." He looked at the woman and closed one eye in a wink. "Everyone's priorities are different. For example, I'd much rather spend money on a diamond that will last a lifetime than fancy clothes I'll wear a few times and donate to Goodwill."

The woman snickered and Nola felt her cheeks warm. Silence settled over the room as the couple perused the tray of rings. Finally the man looked at Nola again. "These are nice, but they're not fantastic. I want my Sweet Pea to have fantastic." He leaned forward and said in a conspiratorial tone, "I wouldn't mind having something custom-made for her, if the stone was the right shape and clarity. I know fancy jewelers almost always keep a store of unset gems, am I right? Surely there's something more suitable in your safe?"

Nola hesitated. Only a few hours ago a shipment of fine unset diamonds had been delivered and was sitting in their vault. Nola knew that Van Nuys planned to show the gems to Kay Daffron, a wealthy widow and one of Fox Hollow's more influential citizens, but she also knew that Kay was a shrewd bargainer and would haggle over every penny. This man seemed quite eager to spend whatever it took to make his "Sweet Pea" happy. Plus, she could surely use the commission this large sale would bring. Abruptly, she made up her mind.

"Wait right here," she said. "I've just the thing."

Nola turned and vanished into the back room, returning a few minutes later with a velvet-covered tray. She set it down carefully on the counter and whipped off the cloth. "Voilà," she said.

Over two dozen diamonds of various shapes and sizes twinkled brightly in the soft overhead light.

Both the man and woman sucked in their breaths. "Well," the man said at last, "this is more like it." He leaned forward, squinting at the stones. "I'm not a betting man, but if I were, I'd bet my whole bankroll these babies are as near to perfect as you can get."

"That's correct," Nola admitted. "These gems are a very select grouping. Most of the larger ones have no inclusions that are visible under ten-k magnification. The others' inclusions are so slight it is even difficult for a skilled grader to see."

The man plucked the largest diamond from the tray and held it up. "They must be worth a small fortune." He turned the stone over in his hand. "How much would you say this whole tray was worth?"

"The preliminary estimate was in the neighborhood of several million dollars." Nola shifted her weight to her other foot. She was beginning to regret her rash action. "Truthfully, I really shouldn't have shown them to you. Mr. Van Nuys already has them earmarked for a customer and—"

"That's a shame," the man interrupted. His hand shot out, clamped around her wrist. "Because we'll be taking these diamonds. All of them."

Nola stared at him, certain she'd not heard him correctly. "Wh-what?"

"He said, we're taking all of them."

Nola's gaze skittered over to the girl, and her eyes popped as she saw the glint of the .38 Smith & Wesson she held in her hand. Instinctively her hand dropped beneath the counter, fumbled for the alarm button that she knew was there, somewhere, but before she could find it the man had reached out, grabbed her other arm, and jerked her around so that her back was pressed against the glass.

"Now, no funny business on your part and no one gets hurt," he rasped. He reached into his back pocket and pulled out a black bag, which he thrust at Nola. "Put all the diamonds in this."

Her hands shaking, Nola did as she was told. When the tray was empty, the woman reached out, snatched the bag from Nola's rapidly numbing fingers. "Nice work," she said.

The man had come around the other side of the counter while Nola was loading the jewels into the bag. Now he produced a length of rope from his other pocket. "Get on the floor," he ordered. Nola sat on the floor just behind the desk and he bound her hands and feet. The woman had been rummaging in the desk, and now she handed him a roll of duct tape. He took it and smiled at Nola.

"This won't hurt—much."

He slapped a length of tape across Nola's lips. The woman came over and tapped him gently on the shoulder. "Got to hand it to PJ. He did his part, all right." She nodded toward Nola. "What about her? She's a witness."

"True—but in another few hours our appearances will have changed and we'll be on our way out of the country, so does it really matter? Besides"—his lips quirked slightly—"I hate the sight of blood."

The corners of the woman's lips turned down. "You've just got a soft spot for pretty redheads," she growled.

He laughed and twirled one of her russet curls around his finger. "You know it, babe. Let's go."

The two linked arms and strolled casually from the store. No sooner had the door closed behind them than the stockroom door opened and Velma walked out shaking her head. "Did Olivia come back? It's the darndest thing, I've been over every inch of that storeroom and I can't find . . . good Lord!" Her eyes popped wide as she caught sight of Nola, and she hurried over to her, bent down and ripped the tape from the younger girl's lips. "What on earth . . ."

"Call the police, fast," Nola gasped. "We've been robbed."

One

Fox Hollow, Connecticut
Ten years later, September 2023

The body hung at a rakish angle out of the Jeep, its legs dangling down, almost touching the driveway. I kicked at a piece of gravel with the toe of my Nike and stood surveying it, my hands on my hips. "I suppose we could try pushing her in," I said.

Beside me, my friend Olivia Niven let out a large sigh. "That might have been a solution on your old show, Shell McMillan," she said, "but I doubt that would work here. Doing that would probably break both her legs."

Mention of my old show made me smile, albeit faintly. Up until recently I'd been better known as Shell Marlowe, the star of *Spy Anyone*, a popular cable TV show. When it had been canceled I'd looked on it as a chance to get a fresh start in life. As fate would have it, my Aunt Tillie passed away a few days later, leaving me her Victorian mansion, a healthy financial portfolio, her cat Purrday—and her business, the Urban Tails pet shop in Fox Hollow, Connecticut.

I heard a loud meow and glanced down to see said white Persian wind his tubby body around my ankles. He paused and looked up at me with his one big blue eye. "Merow," he said again. I bent down and gave the cat a pat on his head. "I'm glad to see you agree with me," I said.

Olivia huffed a dark curl out of her eyes. "You're both wrong," she insisted. "Maybe we should try feet-first?"

I debated this for a moment, and then slowly shook my head. "She still wouldn't fit, unless . . . are the legs removable?"

A bark of laughter sounded behind me. "Honestly, Shell. Are your legs removable?"

I glanced over my shoulder and saw my pal Sue Bloodgood approach, shaking her head. Sue was the sister of my boyfriend, Josh, and the owner of the local secondhand shop appropriately named Secondhand Sue's. "No, of course not," I replied. "Then again, I'm a human, not a mannequin."

Sue laughed. "True. And this might not be just any old mannequin. It could be a vintage Rootstein. After all, he was known primarily for creating mannequins that were not only extremely lifelike but also had a cultural significance."

Olivia and I exchanged a glance and then Olivia said, "Wow, Sue. When did you become a mannequin expert?"

"Oh, I'm hardly an expert," Sue confessed. "I just picked up a few tidbits from Clarissa when we went on that buying expedition to Hartford last week."

I groaned inwardly. My mother, Clarissa McMillan, an ex-stage actress, had recently invested in Sue's secondhand antique shop, a move that had ultimately resulted in her relocating from California to Fox Hollow. Although my mother insisted it was only a temporary move, I wasn't so sure, especially since she'd moved into a cozy bungalow not far from my home that had an option to buy. Suffice it to say the thought of my mother living in such close proximity didn't exactly give me the warm fuzzies. We've always had a volatile relationship, mainly because of my career choices. I was convinced her deciding to partner with Sue masked an ulterior motive: to somehow talk me into moving back to LA and resuming my acting career.

Sue leaned inside the Jeep and flicked the mannequin's mane of ink-black hair off her shoulders. "This baby definitely fits the criteria. It is supposed to be Cher, right?"

"So Leila says," I replied.

"Hmpf." Olivia gave a mild snort. "Figures it belongs to *her*."

I bit my tongue and didn't answer. I'd met Leila Simmons a few weeks ago, when she'd interviewed me for a story for her paper, the *Youngstown Sentinel*, after I'd been instrumental in bringing the killer of a noted director to justice. She'd sort of attached herself to me ever since, although I was personally of the opinion that she found my former costar, Gary Presser, a lot more interesting than me. Gary and Olivia had been dating, and Olivia was more than a little resentful of Leila's flirting with him. As for Gary, well, what can I say? He's always had a way with the ladies, and even though he seemed serious about Olivia, he still enjoyed the casual flirtation. I knew darn well he wasn't about to change, but that was a character trait of his it was better Olivia find out for herself.

Sue had wriggled into the Jeep and now called out, "Cher here looks like she's in pretty good shape. If she does turn out to be a genuine Rootstein, it could be worth several hundred, maybe even several thousand."

Olivia's eyes popped. "Really? That much?"

"Oh, yes." Sue's head bobbed up and down. "Rootstein mannequins are top-of-the-line in quality and durability. Collectors love them, especially the ones that are modeled after celebrities." She paused again and then added, "At least, that's what Clarissa said, and I'm inclined to take her word for it. She's very knowledgeable when it comes to antiques."

I couldn't disagree even if I wanted to. After Shakespeare, my mother's next greatest love was antiques. Her home in the San Fernando Valley in California was filled to the brim with collectibles of every kind, from artwork to coffee cups and everything in between. I remembered my father saying more than once that we didn't live in a home, we lived in a museum. Probably one of the many reasons why he'd divorced my mother and married her best friend in a quickie Vegas ceremony.

"I'm sure Leila will be thrilled with that news," I said. "She told me last night she doesn't think she's going to get that promotion."

"Promotion?" Olivia frowned. "She's in line for a promotion at the paper?"

"The reporter who handled the crime beat announced his retirement at the end of the month, and she interviewed for the job. She thought she had a good shot at it, until she found out Jeremy Jackson was interested."

Sue's mouth dropped open. "Jeremy Jackson! You're kidding!"

I looked at her. "You know who he is? I never heard of him, but from the way Leila said his name, I figured he must be some sort of hotshot reporter."

"He's made a name for himself," Sue said. "He covers the crime beat for the *Post and Courier* in Charleston. Some of his stories have been picked up by the AP and *USA Today*."

"No kidding. Well, according to Leila, he and Parker have been very chatty."

"It seems odd to me," said Olivia. "The *Post* is one of the top papers in South Carolina. Why would he want to leave that paper to work in Youngstown? I mean, it's a good paper and all, but it's still small potatoes compared to where he's currently employed."

"Not necessarily."

We all turned to see Leila striding toward us. I had to admire the way she always looked so put together. Even at this early hour her makeup was flawless, and her auburn hair fell in soft ringlets past her slim shoulders. She wore an outfit that looked perfect for early fall: black leather trousers with matching jacket, and an aqua-colored mock turtleneck for a splash of color. Black leather riding boots with aqua and white appliqué on the sides completed the outfit. I knew that if she were here, my mother would have definitely given it two thumbs up.

Olivia frowned at Leila. "What do you mean?"

"Simple. On the *Post and Courier* he's part of a team of crime reporters. Here, he'd be top dog, with his own column. And if the money's right . . ." Leila shrugged. "Parker's been saying for months now that we've got to improve the *Sentinel*'s circulation. Maybe he thinks that hiring a big name like Jackson would inject new life into the paper." She tugged at a red curl. "If only I could get a big, juicy scoop, I might still have a good shot. Where are criminals when you need them?"

Sue gave Leila a poke in the ribs. "In jail where they belong, I hope. Like those teens who were robbing those houses on the south side of Fox Hollow. Thank goodness they were finally caught."

"They hit some houses in Youngstown too. Another plum story I missed out on," Leila said glumly. "Chip was on hand for that arrest, and where was I? Out reporting on the dog show in Raleigh. Watching Mr. Puffles take top dog honors. Granted, he's an adorable King Charles Cavalier, but—grr." She scrubbed at her face with both hands. "It seems as if everyone's got a better shot at getting that job than I do."

"I wouldn't say that," I said. "Chip just happened to be in the right place at the right time to home in on that robbery story, but as far as getting that beat permanently, I doubt it. He's too valuable as a sports reporter and Parker knows it. I doubt he'll ever get out of that niche. As for Jackson, well, did you ever stop to think that he might be using Parker's interest in him as a bargaining chip with his own paper? To maybe get his own column?"

"I didn't consider that angle," Leila admitted, her gaze thoughtful. "It's possible. Jackson's a shrewd opportunist."

"I didn't realize there was such intrigue on newspapers," Olivia said dryly. "I doubt we have any of that on the *Fox Hollow Gazette*."

"That's because it's practically a one-man operation," Sue cut in. "No one in their right mind wants to work with Quentin Watson."

"Amen to that," I said. I'd had several dealings with the peppery newsman, who could definitely be a handful. "But right now we've got another problem." I gestured toward the mannequin. "How are we going to get Cher to the event?" The event being Appraise for Strays, a fundraiser for the local animal rescue shelter, where people could bring their antiques or any old items and get them appraised for a small fee, which would go toward the shelter.

"Say, maybe Gary has an idea or two?" Leila craned her neck to and fro. "Where is he, anyway? I thought for sure he'd be here."

"Well, he's not," Olivia sniffed.

"He wanted to be," I interjected, sensing the tension between the two women. "But someone had to open Urban Tails. Our assistant manager, Robbie, couldn't come in this morning till ten, but Gary will be at the event as soon as Robbie does get in. After all, I can't man the Urban Tails booth by myself." As cosponsor of the event, my pet shop had a booth where folks could purchase treats and toys for their pets, if they were so inclined.

"Don't worry," said Olivia. "If Gary doesn't show, I can help out at your booth."

"Oh, I hope he gets here," chimed in Leila. "I'm looking forward to seeing him again. He always has the funniest stories. The other night at the Wet Your Whistle, he was telling me about the prank he played on one of your directors last Halloween."

Both of Olivia's eyebrows rose. "The two of you were at the Wet Your Whistle?" The tavern had just opened in nearby Gateville and already had a good clientele, thanks to specialty drinks and a very extensive Happy Hour menu.

"Oh, we weren't together," Leila said with an offhand wave. "I just happened to see him there, so I went over and joined him. He was getting takeout." She bounced an eyebrow. "Not that I'd have minded being on a date with him," she added.

"Really?" said Olivia, her tone icy.

Sue also must have sensed the tension because she cleared her throat and said, "Getting back to more important matters, I'd suggest using Secondhand Sue's van if it weren't in the shop." A Hummer had blown through a stop sign and rammed the van in the rear. No one had been hurt, but the van's rear bumper and axle had been pretty badly damaged. The good news was that the man who owned the local garage had offered to repair the van at cost. The bad news was the only time he had free to work on it was this weekend. She slid me a lopsided smile. "Maybe Shell can talk her mother into using her charm to talk Gerard Antoine into making a house call. After all, she got him to do this fundraiser gratis, right."

"Well, that's my mother," I said. Gerard Antoine was the host of a local antiques appraisal show and had a large, loyal following.

"True enough," Sue agreed. "I'm still boggled at how Clarissa got Antoine to waive his usual fee."

"Yeah? How'd she do that?" Leila asked.

"She found out that he's a huge animal lover and supporter of no-kill shelters. He generously offered to donate his time. I think we're going to take him out to dinner after the event, though," Sue said. "I heard Clarissa on the phone yesterday with Enzio's."

I let out a whistle. Enzio's was an upscale Italian eatery in nearby New Haven. "That figures," I said. "Only the best for Clarissa McMillan."

"Maybe so," said Sue. "I'm just not used to all this fuss, though."

"Better start, if you're going to be in business with my mother. Fuss is a way of life with her." I looked at Cher's glitter-covered backside sticking out of the rear of Leila's Jeep. Suddenly I snapped my fingers. "We're going about this all wrong." I walked over and grabbed Cher's left thigh. "One of you get her other leg, please," I directed. As Leila reached for the mannequin's leg, I motioned to Sue to open the front passenger door.

"Wait, what are you going to do? Stick her feet in front and her head in the back?" Leila demanded. "Once I start driving she could slide backward and crack."

"See, that's the problem. I'm thinking we should lay her flat. She bends at the waist, correct? All we have to do is strap her in the passenger's seat."

Leila almost dropped her half of the mannequin. "Wait—I have to drive over to the community center with the dummy in the seat next to me?"

"Well . . . yes. After all, it wouldn't be the first time you rode with a dummy next to you, would it?" I said with a chuckle.

Leila laughed. "Not by a long shot."

We picked up the mannequin again and maneuvered Cher into the front seat. Once the mannequin was in position I fastened the seat belt over its torso and backed out of the car. I leaned against the hood and made a motion with my hands. "Ta-da. Mission accomplished."

Sue glanced at her watch. "And not a minute too soon. We're going to have to hustle if we want to get everything set up in time." The event was set to run today from eleven until five. We'd planned on getting over to the center around nine to check on everything, but all the fussing with Cher had delayed things a bit.

I reached into the pocket of my plaid jacket and pulled out my car keys.

I waved at Leila. "You go on," I told her. "We're right behind you."

Sue chuckled as Leila backed carefully out of the driveway. "If I didn't know better, I'd think that really was Cher in the front seat. If she drives down Main Street she's certain to attract a lot of attention."

Olivia let out a snort. "I'm sure she won't mind it one bit."

"Oh, I think she would. In spite of what you think, Liv, Leila's really an unassuming type of gal. Which is why she won't take that route," I said. "She'll spend the extra time and take the back road so no one gawks at her."

Olivia shrugged. "If you say so. We should probably get going."

Purrday butted his head against my shin and tilted it up so that his blue eye looked straight at me. "Mrrr," he said. "Mrrr."

"Where are your other kitties?" asked Olivia. "They didn't want to attend the show?"

With that, a beautiful, long-haired red cat appeared next to Purrday. I reached down and gave her a pat on the head. "Purrday and Princess Fuzzypants have become inseparable," I said. "And Kahlua was sleeping, so I decided not to disturb her." Kahlua was my purebred Siamese, a gift from my mother. Princess Fuzzypants was a beautiful Maine coon cat that Purrday had found in the bushes behind my shop. I'd put some ads out but so far no one had claimed the beautiful cat, which was okay with me, and Purrday too, since he'd developed a huge crush on her. The two cats hopped into the convertible and cocked their heads at me as if to say, "Let's get this show on the road."

We all piled into my convertible and I was just about to pull away when I heard a squeal of tires. The next second, a large white van skidded to a stop in front of my car, missing my fender by inches!

Two

"Of all the . . ." I sputtered.

"Who the heck drives like that?" muttered Sue. Both she and Olivia looked pale, and I didn't blame them one bit. As for myself, I was close to boiling mad, and I was pretty sure my flaming cheeks would attest to that.

I tugged on the door handle. "I don't know, but I'm going to find out. Another inch and my front end would have been history."

"Not to mention me and the cats," Olivia called after me.

I was out of my car and making my way over to the van to blow off some steam when the driver's-side window lowered and a loud voice boomed out, "Morning, Shell. Sorry if I scared you."

I stopped in my tracks to peer at the man. "Gus?"

"Yeah. Sorry if I scared you," he repeated.

Gus Morton owned Good Eats, a small diner over on Fox Hollow's south side. I knew he'd been sick last winter with a bad case of the flu, and he'd never bounced back as he'd hoped. Today, though, he looked more haggard than usual. There were deep lines etched in his high forehead and his face. His lips drooped and his jaw sagged, making him look a lot older than his fifty-seven years. I had the feeling stress might be playing a large factor. It was common knowledge that ever since a popular food chain had opened a restaurant on the new super highway, Good Eats hadn't been doing all that well. I walked over and leaned against the van door. "Is everything all right?" I asked him.

His finger tapped impatiently on the steering wheel and he reached up with his other hand to swipe at the bump on his nose. "Wal, now, that depends on how you look at it. Things haven't been all right for quite a while now," he said.

I nodded sympathetically. "Running a business is hard work."

"Yep, and made harder when your customers and your trusted employees all go off to consort with the enemy. Ted Trainor handed in his resignation this morning. He's going to work for the new kid on the block. Gave me a whole hour's notice." He reached up to rub at the bridge of his nose as he continued, "Ted was supposed to work the day shift today. Carmen is out of town, so that means I have to pull a double. Which also means I can't watch *her*."

He flicked his thumb in the direction of the passenger seat. I peered past him and saw the chocolate-colored Burmese sitting regally in her bright pink carrier. She turned her head and blinked her big yellow eyes at me. "Merow."

I smiled back at the cat. "Well, good morning to you, too, Cleopawtra." I looked at Gus. "You do know that cats are independent creatures. They thrive on being alone. Burmese are no exception."

Gus's lips twisted into a rueful grin. "You know it, and I know it, but try telling Inez that. She's got that cat so spoiled . . . I thank God that Marcy lets Inez bring Cleo with her to work, or I'd have had to hire a permanent babysitter."

"A cat-sitter, you mean," I said with a chuckle. Inez worked part-time in the local library, downstairs in the research department. Unfortunately, the library was an old building and up until recently had had a slight rodent problem. Marcy Windsor, the head librarian, had never been a cat lover, but Inez's persistence (as well as the cat's mousing ability) had won her over, and in the end she'd decided that Cleopawtra could be an honorary library employee.

Gus gripped the steering wheel with both hands. "I really hate to impose like this, Shell, but I've got no one else I can turn to. Inez is gone all day visiting her aunt in Emporium. I was supposed to watch Cleo this morning, and then Ida Jenson next door was going to spell me until Inez came home." He ran a hand through his hair. "Then I find out my best employee quits on the day I need him to open, and then Ida calls that her mom is sick and she can't make it either. I don't dare leave that cat alone all day. Inez would kill me." He looked at me, his expression imploring. "Would you mind watching her?" As I hesitated, he rushed on, "I know it's short notice, but honestly, there's no one else I could ask that Inez would approve of. I figure you had to be taking at least one of your cats to this event, right? Cleo could play with him?"

Purrday's head popped up and he tapped his paw against the car window. "Merow."

The Burmese's head swiveled in Purrday's direction. She blinked her eyes at the white Persian. "Mer-oooo," she crooned.

"Well, isn't she a flirt," I said with a laugh.

The next instant the princess's head popped up beside Purrday's. The princess looked at Cleopawtra, and her eyes narrowed a bit. She turned her head to look at Purrday. "Merow?" she said.

I waggled my finger at Purrday. "You watch it now. You don't want to make your favorite playmate jealous, do you?"

Purrday's lips tipped up, and then he leaned over and gave the princess a lick.

"Cleopawtra gets along good with other cats," Gus said in an earnest tone. "They should all be fine. So—what do you say, Shell?"

I sighed. Where animals were concerned I was, as Gary would put it, a pushover. "Okay, fine. I'll take her along."

Gus let out a relieved sigh. "Great. You have no idea what a burden you've lifted from my shoulders." He shot me a sheepish grin. "We both love animals, and I'm pretty fond of that cat myself, but Inez treats her like she's heir to the throne. To be perfectly honest, sometimes I think Inez loves that cat more than me."

He looked so woebegone I felt a rush of sympathy for him. I laid my hand on his arm. "I'm sure that's not true."

"Oh, it is," he said matter-of-factly. "I can't blame her, either, the way things have been lately. I might have a solution soon, though." He leaned forward and said in a low tone, "The former owner's back in town, and he seems pretty anxious to buy the diner back."

I frowned. "You mean Aldo Jenkins? That's surprising. I heard he loved it out in Arizona."

"He does," Gus said with a short laugh. "This is the guy who bought the place before me. Pete Martin."

"Oh. I wasn't aware that anyone owned it in between you and Aldo."

Gus reached up and rubbed at the bridge of his nose. "Well, he didn't own it very long," he said. "He more or less ran it into the ground."

"You mean he bought it for a tax loss?"

"I don't think that was his original intention," said Gus. "To be honest, I think after a few months the thrill was gone, so to speak. He made drastic cuts: staff, the menu, the quality of the food. He got a rep for being habitually late paying his suppliers. I got the place at a real cheap price. That's what enabled me to make all the improvements."

I'd heard from Olivia and my friend Rita Sakowski all about the improvements Gus had made. He'd tried to make the diner into more of a lounge atmosphere by adding a seating area that boasted brown leather chairs with wood tables. He'd also added a small raised stage where the Brogues, an Irish band, played on Friday and Saturday nights. Sunday through Thursday the jukebox in the corner provided Irish tunes, as well as more popular music. He'd even sprung for a liquor license and now the diner boasted fancy liquors and new drafts of beer, including Irish, Chilean and Mexican beer. The diner menu not only featured favorites like burgers and a wide variety of salads and sandwiches, but new favorites like shepherd's pie and Irish stew, and daily specials like Reubens and club sandwiches. Gus had put a lot of blood, sweat, and tears into Good Eats, but mostly what he'd put in was love. And if all those five-star reviews on Yelp were any indication, it showed.

Gus continued, "Anyway, Martin's been back in town about two weeks now, and he's been pestering me night and day about selling the diner back to him. Keeps telling me how much he misses it." Gus ran a hand through his hair, making the ends stick out. "Selling would probably be the smart move but . . . I'm not certain I buy that nostalgia bit of his. There's something else going on, mark my words." He made an impatient gesture with his hand. "I'm sorry to run on like this, Shell. Martin's my problem, not yours." He glanced at his watch. "Golly, I've got to get going. Let me put Cleopawtra in your car for you."

Gus hopped out of the van and walked around to get the cat. No sooner had he slid her carrier into the backseat of my convertible than both Purrday and the princess rubbed up against it. They pressed their faces against the bars, and Cleopawtra did the same. A few seconds later the three of them were exchanging soft meows.

I chuckled. "Looks like the three of them will be just fine," I said. Gus reached up to scratch at his ear. "So, what time is this event over?"

"Five o'clock."

Gus's face fell. "That early? I'm not sure I can get away then, and Inez probably won't be home till well after nine." He cast me a pleading look. "I don't suppose you could cat-sit till then, huh?"

I hesitated and then nodded. "I suppose it could be arranged."

He thrust out his hand, gripped mine. "Thanks, Shell. You have no idea what you're doing for me. You're a lifesaver is what you are." He paused. "About picking the cat up . . . I could stop by your place at midnight, after I close. Or would that be too late?"

"Tell you what. Why don't I drop her off at your house tomorrow morning. The only cat that might object would be Kahlua, and I can keep her in my bedroom overnight."

Gus frowned. "I'll have to check with Inez on that. She gets itchy if she's separated from that cat for too long—excuse me." Gus suddenly reached into his pocket and whipped out his cell phone. He glanced at the screen and the corners of his lips turned down in a deep scowl. He gave me an apologetic look. "Sorry, I have to take this." He moved a bit away from me and I could see from the expression on his face that the conversation wasn't a pleasant one. Finally I heard him say, "Okay, okay. Grimley later, you say? I'll let you know." He slid his phone back into his pocket, and when he turned to face me, I noticed two bright red spots on his cheeks. Impulsively I reached out and touched his arm. "Is everything all right?" I asked.

He ran one hand through his hair. "What? Oh, yeah. Yeah. It's nothing I can't handle. I'll try and get hold of Inez and let you know about the overnighter." His hand shot out and gripped mine. "Thanks again, Shell, for doing this. Anytime you want to stop by Good Eats, your food is on the house."

He touched two fingers to his forehead in a salute, hopped back into his van. As I watched him speed away, my thoughts drifted back to the phone call he'd received. Whoever it had been had certainly seemed to upset him. Really upset him, and Gus was a person who didn't get upset easily.

Sue touched my arm. "Penny for your thoughts," she said. She raised her wrist, tapped at the face of her watch.

"I know. I'm sorry. I was just . . . thinking," I murmured.

"Uh-oh," said Olivia. "There's your first mistake, Shell. No thinking allowed."

"You're right," I said. "Let's just concentrate on having fun."

But as I pulled away from the curb, I couldn't shake the feeling that had suddenly washed over me, like a sense of impending doom. I sincerely hoped I was wrong.

Unfortunately, I wasn't.

Three

It was nearly ten thirty when I parked my car in the Fox Hollow Community Center's parking lot. I didn't see Leila's Jeep, so I figured she must still be plodding along on the back road. We all piled out of the car and I lifted Cleopawtra's carrier out of the backseat. Purrday and the princess trotted along beside me, glancing up at the carrier every now and then. Off to my left in the center's large backyard, I could see the tents that had been carefully erected. The sun was shining, birds were singing, the air was crisp and clear. It was a beautiful early fall day, perfect for a fundraiser.

We made our way around to the rear of the center. The back entrance was unlocked, and we went inside. The first thing I noticed was the large sign above the stage off to the left: *Fox Hollow Welcomes Gerard Antoine.* The long table below it was adorned with a white damask tablecloth and covered with large vases of fresh-cut flowers. I let out a low chuckle. "That's my mother," I murmured.

"It looks great, though," Sue said. She pointed to a large table over to the right and the sign above it that read *Secondhand Sue's. Antiques Bought and Sold.*

Clustered around the table were several large boxes that I presumed held items from Secondhand Sue's. Catty-cornered across from that was another, smaller table with a sign that read *Urban Tails: Everything You Need for Your Pet.* Next to the table was a smaller stack of boxes that held the items Gary and I had decided to display today.

"So," said a voice behind us. "What do you think?"

We all turned to see my mother, elegant in a dark blue suit with a navy dotted blouse and navy and white pumps, grinning ear to ear. She reached out to squeeze Sue's arm. "Isn't it exciting, Sue! We got a lot of interest from that full-page ad I took out in the *Fox Hollow Gazette.*"

Sue's brows drew together. "Ad?"

"Didn't I tell you?" My mother paused to inspect her flawless French-tip manicure, then continued, "I took an ad out last week, spotlighting the fact that Secondhand Sue's was sponsoring Appraise for Strays and that we'd be more than willing to accept items for consignment at the event. My assistant tells me we had a good number of responses."

Now it was my turn to lift a brow at my mother. "*Your* assistant?"

My mother's smile dissolved into a thin line. "Fine. The store's assistant. But seeing as I'm a partner, Iris is my assistant too, correct?"

Hearing her name, Iris's head popped up from behind a pile of boxes. "Hey there," she called out. "If no one's busy, I could use some help arranging the display."

"No problem." Sue gritted her teeth and walked over to where Iris stood and peered into one of the boxes. "What on earth did you bring? The whole store?"

Iris laughed and gestured with a sweep of her arm. "Only those two boxes over there are from our store. The rest Ms. McMillan had shipped in."

"It's nothing much. Just some of my china collection and some Japanese artwork a friend loaned me. There are a few antique jewelry items as well. I wanted to have a broad range of items that I thought might appeal to people so they might want to put their own high-end items with us on consignment." My mother flashed a wide smile at Sue.

"Oh. That sounds like a good idea," Sue murmured. I could tell, however, that Sue wasn't entirely too pleased with the way my mother had taken over, and I found myself wondering again just how long their partnership might last. Because if it didn't . . . I was ready to step in.

As my mother inserted herself in between Sue and Iris, I turned to Olivia. "Let's see if we can find Marianne," I said. I glanced down at the carrier at my feet and the other two cats beside it. "I'd like to get these guys settled in the community center office, and then I need to unpack the boxes and start setting up."

"Good idea. I've got coupons for the dance studio too. Sign up for ten lessons, get eleven and twelve free."

We found Marianne Barton, the director of the Fox Hollow Animal Shelter, seated behind a desk in the community center office. She was on the telephone, but she motioned for us to have a seat. I noted that she looked a bit upset as Olivia and I settled into well-worn chairs in front of the desk. After a slight hesitation, I placed Cleopawtra's carrier on its edge. Marianne completed her call and then regarded us with twinkling eyes. "Don't tell me," she said with a chuckle. "You want Antoine to appraise that cat."

"I'm sure he could, but this happens to be Inez Morton's cat. I got roped into babysitting because Gus was in a bind and couldn't do it."

"I thought that was Cleopawtra." Marianne's gaze wandered to the other two cats, who'd arranged themselves on each side of the carrier. "I take it your cats are Cleopawtra's bodyguards?"

I chuckled. "It certainly looks that way."

Marianne pushed back her chair and stood up. "Well, they can stay in here no problem. You can even let Cleopawtra out of her carrier, if you want. No one should be coming in here other than me today, and I'll make sure the door's closed tight if I have to leave."

"That would be great," I said. "Has Antoine arrived yet?"

Marianne frowned. "That's who I was on the phone with when you came in. He had a bit of car trouble, but it's been resolved and he's on his way. He anticipates his ETA to be shortly before eleven." She bit down on her lower lip as she added, "I know I should be grateful he's coming here at all, but it's going to be cutting it close. I was counting on him getting here early to start appraising all the items left by people who couldn't make it here today."

"Right. The absentee appraisals." Another of my mother's brainstorms that had hit it out of the park. "What about having Antoine fit in some of those during his breaks?" I remembered my mother saying that Antoine had wanted about a half dozen fifteen-minute breaks during the duration of the event. "Ed Halsey set that tent up right behind the refreshment tent specifically for Antoine, right? It's not like he'd be interrupted or anything."

"True," Marianne said slowly, "but he might not want to do appraisals on his free time."

"I'm sure my mother could use her charm to persuade him," I said. "But it might not be necessary. From what I understand, Antoine is very into rescue animals and a big shelter supporter. If doing appraisals on his break time means extra funds for the shelter, I'm sure he wouldn't mind."

"There's a lot of stuff," Marianne cautioned. "Take this, for example." She reached beneath the desk and emerged with a large box, which she placed square in the center of the desk. "Eunice Coulter dropped it off at the shelter last night right before closing. She originally planned to come today but her husband's doctor wanted him to have some treatments in Emporium, so they have appointments set up with him for this coming week. She told me she got the chest at an estate sale in Winfield for five bucks last weekend, and the strangest thing happened. When she was walking to her car, a woman hurried over to her and offered her two hundred dollars for it. She said no, and then the woman offered two hundred fifty."

"Wow," said Olivia. "That's a lot of money for something that only cost five bucks. How come Eunice didn't sell it?"

"She said she didn't particularly like the woman's looks. Hard-looking, she called her. But she was so insistent it made Eunice think maybe the item might be worth something after all, so she thought she'd get Antoine's opinion."

I eyed the box. "What on earth could be worth that much money? Do you mind if I take a peek?"

Marianne stepped back and made an expansive gesture. "Be my guest."

I reached over and peeled back the box flaps. Olivia stepped forward too and we both stared at the object within. Finally I raised my gaze to meet Marianne's.

"Two hundred fifty dollars for *that*," I said, incredulity evident in my tone. "You've got to be kidding!"

Marianne clucked her tongue. "I wish I were."

I reached in with both hands and lifted the object in question out of the box, turned it over in my hands. It was a jewelry chest, and for the life of me I didn't see anything special about it that would warrant someone wanting to pay that much money. The wood was dark walnut and there were several deep scratches on the body and on the box's short, stubby legs. The lid had a nice museum-quality finish though, and there was a flower engraved on it, I wasn't quite sure of the type, Edelweiss perhaps? I ran my finger along its edge. The veneer had faded in some places and there were noticeable chips on the edge of the lid and along the left side. I set the chest on the desk and flipped the catch. It had been definitely designed to accommodate a jewelry lover, that was certain. There were two swing-out necklace bars, a catch pocket, two padded watch pillows. There were lots of drawers—three pull-out ones that ran the length of the box, two vertical pull-out drawers with hooks for necklaces and bracelets. The entire box was lined in a soft chamois yellow that in all probability had once been considered very stylish, but was now ripped and stained in several places.

"I know how you feel," Marianne said as she peered over my shoulder. "I had the same reaction. There's no telling what people can waste money on, though. My sister once spent six hundred dollars for a Nancy Drew book."

I turned my head slightly to look at her. "I wouldn't exactly consider that a waste. Some of the first editions with blank endpapers can go for that much and maybe more, if the book and dust jacket are in pristine condition."

"I guess a vintage children's book collector would view it that way," Marianne said with a shrug. "To a non-Nancy Drew fanatic, though, it seems like a waste of good money. I keep thinking how much cat food and litter that would have bought." Her hand reached out and lightly touched the top of the chest. "So who knows? Maybe to a jewel box aficionado, this particular chest is a rarity. To them it could be worth two fifty . . . maybe more." She paused and then added, "I confess, Eunice's story piqued my curiosity, so I did a little research. Want to see what I found out?"

I grinned. "Absolutely."

Marianne grinned back. "I figured you would." She bent down and pulled up her briefcase. She reached inside and pulled out a sheaf of papers, which she handed to me. "Read that," she said.

Olivia looked over my shoulder as I read what Marianne had printed out. The chest that Eunice had purchased was apparently a dead ringer for one made for Queen Victoria in the early 1900s. The chest had been copied many times over, but after the Queen's death the original chest had gone missing and not been found to this day. I glanced at Marianne sharply. "Oh, no. You don't think . . ."

"No, of course not," Marianne said quickly. "But it was the only reason I could think of why someone would offer so much money for it."

I tapped at my chin. "If this box really did belong to the Queen, it would be worth far more than two hundred fifty dollars."

"Well, I know that. But Eunice said the woman who owned it was supposed to be a world traveler, and she collected quite a few antiques. Who's to say she didn't acquire the original, and somehow that woman discovered that fact. She probably wanted to get her hands on it quick before anyone else found out about it."

I scanned the paper. "It says here the original had a secret compartment built into it, so that the Queen would have a place for her most valuable jewels. Some of the copies have them too." I leaned over the box and tap-tapped along its side. "Nothing sounds hollow to me."

"I did the same thing and had the same reaction," Marianne admitted. "Oh, well, I guess we'll just have to wait and see what Mr. Antoine has to say about it. I'm sure he'll be able to clear up the mystery."

"I'm sure he can." I paused as a thought occurred to me. "Speaking of mysteries, I stumbled onto one a bit more local. What do you know about Peter Martin?"

Marianne had picked up the chest and nearly dropped it when I mentioned the man's name. "Peter Martin! I haven't heard that name in years! What made you ask about him?"

"Gus mentioned he's back in town." I paused and then added, "He's been after Gus to sell him Good Eats."

Marianne looked shocked. "Martin wants his old diner back? That's a surprise. If I remember correctly, he couldn't unload it fast enough." She gave her head a shake. "I hope Gus doesn't sell. He's put so much time and money into that place, it would be a shame. I can't imagine why Martin would want to come back here, anyway, after . . ."

But the rest of Marianne's sentence went unfinished as the office door burst open and one of the teen rescue volunteers burst through. "Hey, guys! You'll never guess who just pulled up in a Jeep! Cher!"

Four

"He appraised this old doll of my Aunt Sophie's at almost four hundred dollars! Can you believe that, Shell! Four hundred!"

I smiled politely at the mammoth woman wearing a sack dress who stood in front of me. She clasped a large doll attired in a deep pink dress and matching hat in her arms, staring rapturously at her. I reached out to pat her arm lightly. "That's great, Molly," I said.

"It sure is." Molly McKinnon's hazel eyes gleamed behind the massive tortoiseshell glasses that took up almost the entire top half of her round face. "Mr. Antoine said this was a genuine antique German bisque head Armand Marseille doll. An Eaton's Beauty, he called it. Apparently they're quite rare, especially in this good condition." Her fingers fiddled with a tag hanging from the doll's wrist. "She still has her original Eaton Red Tag, too. He said the hat and dress might not be originals, but he wasn't positive. He said the wig was original, but it needed a bit of work, and there were some marks on her arms that needed to be removed. If it weren't for that, she'd have been valued higher, much higher."

I nodded. When I'd seen her come in with the doll, I had an idea it might fetch a high price. I remembered seeing similar dolls at a show in LA that had gone for almost a thousand dollars. Molly, recently widowed, worked as night manager at the local QuickCheck and could use the money.

Molly shifted the doll in her arms. "Your mother said that if Antoine gave it a good appraisal, she'd put the doll on consignment for me. I think I might let her."

I gave her an encouraging smile. "If anyone can get top dollar for her, my mother can," I said.

Molly nodded. "That's what I thought. Your mother can be very intimidating, but she's got good business sense. I guess you inherited that from her."

I just smiled. Molly was probably right. My father certainly had no head for business. Besides, there were worse things I could have inherited.

Molly purchased a bone and several cans of dog food for her mutt, Rufus, and then hurried off, humming a little tune. I glanced over at the line of people waiting in front of the table where the noted appraiser Gerard Antoine was seated. Antoine was an older man who resembled a thinned-down version of Santa Claus. He had a white goatee that was expertly trimmed, a ruddy complexion, and bright blue eyes that seemed to twinkle endlessly from behind wire-rimmed glasses that he wore perched on the edge of his short flat nose. Right now he was examining an antique pistol that I knew Darryl Graham's grandfather claimed to have been used by one of his ancestors during the Civil War. I turned away. If Antoine should burst Darryl's bubble by revealing the pistol wasn't the antique heirloom he'd always thought it to be, I didn't want to see the inevitable waterworks. Men crying always seemed to upset me, somehow.

Leila hurried over to me, her eyes alight. "Hey there," she said. She gave a quick look around. "No Gary yet?"

I looked at my watch. "He should be here soon," I said. I studied her flushed face and too bright eyes. "You look very pleased. Did you get good news?"

"I sure did," Leila said, and her grin stretched from ear to ear. "Cher turned out to be a genuine Rootstein mannequin, can you believe that? Better yet, Antoine said he knew of some collectors who might pay upwards of four thousand for her. He's going to give them my number—oh, oh!" Leila stopped speaking abruptly and her eyebrows came together in a deep frown. "What's *he* doing here," she growled.

I glanced over at the long line. "He who?"

"Jeremy Jackson."

"Jackson? Really? Where?" I started to crane my neck to and fro, but I stopped as Leila's nails dug into my forearm.

"Don't make a big deal of it," she whispered. She took a step backward so she was standing behind me, and said in a low tone, "He's the guy third from the end, in the blue sport coat and khakis."

I turned my head slightly so I could observe out of the corner of my eye. To say Jackson was handsome would be an understatement. Of course, all I could see from this angle was his profile, but it reminded me of photographs I'd seen of Greek gods in history books. He had a high forehead, a firm chin, and he appeared to fill out his sport coat and pants very nicely. I shot my friend a mischievous glance. "Not bad. He'd certainly be good eye candy around the paper."

Leila let out a snort. "Oh, yeah, that's just what we need around that place. I guess I might as well say bye-bye to any hope of promotion. Jen White told me that he and Parker were holed up in Parker's office for two hours last night, and they were both smiling when they came out. And it takes a lot for Parker to smile." She cast another furtive glance in the reporter's direction. "I think I'll head over to the refreshment tent. Want anything?"

"I'm good, thanks."

"Okay. Catch you later."

Leila hurried off in the direction of the other tent. I stood and surveyed the line a few minutes longer. Jackson seemed preoccupied with a flyer he held in his hand, so I let my gaze wander toward the rear of the tent. There was a man standing there. At first glance he appeared to be interested in the newspaper he was holding, but a few seconds later I saw his head turn slightly and his gaze fasten on Jackson. "Curious," I muttered.

"What's curious?"

I jumped and whirled around, bumping into the chest of the handsome, dark-haired man who stood very close behind me. I caught the amused twinkle in his blue eyes and shook my finger in his face. "Geez, Gary," I cried. "Don't do that. You scared the daylights out of me."

"Sorry," he said, but his grin belied his apology. "So, are you going to tell me?"

"Tell you what?"

Now it was Gary's turn to shake his finger at me. "What's got you so curious. Spill."

"Okay. There's a guy standing over near the back of the tent who seems pretty interested in Jeremy Jackson."

Gary looked in that direction and frowned. "Yeah? He couldn't have been that interested. There's no one there."

I stole a quick glance over my shoulder and saw he was right. There was no one there now. "He was there before," I murmured.

Gary shrugged. "Maybe he decided Jackson wasn't worth spying on."

"I didn't say he was spying on him. I said he seemed interested in him. Maybe he's a fan or something."

I gave him the lowdown on the promotion situation and what Leila had told me about Jeremy Jackson having the inside track. When I finished, Gary's lips puckered. "I somehow can't picture a big-shot reporter like Jackson working on a small-town paper. No offense to Leila's paper, but . . ."

I held up my hand. "I know. I said the same thing. Leila mentioned something about the fact that here he wouldn't just be a little fish in a big pond, he'd be the big fish."

Gary shrugged. "Maybe."

I hesitated, then said, "Leila mentioned that she had a drink with you at Wet Your Whistle the other night."

He frowned, then his expression cleared. "Oh, yeah. I stopped in for some takeout and ended up having a beer at the bar. She came in, saw me, and invited herself to join me." He leaned closer to me and said in a low tone, "Just between you and me, Shell, I think the woman has a crush on me."

I widened my eyes and tried to look surprised. "No! You don't say!"

If he noticed the sarcasm in my tone he ignored it. "Yes. I suppose I'll have to let her down easy. She's really not my type."

"That's odd. I thought every woman was your type."

He made a face at me. "That might have been true once, but I've changed my ways."

"Do tell. Does that mean you're a one-woman guy now?"

He chuckled. "I could be. Anyway, I was never the man about town those gossip rags painted me as, either. Most of that was courtesy of our former agent, Max Molenaro."

"Well, my mother still thinks you're a shameless flirt who's using me for free room and board."

"As long as you don't think that, I'm good," he responded. "Seriously, though, I've got to get Leila off my back. I'd hate for her, or anyone else for that matter, to get the wrong idea."

"Too late. Olivia already has the wrong idea."

He rolled his eyes. "Oh, no. She told Olivia about having a drink with me?"

"She told all of us." I batted my eyelashes in my best Scarlett O'Hara Southern belle style. "She is quite enamored of you and your many charms."

"Swell," he moaned. "I'll have to do something super nice for Olivia. Any suggestions?"

"Lots. I'll tell you later. While you handle things here, I want to check on the cats—see if the three of them are behaving themselves."

Gary goggled at me. "The three of them? Did you decide to bring Kahlua too?"

"No, Kahlua's having a peaceful snooze at home. Gus Morton sorta kinda needed a cat-sitter for Cleopawtra, so . . ." I spread my hands. "I volunteered. Or more to the point, Gus volunteered my services."

Gary shook his head. "I'm shocked Inez let you take Cleopawtra. She's a bit of a fanatic about that cat."

"Inez doesn't know. She thinks Gus is watching her, but he ran into some difficulties. I'll fill you in on everything later."

I left Gary sorting through an assortment of catnip sticks and walked to the community center office. Marianne was seated at the desk, her head bent over a large mound of papers. She looked up as I approached and her smile morphed into a disappointed look. "Oh, hello, Shell. Sorry, I thought you were Jen with some items I asked her to bring."

"Sorry to disappoint you," I said. "I just wanted to check in on my cats." I saw Cleo's carrier was empty and I glanced around the room. No sign of any of the cats. "Where are they, by the way?"

Marianne frowned. "Oh, why. I don't know. I've been so preoccupied with my paperwork I wasn't paying attention. But they have to be here somewhere," she added quickly. "They couldn't have wandered off anywhere. Cats are very good at hiding, you know."

I frowned. "I'd better look for them. Inez will just die if anything happens to that cat."

Marianne glanced at her watch. "Tell you what, I need a break myself. Suppose I run over to the shelter tent for the rest of the donations, and you stay here and look for them. I won't be long."

"It's fine with me," I said. "Gary's manning our table right now. Take all the time you need."

Marianne shot me a grateful smile and left, and I started to walk slowly around the room, calling out the cats' names. Suddenly I heard a rustling sound. I whirled around and saw Purrday, Princess Fuzzypants and Cleopawtra all jump onto the desk. I placed my hands on my hips and gave them a stern look. "And where did you all come from may I ask."

Purrday let out a sharp yowl, while the princess and Cleopawtra each stretched a paw out toward the jewel chest. "No, girls," I said sharply. Both cats turned to stare at me. I walked forward slowly, shaking my head. I reached out and picked up the jewel chest. "This isn't a toy. You wouldn't want to knock it off the desk and damage it, would you?"

Both cats looked at me for a few seconds, and then let out soft meows. Purrday swatted at Cleopawtra with his paw, and the two of them jumped off the desk and trotted off into the far corner, the princess in hot pursuit. I picked the cardboard box up off the floor and set it on the desk. I was just about to slip the chest into it when I heard a soft footfall behind me. I whirled around to see a man only a few inches taller than me with close-cropped red hair, wearing jeans and a checked shirt, standing in my doorway. "Pardon me," he said. "Is this where the antique show is being held?"

I frowned. The man must have entered through the rear door and not the front one, which would have brought him directly into the community center. I forced a pleasant smile to my lips and said, "I'm sorry, it's not a show. It's a fundraising event for the shelter." I pointed to the sign in the hall that read *Appraise for Strays*. "For a fee, people can have their items appraised and find out if what's been languishing in their cellars or attics for years might actually be worth something."

His dark red brows drew together in a deep frown, etching deep lines in his high forehead. "Oh, my apologies. I thought it was a show."

"No, sorry, it's not. But if you have anything you'd like appraised, the fee is three dollars for one item and ten dollars for three. All proceeds go to the shelter. If you'd like, I'd be glad to walk you around back to the event."

He waved his hand. "That's okay," he began, and then stopped abruptly as his gaze fell on the jewel chest on the desk. He pointed a stubby finger at it and said, "Say, that looks like a Queen Vic box. Is it?"

I hesitated. "I really don't know. One of the patrons left it here to be appraised."

"Do you mind?" Before I could utter an objection, he'd stepped all the way into the office and over to the desk. He peered down at the box and nodded. "Yep, that's a Queen Vic, all right. My mother's always wanted one of those." His hand dipped into his pants pocket and he withdrew a fat wallet. "Tell you what. You can make a nice little profit for the shelter right now. I'll give you a hundred and fifty dollars for it, what do you say?"

I maneuvered around him, picked up the chest and slid it inside the cardboard box. "I'm sorry," I said in a firm tone. "I don't work here, but even if I did, none of these items here are for sale. They were left here by shelter patrons who wanted them appraised."

The man let out a sigh. "Okay, okay. I'll make it worth your while. Two hundred." When I didn't respond, he pulled more bills out of his wallet. "Fine. Three hundred, and that's my final offer. What do you say?"

I struggled to keep my tone even as I replied, "Apparently you didn't understand me. Nothing here is mine to sell. However, if you want to leave your name, I'll tell the shelter director about your offer. She can contact the owner, who will make the final decision, after the item's been appraised, of course."

The man's brows drew together in a fierce scowl. He glanced over at the poster bearing Antoine's likeness and then back at me. "You really like to play hardball, don't you?" He whipped another bill from the wallet and waved the stack in front of my face. "Okay, four hundred. And that is definitely my final offer."

Gosh, this guy was thick! And definitely getting on my last nerve. "I'm sorry," I said, and this time I didn't even try to keep the irritation out of my tone. "I'm not playing hardball. This item isn't for sale, at any price."

"Yeah?" he growled. He shoved the bills back into his wallet. "Well, we'll see about that. Everyone has a price. I just haven't hit yours yet." With that, he turned on his heel and marched out the back door, letting it slam behind him. I stood for a moment, hands on hips, and let out a slow breath. I felt something furry touch my ankle and I looked down to see Purrday at my feet. He looked up at me, his eyes wide. "Merow?"

I picked the cat up and he butted my chin with his head. I dropped a kiss on his forehead. "I'm more curious than ever to see what Antoine has to say about this box now," I murmured. "There must be something special about it for not one but two people to offer so much money." I looked the cat straight in the eye. "You know, I'm starting to think this little item is more valuable than we think. Why, for all we know, this really might be Queen Victoria's jewel chest."

I felt around in my tote bag and pulled out three catnip balls. I set them on the floor. Immediately all the cats started to nose at them. "That should keep you occupied," I said. I heard the back door open again and I steeled myself for another confrontation with the stranger, but the newcomer was Marianne, a baby doll tucked under one arm and an ebony walking stick in the other. She set down the items and looked at me. "What on earth did he want?" she asked.

I stared at her. "You mean the man who was just here? Do you know him?" I asked.

Her answer startled me. "Of course I do. That was Pete Martin."

Five

I stared at Marianne. "Pete Martin? Are you sure?"

She looked a little insulted as she replied, "It's been awhile, true, and he's put on a few pounds, but I never forget a face. I'd know him anywhere. A fundraiser is the last place I'd ever expect to see him. What did he want?"

I opened the box flaps and pulled out the jewel chest. "Believe it or not, he wanted this."

Marianne's jaw dropped. "Eunice's jewelry chest! He wanted that? Why?"

"I have no idea. He called it a Queen Vic box, and he offered me four hundred dollars for it."

Marianne put a hand over her heart. "Four hundred!"

"Yes. Have you any idea why he'd offer so much money for it?"

"None." She looked at me. "Are you sure you heard correctly, Shell? Martin never had four hundred dollars in cash on him in his life, and if he did, he'd never spend it on a jewel box."

I shifted the box in my arms. "He said he wanted it for his mother, that she'd been looking for one just like it."

"What a load of poppycock!" Marianne let out a loud snort. "For one thing, his mother passed away years ago. He's divorced and has no family to speak of, at least none that I know of. I can't think of one good reason why he'd want that box."

"And don't forget the woman who offered Eunice two hundred and fifty for it. It would be understandable if this box really did belong to Queen Victoria, I suppose, but somehow I just can't see it."

"Me either," said Marianne. "Antoine should be on his break now. I need to take some more items over there anyway. Maybe he can shed some light on just why this jewel box is so popular."

Marianne gathered up the walking stick and the doll, and I took the jewel box. But when we got to the break tent Antoine wasn't alone. My friend Rita Sakowski sat beside him. There was a platter of blonde brownies on the long table in front of them, and the fragrant smell of hazelnut coffee emanated from the large mugs they both held in their hands. Antoine looked up with a smile as I approached.

"Ah, the lovely Shell Marlowe—sorry, I mean McMillan. I was

wondering when I might meet you. I have heard much about you from your most charming mother."

Wow, I could just imagine what an earful she'd given him. I extended my hand, and Antoine took it. "It's a pleasure to meet you, Mr. Antoine," I said. "Thank you so much for doing this."

He smiled. "Ach, how could I refuse for charity? Besides, your mother was most persuasive. And I am being treated very well." He threw a beaming glance at Rita and reached for another brownie.

Rita grinned at me. "He's such a flatterer. It's easy to see why he has so many female fans."

"Well, I'm definitely one of your fans now," Antoine said. He bit off another piece of blonde brownie, chewed it deliberately, and made little sighing sounds deep in his throat. "I have never tasted anything so delicious. If you weren't already married, Rita, I'd be tempted to propose." He took another bite of the brownie and looked over at Marianne. "One of your volunteers was telling me about all the rescue kitties you have at your shelter. She mentioned one in particular, a Siamese?"

"Yes, an adorable seal-point female. Her name is Fauna." Marianne shot him an appraising glance. "Are you interested in adopting her?"

"As a matter of fact, yes. I had rescue pets growing up. Two shelties and a Siamese that I loved dearly. Lately I've been thinking the time might be right for me to have a pet again." He smiled faintly. "Now that I have a cable show I don't need to travel as extensively, and when I do it's not that far. People come to me now," he said with a chuckle.

"Speaking of that, we've brought some more items for appraisal." Marianne gestured toward the low table where we'd set the items. "There's a baby doll that I believe could be an authentic Bru, a walking stick, and a jewel box."

Antoine looked at his watch. "Would it be possible if I held off examining them until my next break? I would love to continue chatting with the lovely Mrs. Sakowski." He reached over and gave Rita's hand a pat before he continued, "Don't worry, worst case I'll stay a bit later after the event ends to finish." He turned to me and closed one eye in a wink. "I am sure your charming mother will not mind if we are a bit late for that fancy dinner she wishes to treat me to."

"No problem, Mr. Antoine," said Marianne. Antoine tossed us a beaming smile before turning back to Rita. We moved back toward the table, and Marianne looked at the items with a frown. "It seems like a waste to keep carting them back and forth. Why don't we just leave them here. Lois Klein is manning the refreshments. I can ask her to keep an eye on them."

"I'd feel better if we found another spot for the jewel box," I said. "There seems to be entirely too much interest in it."

"True," sighed Marianne. "I guess we could put it back in the community center office, but the lock's been jamming."

I gave a quick glance around the tent, saw a small table in the far corner that had some empty boxes piled on top of it. The table was draped with a white tablecloth that reached all the way down to the ground. I pointed to it. "What about that table? If we shove the box underneath and pull the tablecloth all the way down, no one will see it. It should be safe there until Antoine's ready to look at it."

"Fine," said Marianne. "I'll leave you to it, and I'll meet you back here in an hour and a half, for Antoine's next break."

Marianne left and I went over to the table. I wiggled the box underneath the table, then made sure the tablecloth facing the entrance to the tent was pulled all the way down. Once the box was safely concealed my stomach let out a loud growl, reminding me I hadn't eaten anything since I'd wolfed down two pieces of dry toast this morning. I decided a quick visit to the refreshment tent was in order.

I had to admit, Ed Halsey had done a stellar job setting the tent up. There was a counter with a glass case to display the goodies along one side. A mini-fridge was in back of the counter, along with a small sink, a microwave and a coffeepot. He'd set up a dozen tables with folding chairs so that folks could sit for a spell and enjoy coffee, tea and a baked good while they were waiting to get their items appraised. The line wasn't all that long, four people, so I went over and dutifully got on the end. There was only about a five-minute wait before I was next. Ardis Jackson, who worked in Rita's shop on Monday and Friday afternoons, smiled at me.

"Well, well, Shell. Come for a treat?"

"Absolutely." I peered at the goodies stacked inside the glass case and pointed. "Is that a pumpkin muffin?"

"Sure is. Want one?"

"Yes. Heated with butter, please. Lots and lots of butter."

"I've gotten that request a lot. Looks like folks aren't worrying about cholesterol today. Anything else?"

"A pistachio muffin and two coffees, please," I said. By this time Gary could probably use some sustenance too.

Ardis got the muffins out of the case, sliced them in half, and popped them in the microwave. She glanced at me over her shoulder. "Quite a turnout today."

"Yes, there is," I agreed. "It was good of Rita to donate all these treats."

"Yeah, well, she always seems to garner a lot of new business after one of these events, so her motives aren't entirely selfless." Ardis pointed to an empty cardholder on the front of the counter. "Had a hundred cards in there when we started, and now they're all gone. People from neighboring towns that came to this event told me they're going to make regular stops at Sweet Perks from now on."

The microwave beeped. Ardis removed the muffins, slathered butter on them, and placed them on plates on a brown plastic tray. She moved over to the coffee machine and deftly filled two cups to the brim. As she arranged them on the tray she remarked, "To tell you the truth, I thought we were going to be late getting here," she said. "That guy who owns the diner and some other man I've never seen before decided to have a shouting match just as we were getting ready to leave. I thought Rita was going to have a fit."

My head jerked up. "You mean Gus Morton?"

"Yeah, that's his name. I should have remembered. He and his wife are two of our best customers. Gus stops in every day for a decaf and Inez always comes by on Fridays for lunch."

I frowned. Gus had to have stopped at Rita's right after he'd dropped off the cat with me. "They didn't get violent, did they?" I asked.

She shook her head. "No, just loud."

"What were they arguing about?" I asked casually.

"Dunno." Ardis's shoulders lifted in a shrug. She pushed the tray in front of me. "I wasn't paying that much attention, to tell you the truth. I could see, though, that Gus seemed really upset. He shook his fist right in the other guy's face and said, "I'm tired of all this. I don't need you pressuring me too." Then the other guy said, "If you don't do this, you'll regret it big-time," and then the two of them had a sort of staring contest for a few minutes. Rita was just getting ready to throw the two of 'em out on their rears when the strange guy stormed out. Then Rita went over and said to Gus, 'the next time you want to have a fight, don't do it in my shop.' Gus apologized and then he left too."

"I see." I dropped two sugars into my coffee, gave it a quick stir, and then asked, "What did this other man look like?"

I fully expected Ardis to describe Pete Martin, so I was somewhat taken aback when she said, "Close-cropped blonde hair. Clean-shaven. Nice pressed jeans and a tailored shirt. He looked pretty respectable, if you ask me." She wrinkled her nose. "I prefer men with beards, myself. Or a nicely trimmed goatee."

I chatted with Ardis for a few more minutes before picking up my tray and heading to a small table at the rear of the tent. As I sipped my coffee, I thought about Gus's earlier phone conversation. Maybe the man who'd called him earlier wasn't Pete Martin after all, but this other man. Someone else interested in buying Good Eats? Or something else? I was so deep in thought that I didn't notice the shadow that fell across the table, or realize anyone was behind me until a hand fell on my shoulder. I yelped, jumped up, and dropped the rest of my muffin on the floor before I fell straight into Josh Bloodgood's outstretched arms.

"Sorry, Shell," Josh said. "I didn't mean to startle you." He looked down at the remains of my muffin. "Want me to get you another?"

"No, thanks." I met his clear blue gaze and resisted the sudden impulse I had to run my fingers through his thick, curly hair. I snuggled a little closer in the circle of his arms. "To what do I owe this honor? I didn't expect you until around three," I said, my voice muffled against his shirt. "Sue said you had to work." Josh was a homicide detective on the Fox Hollow police force.

He tilted my chin back so he could look into my eyes. "I'm apologizing in advance."

I frowned. "In advance? We didn't have anything scheduled for today, did we?"

"No, but remember when I said I'd be free on Monday night, and we could go to dinner?"

"Oh, no!" I didn't even bother to hide the peevish note that crept into my tone. "I thought you said the captain gave you some time off, that you'd finished your consult with the detective in Emporium?"

"I did, but now something else has come up, something the captain thought maybe I could help with. Unfortunately, this new project looks like it's going to be very time-consuming."

"Another consult?" At his nod, I sighed. "Swell. So, where's this one out of? Stamford? New Haven? Hartford?"

"Actually, it's right here in Fox Hollow." He paused. "It's a cold case. Ten years old. I've got a meeting with an FBI agent in a half hour, so I figured I'd stop by and fill you in."

I sucked in a breath. "Wow, FBI, that's really impressive. Are you permitted to share any details?"

He cocked a brow at me and his facial expression clearly said, "you know better than that, Shell," but what he actually said was, "What I can say is that it concerns a local crime. They've gotten a good lead, and that's all I can say on the subject." He dropped a kiss on the top of my head. "I've got to get going. I'll give you a call tonight."

I blew him a kiss back and then paused, assailed by an odd feeling that I was being watched. I turned my head ever so slightly and frowned.

Jeremy Jackson was seated at a small table about ten feet from mine. The reporter seemed absorbed in a paper spread out in front of him, but I wasn't buying it. I had the feeling he'd been eavesdropping on my conversation with Josh. Leila had said that Jackson had a nose for news and could sniff out a story from ten miles away. Had that been the case now?

Jackson abruptly pushed his chair back, stuffed the paper under one arm, and headed for the exit. As he strode away, another more disturbing thought popped into my head. What if Jackson had known all along about Josh's cold case? Could that be what had brought him to Fox Hollow? I frowned. Whether he was considering a career move here or merely trying to secure a better slot for himself on his current paper, what better way than to crack a case that had baffled the FBI for ten years?

Six

"You've been awfully quiet, Shell," said Gary. "Penny for your thoughts?"

I paused, my coffee cup halfway to my lips, and regarded Gary over its rim. After Josh had left, I got fresh coffees and returned to the Urban Tails table, where I found Gary deep in conversation with Olivia. I'd given Olivia my coffee and half listened while she related how pushy my mother was over at the Secondhand Sue table and how poor Sue had nearly bitten her tongue off trying to keep silent. Gary, of course, had noticed I wasn't joining in the conversation. I looked at him. "They're worth much more than a penny," I said. "A quarter, at least."

Olivia reached into her pocket, pulled out a quarter and handed it to me. "We're all ears," she said with a grin. "Although I can probably guess what's on your mind. That jewel box Gary told me about."

"Yes, but that's only part of it." I leaned back in my chair. "Josh stopped by to tell me that he's been tapped to consult with the FBI on a cold case. It concerns a crime that happened in Fox Hollow ten years ago. Do you remember any local crime that the FBI might have taken an interest in?"

"Hm, that's a very good question." Olivia's usually smooth brow furrowed as she thought. Suddenly her eyes lit up and she snapped her fingers. "Wait! There was something, ten years ago this very month, I think. A robbery."

"A robbery?" I couldn't keep the disappointment out of my tone. "I thought it might have been something more exciting, like a kidnapping, or a murder."

"Well, hold on now. This wasn't just any robbery. It was a diamond heist. Several million dollars' worth, in fact."

My eyes popped. "You're kidding!"

"Nope." She pulled out her iPhone, fiddled with it a few minutes, then passed it over to me. "See here—that's an article from the *Fox Hollow Gazette*. Notice the reporter's byline."

I looked at the screen and made a face. "Quentin Watson. Figures. That must have been right before he bought the paper."

"Right. It's a pretty detailed story."

I skimmed the article. The Van Nuys Jewelry Store had a shipment of valuable unset diamonds that had just been delivered. Kay Daffron, the society maven, had them on special order for some pieces of jewelry she'd wanted custom-made. A man and a woman came into the store and wanted to look at engagement rings. The accommodating clerk was then threatened at gunpoint, tied up, and the two made off with the gems. I looked up from the phone. "It says here the jewels were never recovered. They were worth two million at least, maybe more."

"Yep." Olivia reached for her phone as I passed it over. "I bet Quentin Watson could tell you more details."

I made a face. "I'm sure he could, if I want to put myself through that torture."

Gary had taken Olivia's phone and was also scanning the article. He set the phone down on the table. "Sounds like it might have been an inside job."

"I guess the police thought so too. The article said they investigated the two sales clerks, as well as the floor manager. They all checked out." I tapped at my bottom lip with my nail. "I bet this is the cold case Josh mentioned. I wonder what could have surfaced after all this time to prompt the FBI to reopen the case?"

Gary shrugged. "It could be anything. One thing's for sure, Josh will never tell."

"You got that right," I agreed. "Jeremy Jackson was sitting nearby when Josh was telling me about it," I said. "I could just tell from his manner that he'd been listening to our conversation."

"So what?" Gary asked. "You think that's why Jackson's here? Not to interview for that job, but to cover this cold case?"

"It wouldn't surprise me." I lifted my hand to brush back a wisp of hair from my eyes and suddenly gasped. I pointed to my bare wrist. "Oh, no! My watch is gone," I cried.

"Not the one your aunt gave you when you graduated college? The one with the tiny diamonds around the face?" Olivia cried.

"Yep. I put it on this morning, and I did have a little trouble with the clasp. It must have fallen off my wrist somewhere."

"Didn't you fasten the safety?" Olivia asked.

I bit down hard on my lip. "I forgot. I'm not used to doing that."

Olivia put her arm around my shoulders. "Take a deep breath, hon, and think. When did you see it last?"

I closed my eyes and started to retrace my steps in my mind's eye. My eyes flew open and I looked at my friend. "I remember glancing at it when I put the jewel chest back in its box. It could have slid off my wrist then. I'm just going to run back to the break tent and have a quick look."

"I'll go with you," Gary said, but I waved him away. "No, you stay here with Olivia and finish your coffees. Enjoy some quality time," I added with a wink. "I'll be back in a flash."

Gary and Olivia exchanged a look, and then Olivia smiled. "Okay, Shell, if you insist."

"I do. I'll be back in ten minutes, maybe less. If I'm not, feel free to come looking for me."

"Don't think we won't," Gary called after me.

I was halfway to the break tent when I saw Lois walking swiftly toward the restroom area. I frowned. Had she left the tent unattended? I quickened my steps and was just about to walk inside the break tent when I halted. Was I imagining it, or did I hear voices? I crept closer and pressed my ear to the flap. Yes, indeed, there were voices—muffled—coming from inside. I peered through the small opening and saw a man in pressed jeans with neatly combed blonde hair standing beside the table in the far corner. A thin dark-haired woman, her back to me, was sliding the cardboard box out from underneath the table. The man bent over, pushed back the flaps and let out a little cry.

"Here it is!" he said triumphantly. "At last."

As the man started to pull the jewel chest out of the box, I stepped into the tent and cleared my throat loudly. They whirled around, and I crossed my arms over my chest, fixed them both with a stare. "Just what do you think you're doing?"

Even though I was looking straight at the man, it was the woman who answered. "We're doing nothing wrong," she said in a clipped voice.

I switched my gaze to her. "Really? Because it looks to me like you're trying to steal something here."

"We're doing nothing wrong," she repeated. "We have a right to reclaim our property."

I raised an eyebrow. "I'm sorry? *Your* property?"

"Actually, it's neither of ours," the man said smoothly. He flashed me a smile best described as oily. Something about him set my antenna rising, but I couldn't pinpoint just what it was. "My sister and I have spent quite a good deal of our valuable time tracking this down."

The woman tossed her head so her dark hair spilled over one shoulder. "I don't know why we have to explain ourselves," she said indignantly. Her gaze raked me head to toe. "Who are you, anyway?"

I raised my chin and returned her stare. "I'm Shell McMillan. I run Urban Tails, the local pet shop."

"I see," the woman said. "And that gives you what sort of authority here?"

"My mother and my friend Sue's store is sponsoring this event for the shelter, so it definitely gives you more authority here than you," I shot back. I gestured toward the box. "This item was brought in for appraisal. The woman bought it at an estate sale last week."

"I know," the woman snapped. "She beat me there by five lousy minutes. Then she turned me down flat, wouldn't even listen . . ."

I stared at her. "*You're* the person who offered two hundred fifty dollars for it?"

"Yeah. Most people would have jumped at that offer, but not that woman." The brunette's lips curled in a snarl. "All this could have been avoided."

"All what could have been avoided? You barging in here and helping yourself to someone else's property?"

"Well, after all, it's not like we're stealing it," the woman rasped. "It . . . it belongs to our grandmother."

I stared at her. "Excuse me?"

"She's right." The man put a hand on the woman's arm, squeezed it lightly and then turned to me. "It's all a misunderstanding," he said smoothly. "The item was sold in error. It shouldn't have been. We've been going crazy trying to find this and get it back for Granny."

That story smelled worse than a day-old salmon. I walked over, bent down, and lifted up the box. I set it on the table and stood, one hand resting on its flaps. "How did your . . . *granny* happen to lose it?"

"She didn't lose it, not exactly," the man replied. "Her friend was going on a long trip, and needed something to take her jewelry in. She thought that chest would be perfect, so Granny, dear soul that she was, loaned it to her."

"Yes." The brunette bobbed her head up and down. "So while this woman was on her trip, Granny had a stroke, and had to go to the rehabilitation center." She pulled a Kleenex out of the pocket of her dress, dabbed at the corners of her eyes. "It was a while before she recovered, and what do you think she asked about first? This jewel chest. Of course, in the meantime her friend couldn't locate her, and then she moved, and then . . ."

well, the woman died."

I'd heard fishy stories from clients in the past, and this one recked. "What was this woman's name, the one your grandmother loaned the box to?"

The man and woman exchanged a look, and then the woman said in an indignant tone, "We only knew her as Mrs. Johansen. I don't know her first name."

"Yes, and once we learned of that estate sale my sister went there immediately to reclaim Granny's property, but . . . it had already been sold." The man's teeth flashed a quick smile. "So now that you know the details, surely you understand our position."

"I'm not sure I do," I said. "That chest was bought in good faith and left to be appraised. Even if I wanted to, I have no authority to turn it over to you."

"A mere detail," the man said, waving his hand in the air. "I'm sure we can reach an understanding. We're quite willing to reimburse your patron for the box, and tack a tidy profit on besides."

"That may well be, but I don't believe she wishes to sell . . . at least not until she finds out the appraised value."

"Which, I'm sure, will be nowhere near what we can offer her for it," the man said, reaching into his breast pocket. He withdrew a fat billfold, opened it, and plucked out three bills. "Three hundred dollars. Cash."

He held them out to me, but I made no move to take them. I looked him right in the eye and said, "I should tell you that I've already been offered four hundred for this box today by someone else."

"Four hundred!" The man and woman exchanged a look. "By who?" the man finally asked.

"There was another man here earlier," I said. "His mother has been looking for a similar jewel box and he offered four hundred for it. I turned him down as well." I fixed them both with a stare. "You can see why I'm a bit skeptical of your story."

Another look passed between the man and woman and then the man said smoothly, "Of course. This other man is probably our cousin. His mother has always coveted that jewel box, and this is just the sort of underhanded, sneaky trick he would pull to try and get it. You were right to refuse him. We're telling you the truth." He plucked two more bills from his wallet. "I'll give you five hundred. Cash." He waved the bills in the air. "You can't beat that."

"You're missing the point, as did the earlier gentleman," I said, my temper rising. "This isn't an auction, and this box isn't mine to negotiate with. I happen to know that the owner wants to get Mr. Antoine's appraisal before she'll do anything. So I'll tell you the same thing I told him. If you'll leave your name and number, I'll be glad to relay your message to the proper people."

"I think *you're* the one missing the point." The blonde man took a step closer to me. With his set jaw and brows drawn together, he looked quite menacing. "This box wasn't supposed to be sold. It was a mistake. My grandmother is the owner of this box. Technically, I don't have to offer you a dime for it."

"I beg to differ."

We all turned to see my mother standing there. "Another country heard from," the woman cried. "Now, who are *you?*"

My mother leveled the two of them with her best Lady Macbeth stare. "I am Clarissa McMillan, and I am one of the sponsors of this event." She moved forward, her gaze riveted on the two intruders. "I couldn't help overhearing your little discussion with my daughter. Suffice it to say that unless you can come up with some sort of proof that your grandmother did indeed own that box and it was in Mrs. Johansen's wrongful possession, I'm afraid you're out of luck. Unless, of course, our patron does decide to accept your cash offer, or that of the other gentleman, which would be entirely up to her." My mother slitted her eyes and raised her chin as she added, "I'm afraid I'm going to have to ask you to leave, now . . . or I will call the police and have you arrested for attempted theft."

The brunette raised her chin and said haughtily, "You wouldn't dare."

My mother's chin went up as well. She removed her cell phone from the pocket of her Armani jacket and waved it in the air. "Try me."

My mother and the woman stared at each other for what seemed an eternity before the brunette finally looked away. "Fine, fine," she barked, plucking at the man's arm as she did so. "Let's get out of here."

The man looked at me and snarled, "You want proof of ownership? We'll be glad to provide it." He looked over at the jewel box, then back at us. "Trust me. This isn't over."

"It is for now," my mother said, an edge to her tone. "Do not come back here unless you have concrete proof of ownership."

With a final black look at us the two exited the tent. Once they'd gone, I let out my breath in a giant whoosh. "Wow, Mother," I said. "You were great!"

My mother blew at the tips of her fingers. "Naturally, darling, I've had years of practice. I just channeled my inner Lady Macbeth."

I frowned. "Their story sounded like a load of bullcrap to me. Aside from knowing the deceased's name was Johansen, I doubt anything else they said was true."

My mother wrinkled her nose. "Frankly, I didn't like their looks, especially the man."

"I agree. There was just something about him. I can't describe it, it's just a feeling. The woman was a piece of work too. I wouldn't trust either one of them."

"Well, hopefully we've seen the last of them," she said. "Although it wouldn't surprise me if they came back with some sort of bill of sale for that jewel box."

"Me either," I agreed. "Considering what's happened, I don't want to leave this jewel box here."

"I don't think that's wise." My mother snapped her fingers. "Antoine's line wasn't too long when I left. Come on. Let's take it to him right now."

Seven

"Agreed," I said. "I think the sooner we get this item to Antoine, the better. But I don't particularly want to take it out in the open. I'd much rather he examined it in private."

My mother frowned. "I can understand that. But where do you want him to appraise it? Surely not here."

"No. How about the community center office? Do you think you could get Antoine to go over there, Mother?"

My mother tossed me one of her famous *are you kidding* looks. "I'll have him there in fifteen minutes," she said. She paused. "Might I ask what you were doing in here in the first place, Crishell?"

"Looking for the watch Aunt Tillie gave me. It slid off my wrist. I think I saw it just before I tucked the jewel box away." I paled as a sudden thought struck me. "Oh, no. That man had started to remove the jewel chest from the box. I hope he didn't find my watch. If he did, I can kiss it goodbye for sure."

"Not if I find him first," my mother said. We opened the box and removed the chest. Nothing else was in the box. I opened the jewel chest and gave a quick look. Nothing inside either. Then I knelt down and looked underneath the table. "Here it is," I cried. I spied the watch lying in a heap by the table leg. I snatched it up and clipped it back on my wrist, this time making sure the safety was on. "Thank goodness."

My mother hurried off toward the main tent to get Antoine and I headed in the direction of the community center office, the jewel box clasped in my arms. I slipped inside, went straight to Marianne's office and laid the jewel box on the desk. Then I settled myself into the well-worn leather chair behind the desk to wait. I didn't have long. About ten minutes later I heard the outer door open and my mother call out, "Crishell? Where are you?"

"In the office, Mother."

I heard the rapid click-click of my mother's heels against the polished wood floor, and then the door opened and my mother walked in, followed by Gerard Antoine. He smiled when he saw me and made a little bow. "Your mother tells me you have a very urgent appraisal," he said.

"Yes, if you don't mind, Mr. Antoine. It seems there's been a great deal of interest in this particular piece."

I rose from the chair and Antoine slid into it, withdrew a pair of latex gloves from his jacket pocket and snapped them on. I lifted the jewel chest out of the box and set it in front of Antoine. The appraiser's eyes widened and he reached for it, turned it over in his hands. He was silent for several minutes, then said, "Definitely walnut," he said, "and a good grade at that. Of course, you can see there are a few flaws in the grain, but not many." He opened the top compartment carefully. "Hinges seem to be solid. The lining is good, although you can see a few spots—maybe someone left this open in the sun. There are a few rips and tears, but nothing too drastic." He ran his finger along the wood carving on the top. "Carving's nice and neat, and looks to be pretty expertly done. All in all a pretty nice piece of work." He pushed his glasses a bit further up on his nose and added, "Before you ask the inevitable question, no, this is not the original chest owned by the queen of England."

I couldn't help the cry of disappointment that escaped my lips. This chest turning out to be the original would have explained a lot. "Are you absolutely certain?" I heard myself ask.

Antoine shot me what I could best describe as a reproachful look. "As certain as one in my line of work can be," he returned. "I've seen many replicas of that box over the years, and to be quite honest, this one is in the best shape." He motioned for me to come closer, and then he pointed at the lining. "The original had deep purple lining, not faded yellow. And see these hinges?" He tapped at them with a gloved forefinger. "They're definitely mid nineteen thirties—possibly late nineteen twenties. Most telling, though, is the carving on the top. The flower stem on the original is straight. This one curves off at an angle . . . see?"

I followed his finger and let out a sigh. "What about a secret compartment? I've heard some of these chests had them."

"Yes, a drawer cleverly constructed to appear like part of the bottom molding. However . . ." He picked up the chest and tapped at the bottom. "This wasn't one of them. Still, if there weren't so many nicks in the wood, and the hinges were a bit stronger, I'd value it at a hundred, maybe two. As it is now . . . I'd say between fifty and sixty dollars."

I felt a twinge of disappointment surge through me. "Really? That's all?"

Antoine looked offended. "It is my professional opinion," he said, sounding a bit hurt. "And I assure you, I've valued many boxes similar to this."

"I didn't mean to imply anything," I said quickly. "It's just that there has been an inordinate amount of interest in this particular box today."

Antoine shrugged. "I could understand that. Despite the flaws it's still a nice piece."

"Nice enough for someone to offer four hundred dollars for it?"

"Four hundred dollars?" Antoine's skeptical gaze went from me to the box and back to me. "You're joking?"

I shook my head. "I'm afraid not."

"It's definitely not that nice a piece." Antoine stroked at his goatee. "Perhaps they think that this is the original chest, or they believe it could be passed off as such. The original would fetch far more than four hundred, I assure you." He gave me a considering look. "I admit items like this aren't my specialty. I do know some people who are far more experienced in this area than I. If you wish, I could take the chest with me and contact them, see what they have to say."

"That's a very kind offer, Mr. Antoine, but since the chest isn't mine I'll have to pass. I'll have Marianne tell the owner about your offer, though. Maybe she'll want to take you up on it."

"As you wish." He glanced at his watch and then at my mother. "I suppose we'd best get back. There's only a half hour left, and there was quite a line when you pulled me away for your emergency." He paused. "I still have a few excess items to appraise, as well. Perhaps you should bump that dinner reservation back to six thirty."

"Let's see how it goes," my mother said, linking her arm through Antoine's. "The restaurant is only a ten-minute drive from here. You'll love it, I'm sure. I'm told their veal scaloppini is to die for."

Antoine and my mother left. I put the jewel box back in the box and sighed. I knew the appraiser hadn't been wrong, but it made the chest all the more mysterious. Why on earth would those people offer hundreds of dollars for a jewel box only worth fifty? It made no sense.

Since the box wasn't all that valuable, I had no qualms about putting it back in the community center office; besides, I wanted to check on the cats again. I stopped to pick up my tote bag and then continued to the office. I heard scuffling sounds as I approached and frowned. "Purrday, Princess Fuzzypants and Cleo," I called out. "What are you guys doing?"

I saw the minute that I opened the door what was going on. Apparently instead of making them sleepy, the catnip had invigorated them. The cats raced around the office at breakneck speed, jumping on and off the desk, the file cabinet, and whizzing around the room like the Flash on steroids. Well, I'd been through this before. It was best to let them wear themselves down. Then I could put Cleo in her carrier and head home. I wondered idly if Gary had made plans for the evening with Olivia; if so, I'd have to cook something, unless I could somehow finagle an invitation to Enzio's with my mother, Sue and Antoine. I was dying to try their gnocchi and veal parm–flavored meatballs, their signature dish. Of course, worst-case scenario, I could always stop in at Bottoms Up and grab their signature dish, a 1950s-style burger. Maybe I'd even run into Josh there. The pub was near the station and a favorite of his.

Thinking of Josh made me think of his latest case. I set the jewel chest on the file cabinet and went over to the desk. I slid into the chair, pulled out my phone, and was just about to type in *Fox Hollow Diamond Heist*, when all of a sudden a white form streaked right past me. A second later a sleeker dark form whizzed by, followed by a loud thump and a crash! I whirled around and my gaze went first to the file cabinet.

No box. No jewel chest.

I rose from my seat and walked slowly around the desk. Sure enough, the box had split open and the jewel chest was lying on its side on the floor. The top was open at an angle, and two of the drawers were hanging open. The cats had stopped their mad dashes and were sitting a few feet away, staring at it.

"Great," I said in as stern a tone as I could muster. "See what you guys did?"

Three pairs of limpid kitty eyes turned my way. "Merow," they chorused. I had to admit they did sound pretty mournful.

"Okay," I grumbled. "It's partially my fault too. I should have left the jewel chest on the floor, not somewhere it could be knocked down so easily."

I reached for the box, and as I did so, I gave a little gasp. A portion of the wood on the box's left side seemed to have detached and was hanging loose, and something was protruding slightly from it. I stared, openmouthed. So the box did have a secret compartment after all! It was on the side of the chest, not underneath. Perhaps that was how Antoine had missed it. "He said it wasn't his area of expertise," I muttered as I reached for the chest. As I lifted the box up, two objects fell to the ground. One was a small, folded piece of yellowed paper and the other . . . I blinked, rubbed at my eyes, then blinked again.

Was I wrong, or was that a diamond twinkling up at me?

Eight

I waited a few minutes for the hammering in my chest to subside before I picked up the stone. It sparkled in the overhead light. Heck, it looked like a diamond, but then again, I'd seen cubic zirconia on shopping channel shows that sparkled like the real deal. And Lord knew jewelry wasn't my area of expertise.

Still clutching what might or might not be a diamond, I unfolded the paper. It appeared to have been cut from a newspaper. On one side was an advertisement for cabinet refinishing. The other appeared to be a snippet of a news article. I looked at the date on the side of the page: September, 2013. The title of the article stood out in big, bold black lettering: *Local Man Sentenced to Prison Term.* The first two sentences were intact, but the rest was obliterated by a jagged edge.

I looked first at the article, then at the stone clutched in my other hand. It was an amazing coincidence I should find what appeared to be a diamond right around the same time the FBI was reopening an investigation into a ten-year-old diamond heist, wasn't it?

Then again, I'd never believed in coincidences.

The door opened suddenly and Marianne stood framed in the doorway. "Shell?" she asked. I hastily scooped up the stone and the slip of paper and crammed them into my tote bag as she stepped all the way into the office. I heard her sharp intake of breath and then she cried, "My goodness! What happened?"

"Sorry. It seems the two cats overdosed on catnip," I said with a little laugh. I walked around the side of the desk and picked up the jewel chest. "It's my fault. I had it on top of the file cabinet. They were having themselves a nice little chase and the box turned out to be a casualty."

"Oh my gosh. Is it damaged?" Marianne's eyes were wide as she stared at the chest, which I'd now placed on top of the desk.

"I don't think it's badly damaged," I said. I slid the drawers in and out. "See, the drawers appear to be all right, and the cover opens and closes just fine."

Marianne pointed to the wood sliver hanging from the chest's side. "What's that? It looks as if the wood has separated."

I picked the chest up in both hands and held it above my head. "Antoine was wrong. He didn't think this chest had a secret compartment, but it does. I guess he didn't expect it to be on the side of the box, not underneath."

Marianne stepped forward, her features screwed into a pensive expression as she wriggled the sliver of wood with her finger. "It's pretty loose. Do you think you could pop it back into place again?"

"Maybe I could, if I knew just how it popped out in the first place. The fall jarred it loose, somehow. It must have been in there pretty tight." I fiddled with the piece of wood, moving it first forward and backward, then side to side. "It doesn't want to slide back in to wherever it slid out from," I said at last.

Marianne's frown deepened. "Well, we certainly can't give it back to Eunice in this condition. Your mother told me what Antoine said. Even though it wasn't appraised for a large amount, I know she was considering giving it to her niece for her birthday. And it's not as if she can take it back to where she bought it from and exchange it."

I turned to the cats and waved my finger in the air. "You know you did a bad thing, right?"

All three cats hung their heads.

Scolding completed, I turned to Marianne. "I could call Antoine," I suggested. "Tell him what happened. He might know someone who could fix it, or maybe I'll get lucky and find something online. Worst-case scenario, I'll just apologize to Eunice and offer to have a professional repair it and foot the bill."

"Maybe you should just forgo online research and find someone decent to repair it. If they do a good job we wouldn't even have to tell Eunice. She's not expected home till late Monday." Marianne let out a sigh. "It's too bad Sam Weatherly died a few months ago. He owned a small furniture repair store in town."

"I've heard his name mentioned," I said.

"It's a sad story. His wife left him, claimed all he did was work and said he didn't care about his family. She took their only child with them, a boy. Wouldn't let Sam have any contact with him. Sam started to drink a bit after that, but he never stopped working. Turned out quality stuff, too. An odd man, and a secretive one, but a genius with wood." Marianne pointed at the box. "He could have fixed that with his eyes shut, I'm sure."

I pointed to the ruined cardboard box. "You wouldn't happen to have a box this would fit in, would you?"

"I think I might. Let me check."

Marianne left, and I whipped out my phone and typed in *Queen Victoria Jewel Boxes*. Just as Antoine had said, some of the later copies had secret compartments built in, but most of them were situated either underneath the top tray or underneath the box's bottom. I didn't find any mention of any boxes with secret drawers built along the side, as this one seemed to have. I paused to regard the cats, who were curled up alongside my chair. Both Cleo and the princess had their heads on their paws and eyes closed, but Purrday's good eye was wide open. He lifted his head and shook it. "Merow."

I looked at my watch. It was a few minutes past five. "Yes, we'll be going home soon," I said. "I just need to make one call." I had Eddie Laverty's number on my speed dial. He answered on the second ring.

"Hey, Shell. How did everything go today?"

"Just fine, Eddie. The event was a huge success, and those tents you set up were great."

"Good. I'll be by sometime tomorrow to take 'em down. Had a big job over in Emporium today or I would have stopped by for an appraisal myself. I've got that big chest of antique tools my granddad left me."

"You could have left them with us, Eddie. Lots of folks did."

"Yeah, Sue told me I could, but I felt guilty They're way too heavy for women to be lifting," he demurred. "Don't worry, I heard this was a big success. Maybe you'll have another one in the spring. Or maybe I'll take it to one of Antoine's shows myself, although I hear the lines get really long at those."

"I'd wait on attending one of Antoine's shows. They are super crowded, and it's not a bad idea to have a repeat of this fundraiser in the spring. Antoine was certainly amenable to a return visit. Actually, I had another reason for calling you. Do you still dabble in woodworking?"

"Once in a while, if I find something that interests me. Why?"

I explained about Eunice's chest. "I was wondering if you could take a look at it tomorrow, and see if you think you might be able to fix it, or maybe recommend someone who might."

"I love a challenge," Eddie said with a laugh. "Sure, I'll take a stab at fixing it. I always loved those Hardy Boys mysteries. I'd love to see a jewel box with a secret compartment. Drop it by my house anytime."

I thanked Eddie and told him I'd be by tomorrow. The cats started twining around my ankles as I hung up. "Yes, I know you're hungry. I am too. I suppose I should see if Mother would mind me tagging along to

Enzio's."

Marianne came in bearing a large box. "This was all I could find," she said.

"That's great, thanks." I slid the jewel box inside, then said, "I called Ed Laverty. He said he might be able to fix it. I'll take it to him tomorrow."

"Great. That would be a relief," said Marianne. As I started to leave with the box she called out, "Oh, I forgot to tell you. Antoine's decided to stay at the Hilton on the highway overnight, so he can pick up his adopted rescue cat tomorrow morning. He said he'd do the remaining items then."

I bit down on my lower lip. "So they've left for Enzio's already?"

"Yes, about ten minutes ago. Your mother said to tell you she'd call you tomorrow."

So much for my tagging along to Enzio's. I sent Gary a quick text: *Got plans?* A few seconds later I got back an answer: *Olivia and I are going to Wet Your Whistle. You're welcome to join.*

I figured the last thing they needed was a third wheel, so I sent back my answer: *No, you kids have fun. C U later.*

I looked at the cats. "Looks like burgers from Bottoms Up it is," I said. "But let's get you guys home first." I put the box containing the jewel box in my trunk, and while Purrday and the princess made themselves comfortable in the backseat, I got Cleopawtra into her carrier and put her in the front next to me. The ride home was uneventful, but Kahlua regarded the pink carrier warily as we stepped into the kitchen.

"Relax, she's just here for . . . gee, that's a good question." I suddenly realized that Gus had never gotten back to me on whether or not it was okay for Cleo to spend the night here. Kahlua meowed loudly, and then Purrday and the princess joined in. "Okay, okay. I'll feed you," I said. I spooned tuna into their dishes and put some on a plastic plate and set it inside Cleo's carrier. I didn't want to give her too much, because I didn't know what sort of diet Inez might have the cat on. As they wolfed down their food, I started to look up the number of the Good Eats. I'd just located it when my phone buzzed and I saw Inez Morton's name pop up on the screen. Talk about timing! I swiped the answer icon and said, "Hi, Inez."

"Hi, Shell," the woman said cheerily. "I understand my husband managed to talk you into babysitting Cleo today."

"It wasn't a bother, really. She spent the day playing with Purrday." *And busting up jewel chests.* "No trouble at all."

"Well, I appreciate your doing that. I suppose one of these days I'll get over being so overprotective." Inez managed a nervous laugh. "Anyway, the reason I'm calling is since I'm home now, I was wondering if I could swing by the community center and pick her up. Gus mentioned you had plans this evening, and to be quite honest, I don't want to wait until tomorrow to see my baby. Besides, I'm sure she'd much rather be in her nice fleece bed."

"The event's ended, Inez. Actually, I have Cleopawtra at my house." I paused. Inez's house was on the way to Bottoms Up. "I could swing by you and drop her off, if you'd like."

"Oh, that would be wonderful, but I hate to impose."

"It's no bother, really," I said. "I'm headed out that way anyway. I can be there in about twenty minutes."

"Perfect. I can't wait to see my baby," she crooned.

I disconnected and looked at my cats. "Sorry, gang, but company's going home. Say goodbye to Cleopawtra."

Kahlua sniffed, minced over to her fleece bed in the far corner of the kitchen, curled into a tight ball and closed her eyes. The princess let out a sharp meow and Purrday sat up on his haunches and pawed at the air.

I chuckled. "I take it you two want to go along?"

The cats looked at each other, then gave loud yowls of assent.

I sighed. "Fine—but you've got to behave yourselves."

If ever a cat could look angelic, it was those two.

I put all the cats in the backseat and started off toward Main Street. The Mortons lived across town, about a half mile from where Good Eats was located. My stomach growled loudly, reminding me that all I'd had to eat today had been that pumpkin muffin. As I approached Main, I could see a ton of red taillights, a sure sign of Saturday night traffic. Abruptly I made a right-hand turn.

"Guess what," I said to the cats. "We're going to take the shortcut to Cleo's house through Grimley Woods. Otherwise, we'll never make it there in twenty minutes, and Inez will probably call the cops."

Grimley Woods was named for the man who'd owned that particular stretch of land and then donated it to the county to use as a park when he passed. I turned my car down the back road that cut through the park. I was glad of the company, even if it was the four-footed variety. There's always been something about woods at night that has spooked me, ever since I was a kid and saw the part in *Snow White and the Seven Dwarfs* where she's trapped in the woods overnight with the talking trees. I'd had nightmares about giant elms chastising me for weeks afterward.

I drove slowly along the winding path and suddenly, out of the corner of my eye, I saw Purrday leap into the passenger seat. His shoulders hunched forward and his head raised slightly, ears flat against his skull.

"Purrday?" I said, my tone sharp. "What's the matter?"

He pressed his nose against the passenger window and let out a soft whimper. I pulled over to the side of the road and leaned across the passenger seat so I could look in the same direction as my cat. A few seconds later, I saw a figure emerge from the woods. At this distance I couldn't see very clearly, but I could tell from the build it was a man. As he moved farther out of the circle of trees and into the clearing, I frowned. There was something familiar about the man, about the way he carried himself—slightly stooped, the same way Gus Morton walked. But this man couldn't be Gus. He was supposed to be working at the Good Eats until well after midnight.

The man moved rapidly now, almost as if he were frightened of something, or someone. He paused every few feet to glance over his shoulder, as if he were afraid someone were following him. Midway across the clearing he stumbled over a rock and almost went down, but he righted himself quickly. A few minutes later he'd turned onto one of the hiking trails and vanished from view.

I reached up to swipe at my forehead. "Goodness. I wonder what that was all about?"

I heard a soft meow, and then a whirr. I looked back at the passenger seat and bit back a cry of dismay. My enterprising cat had put his paw on the automatic window button and the window was now all the way down. I saw Purrday's rear end wiggle and I knew what that meant.

"Don't you dare!" I cried. My hand shot out but I wasn't fast enough. Purrday sprang forward and sailed gracefully out the window, landed with all four feet on the ground and then took off like a shot toward the woods.

"Oh, great," I muttered. "Just great." I slammed the car into Park. The princess was dancing around in the rear seat, her nose pressed up against the window, looking in the direction Purrday had taken off in. "Merow?" she said.

I sighed. "Okay. You can come with me to find him."

After making sure Cleo was secure I locked the car and then Princess Fuzzypants and I hurried off in the direction that Purrday had taken. Finally I saw a white blur. He was over by the rock the man had stumbled over, and he was pawing at the dirt. I hurried quickly over to him. The cat looked up as I approached, and I could see he had something clenched between his paws. I knelt down and saw the object was a button. I reached down and gently disengaged his prize, held it up. The button was made of thin, cheap plastic and had the design of a sailing ship carved into it. It didn't look much the worse for wear, so I reasoned it couldn't have been lying outside very long. I thought about the man I'd seen. Could this button have come from his jacket when he stumbled?

I tensed, suddenly, assailed by the feeling that I wasn't alone here in the woods. I glanced swiftly to my right. A dark shape moved slightly, and then seemed to blend back into the shadows. I blinked rapidly, not sure if it had been my imagination or if I'd really seen someone. "Come on, kids," I said, my voice hoarse. "Let's get out of here."

Purrday suddenly let out a soft *grr*, then sat up straight, ears flicked forward, lips peeled back. His backside wiggled like a bowl of jelly; the next minute he launched himself forward and took off into the woods like a streak of greased lightning. I shoved the button into my pocket and took off at a swift cantor after him, Princess Fuzzypants at my heels. I hurried down the beaten trail, craning my neck to and fro until I finally caught sight of him. He was perched on a large rock, sitting ramrod straight, ears flattened against his skull, his tail swishing like a banner waving in the wind. His gaze was fixed on something just beyond the rock, and as I drew closer I saw what had captured his attention.

The edge of a man's shoe.

Steeling myself, I peered cautiously around the side of the rock. Yep, it was a shoe, all right, and what's more, it was attached to a body, and one I'd seen very recently.

It was Pete Martin's body, and he wasn't moving.

Nine

Purrday looked over at me and meowed loudly.

"Yes, yes, Purrday, I see him," I said. I picked my way carefully over to where Martin lay slumped against the rock. He was dressed the same as I'd seen him earlier, in jeans and plaid shirt, but now he had a khaki windbreaker on as well. His eyes were closed, and his neck sagged to one side. Leaning forward, I touched the side of his neck with two fingers. His skin felt cold to the touch, and I could feel no sign of a heartbeat.

Yep, he was dead all right.

As I drew my hand back, I could make out what appeared to be blood on the collar of his jacket. There was also some sort of ragged hole just behind his right ear. I leaned in for a closer look. Was that a bullet hole? My stomach clenched and I felt something bitter in the back of my throat. I couldn't help but remember the odd phone call Gus had received earlier today. I was almost positive he'd mentioned Grimley Woods. Had it been Gus I'd seen, and had he met Martin here in the woods? "No," I said through clenched teeth. "That's ridiculous. Gus was annoyed but he'd never kill someone. I don't even think he owns a gun."

Princess Fuzzypants rose from her sitting position and took a few steps toward the body. Purrday immediately crossed in front of her and he nudged her with his shoulder. The princess paused, looked at Purrday, and then up at me.

"Purrday's right, Princess," I said. "No touching. If Josh thinks we tampered with anything, he won't be too happy. And speaking of Josh . . ."

I fumbled in my pocket for my phone and punched in 911. When the operator answered I said, "This is Shell McMillan. I've found a body in Grimley Woods. Can you send someone out here right away?"

I gave the operator my exact location and she promised to have someone out there within fifteen minutes. Then I called Inez. When she answered, I told her that I was stuck in a traffic jam, and I'd get Cleopawtra out to her as soon as I could. That done, I slid my phone back into my pocket just as Purrday let out a sharp merow. He raised his paw and pointed at Martin. I squinted down at the body and frowned. "What's the matter, Purrday? Is there something you want me to see?"

The cat waved his paw more imperiously and I leaned over a bit further. Then I saw it: there was a button missing from the jacket. I reached into my pocket and pulled out the button I'd found earlier, held it up to examine it against Martin's.

No match.

"Nice try, boy. But no sale." I slid the button back into my jacket pocket just as the wail of a police siren reached my ears. I hurried down the trail and into the clearing to meet them. Josh wasn't one of the two officers I saw striding toward me. One was Denny Miller, another regular at Urban Tails for treats for his cocker spaniel, Chumley, and the other I'd never seen before. He looked older than Denny, and as he approached I saw that he sported a buzz cut and a serious expression. He carried himself ramrod straight, making me think he might possibly have some sort of military background. He stopped in front of me and gave me a curt nod. "You made the call?"

I nodded. "Yes. The body's a few yards down, just off the trail behind a large rock."

Denny came up and touched two fingers to his forehead. "Evening, Shell. So you've found another one, eh?"

I shot him a rueful smile. "It looks that way."

Denny shot his companion a look, and then jerked his thumb at me. "Shell here has the instincts of a bloodhound when it comes to bodies," he said. With a quick wave he started ambling down the trail.

The other officer shot me a dubious look, and then whipped a notebook and a pen from his pocket. "Mind telling me how you happened to find the victim?"

Before I could answer, Josh emerged into the clearing. He had on charcoal trousers and a gray and white sport coat over a white shirt and a gray and white striped tie, and he looked pretty darn good. He walked over to me and stood, arms crossed over his chest. "I heard the notice on my scanner," he said. "But I didn't expect to find you here."

"Yeah, well, I didn't exactly expect to be here either," I said.

Josh pulled out his notebook and pen. "Can you tell me what happened?"

I related the events leading up to my finding Martin's body, omitting the part about seeing Gus, since I wasn't absolutely certain it had been him. When I finished, Josh was silent for a few seconds and then asked, "You didn't touch anything, right?"

I swallowed. "I felt for a pulse, and when I pulled my hand back, I touched the top of his jacket collar." I paused and then added, "I saw a wound behind his right ear. It looked like a bullet hole."

"We'll let the coroner make the decision on cause of death," Josh said. As he started to slide his notebook back into his pocket, his gaze focused on a point just beyond my left shoulder and he let out an annoyed sigh. "Swell. We've got company."

I turned and bit back an annoyed exclamation myself as I saw Jeremy Jackson striding purposefully toward us. I noticed the reporter had changed clothes since I'd seen him last. Now attired in black slacks, black turtleneck and a black jacket that looked to be cashmere, he looked quite somber indeed. The reporter walked up to us as casually as if we were meeting at a football game and not a crime scene.

"Jackson," Josh said with a brief incline of his head. "What are you doing here?"

Jackson flashed a quick, toothy smile. "Like any good reporter, I have a nose for news. I happened to be driving past when I spotted the police vehicles parked along the road."

Josh's eyebrow lifted. "I see. You were just driving aimlessly through a deserted stretch of woods?"

Jackson's lips quirked slightly. "Well, no. I have to admit that I have a police scanner. I heard there was a dead body found in the woods, so I thought I'd swing by and check it out." He gestured toward the woods. "Has the victim been identified yet?"

"Pete Martin," I blurted before I thought, and then added quickly, "I mean, there's a good chance that's who he is."

Josh's gaze was cool as he regarded Jeremy Jackson. "There's been no positive identification yet," he said. "The victim's name will be released to the media once any surviving relatives are notified."

"Okay," Jackson said, almost cheerfully, "so he's John Doe for now." He reached inside his jacket pocket and pulled out a small notebook and a pen. "Can you comment on whether or not this death was accidental?"

Josh flashed me a swift glance that said more plainly than words: *keep your mouth shut*. Then he turned to Jackson. "I have no comment at this time," he replied. "The cause of death will be made public once the coroner finishes his examination. As a crime reporter, Jackson, you should be familiar with protocol."

"Oh, I am," the reporter said with a careless wave. He started to turn away, then stopped and looked straight at me. "I'm guessing you found the body," he said. "But what about the other man? Did you see what happened to him?"

Josh's frown deepened. He looked from Jeremy Jackson to me and back to Jackson. "Other man? What other man?"

"When I was driving over here, I saw a man cut through the woods not far from this clearing. Next thing I knew, this white van comes roaring out of some bushes, cuts in front of my car and takes off that way—" Jackson made a sweeping gesture with his arm and then pinned me with his gaze. "Did you see anyone else lurking around here?"

I couldn't very well lie about it now. I turned to Josh. "Yes, I did see someone come out of the woods," I admitted. "Actually Purrday saw him first."

Jeremy's brows knit together. "Purrday?"

"My cat," I said to Jackson. I turned back to Josh and said, "I can't really tell you much about the man. I was still in my car at the time. I was too far away to make out anything more than a shape. I could tell you that he was tall and appeared to have a muscular build, but that's about it."

"Well, I got a good look at him when he almost smashed into my front end," ventured Jackson. "I'd place him, oh, late fifties, close to sixty, gray hair slicked back from a high forehead, prominent chin. He might have been a fighter at one time. His nose had a bump on it, like maybe it had been broken once or twice."

I flinched. Jackson had described Gus Morton to a tee. I slid Josh a glance and could tell from the expression on his face it had registered with him too. "Anything else?" he asked the reporter.

Jackson shrugged. "That van had lettering on the side. It whizzed by too fast for me to see exactly what it said, but I could swear one of the words on it looked like *eats*."

I bit my lip. Talk about putting nails in someone's coffin. I stole another glance Josh's way but his expression was what I expected: bland, unreadable. One thing I'd learned about him these past few months was that he was excellent at putting on a detective face. He was very good at not letting anyone know what he was thinking, a trait I found more than a little frustrating.

"Okay." Josh finished scribbling, jammed the notebook and pen back into his pocket. He glanced briefly at Jackson then let his gaze slide to me. "Thank you both for your cooperation."

"You're welcome." Jackson flashed a smile I figured was intended to be ingratiating. He slid his notebook back into his pocket. "I don't suppose my cooperation will earn me any extra points as far as garnering information is concerned?"

Josh shook his head. "Afraid not. Now I'm going to have to ask you to leave, since this is an active crime scene." With that, he turned and stalked off without a backward glance at either of us. I watched until he was swallowed up by the bushes, then turned and started back toward where I'd parked my car, Purrday and the princess trotting along beside me. A few minutes later I heard the pounding of footsteps, and then Jackson cut in front of me. "Detective Bloodgood is rather by the book, isn't he?"

I kept on walking, my eyes on the ground, and didn't look over at him. "Josh is a very good detective."

"So I've heard." I quickened my steps but it didn't seem to faze Jackson. His long-legged stride brought him next to me once again. "We haven't been formally introduced. I'm . . ."

I raised my head and cut him off with a curt, "Jeremy Jackson. I know who you are."

His lips quirked upward. "I know who you are too. You're Shell Marlowe, former star of *Spy Anyone.*"

I stopped dead, causing the cats to tumble into one another. "Actually these days I'm known as Shell McMillan. I run the Urban Tails Pet Shop in Fox Hollow."

"Yes, I'm aware of your career change." He cocked a brow at me. "So your cat's name is Purrday? That's a rather unusual name."

"Well, he's an unusual cat," I responded, and quickened my steps. Jackson quickened his as well. "I understand your mother is involved with the local antique store, and she and her partner sponsored that event today, which was lovely by the way. It drew quite a crowd."

I placed a hand on my hip. "Quite honestly, I'm surprised you were at the event, Mr. Jackson. I wouldn't have thought that was your speed."

He looked amused. "Oh? And just what do you think my speed is?"

"I'm not sure. Maybe you like murder cases." I paused. "Or better yet, cold ones."

To my consternation, he grinned at me. "Maybe I do," he said. "From what I hear, you're rather good at solving puzzles yourself. Maybe you'd like to team up with me? I have a feeling that together we might be able to crack almost anything."

I stared at him. "Not on your life," I said. "Now, if you'll excuse me, I have to go."

"I'm staying at the Fox Hollow Inn, room 505. Think about it."

"Nothing to think about," I flung back. I quickened my steps and a few minutes later reached my car. The cats leapt inside and I slid behind the wheel and started up the engine. As I pulled away I glanced out the window. Jackson stood at the end of the trail. As I passed him, he lifted his hand and gave me a thumbs-up.

"Leila's right. That guy thinks a lot of himself," I muttered. "And thanks to him, Gus is probably now on Josh's radar."

Both Purrday and the princess meowed their assent. Then Purrday's paw snaked out, patted at my jacket pocket.

"Right. The button." I frowned as I tried to remember the jacket Gus had worn. Did it have a zipper or buttons?

As I exited the woods, I'd made up my mind. "We're taking Cleopawtra home," I said to the cats. "And then we're going to Good Eats and pay Gus a visit. Here's hoping his jacket doesn't have buttons, but if it does, cross your paws that none of them are missing."

Ten

Lights were blazing in the Morton house when I parked my car right in front. Inez came out the door almost immediately. She was dressed in what looked like a comfortable powder blue sweat suit, and she had little violet-colored sock booties on her feet that had drawings of kittens on the sides. She raced down the steps and practically snatched the cat carrier out of my arms. She held it at eye level and pressed her face against the mesh. "Cleopawtra, Mommie's baby," she crooned at the cat. "Did you have a good time today with Shell's kitties? Did you miss Mommie?"

"She was very well behaved," I assured Inez.

"Oh, I'm sure she was. She's such a good kitty. Gus thinks I spoil her, but we know that's not true, don't we, lambikins?" Inez's lips drooped down a bit as she added, "I'm sorry that Gus foisted her on you, though. He could have made arrangements, it's just that this thing with Pete Martin has him so upset, he doesn't know if he's coming or going."

"Yes, Gus mentioned that Martin made him an offer to buy the diner."

Inez's eyes flashed. "Can you believe it? Pete Martin was always bad news. Now he comes back after all these years, bragging about his newfound wealth—"

"Newfound wealth? I was under the impression he didn't have much money."

Inez shifted a bit. "I guess I misspoke a bit," she admitted. "He doesn't have money—yet. He told Gus he expected a windfall any day now. I told Gus not to believe one word that came out of that man's mouth. A man like that doesn't change." Still clutching the cat, she leaned closer and whispered in my ear, "Not too many folks know this, but Pete was a gambler. Bet on everything from football games to the ponies, and everything in between. I know this for a fact. I used to be friends with his ex-wife. The last straw for her was when he started spending what little money they had left on that little tart he had on the side."

"I heard she caught him in a compromising position?"

"Hah, that's putting it mildly. She caught 'em both half naked, wrapped in each other's arms in the diner's cellar. They thought no one would ever think to look for 'em down there, but Jeanie knew every inch of that diner and she was determined to catch him in the act. Hired a PI to trail 'em, and when he called her and told her he'd tracked them down to the diner, she grabbed her video camera and hotfooted it right over there. Oh, there was quite a scene. Pete's girlfriend ended up moving away right after Pete took off. She never showed her face around Fox Hollow again, and who could blame her? Jeanie was ready to drag her through the mud and take that worthless piece of scum she married for everything he had. Then he up and sells the diner for cash and takes off, vanishes so she couldn't get the satisfaction. Poor Jeanie. She deserved far better than she got. Lord knows my Gus has a temper! He's gotten better over the years, but when he gets mad, watch out!" She waved her hand in a circular motion. "It's like releasing a floodgate!"

"Really," I said. "Gus always seems so calm. I never imagined he has a temper."

"Oh, he does. Anyway, my point is, if you thought Gus had a temper, well, you should have seen Pete Martin when he got riled. He could give Gus a run for his money in that department, all right." Inez let out a breath. "I've got to tell you, Martin was the last person on earth I ever expected to see back here in Fox Hollow. The man's brazen, I tell you. He came here one afternoon last week, just as cool as you please, looking for Gus. I told him in no uncertain terms to clear out, that the likes of him weren't welcome here and that people still remembered the awful things he'd done. I said if he knew what was good for him, he'd leave and never come back, before either Gus or I did something we'd probably regret." Her lips twisted upward. "I don't think he believed me, but in the end I got Gus's .45 out from under the bed, and when I cocked the trigger, he took off like a wasp had gotten into his shorts."

I stared at her. "Excuse me, did you say Gus's gun? He knows how to shoot?"

She snorted. "He thinks he does. Gus couldn't hit the broad side of a barn. Now me, on the other hand, well, I grew up in Texas. Kids are raised with guns under their pillows." She paused to brush an errant strand of hair from her eyes. "It's all moot, anyway. Martin's not buying the diner. That line he handed Gus about a windfall was just that—a line."

"How can you be so sure?"

"Because I know Pete Martin." She paused and took a deep breath, exhaled slowly. "I'm forgetting my manners. Would you like to come in for a cup of tea?"

I shook my head. "No, I really must be going."

My thoughts were racing, though, as I walked the short distance to my car. The news that Gus owned a gun wasn't particularly encouraging, even though she'd said he wasn't a good shot. The part she'd said about Martin expecting a windfall particularly intrigued me. What sort of windfall? Money from the sale of stolen diamonds, perhaps?

• • •

Good Eats was virtually empty when I arrived. There were plenty of open tables and only three people at the counter. I waved at Mikey Larimer behind the counter, who was mixing up a delicious-looking root beer float. I slid onto a stool at the far end of the counter and picked up a plastic menu. A few minutes later Mikey approached, his towel slung casually over one shoulder. He flashed me a shy smile. "Evening. It's Shell, right? You took over Tillie's pet shop?"

"That's right." I returned his smile with one of my own. "And you're SueAnn's husband. And Gormley's father." Gormley was their Scottish terrier. I'd ordered the special treats the terrier liked a number of times for SueAnn.

"Right." He rubbed his hands together. "What can I get you? Got a craving for a milkshake or a root beer float? They seem to be popular tonight."

"Sounds good, but I was thinking of something a bit more substantial to go. I haven't eaten dinner yet."

"We've got the usual fare . . . hamburger, cheeseburger, chicken wings, tuna melt, garden salad. And then there's the daily specials." He inclined his head toward a blackboard on the far wall. "Today's Saturday, so the cook goes all out. We've got Irish stew, beef stew, kidney stew, shepherd's pie, chicken pot pie and sausage and peppers. He makes it all fresh, too."

My mouth watered at the thought of chicken pot pie, but if it were made fresh it would probably take a while, and I didn't want to leave the cats alone in the car for too long. Right now they were both sleeping, but I was pretty sure it wouldn't be long before they woke up. "It all sounds yummy, but I think I'll have just a burger tonight," I said. "Medium rare, and can you give me sweet potato fries instead of regular fries?" I rubbed my hands together in anticipation. "And extra coleslaw?"

"No problem." He scribbled the order down on a pad. "So, did Antoine uncover any valuable treasures at your event? I remember once on one of his shows he appraised a coin that some guy's grandfather left him at ten thousand dollars."

"Nothing that valuable today, I'm afraid, although several folks who left items will have a nice surprise waiting for them."

"Oh, yeah? How did Eunice make out? She saw SueAnn at the QuickCheck and she told her all about the jewel box and how some woman offered her a bunch of money for it. She was hoping it might really be worth something."

Hm, apparently Eunice had told quite a few people about her experience. "Well, it turned out to only be worth a nominal sum," I said. "I don't suppose SueAnn knows just when Eunice is coming back? I have her jewel box, and I'd like to know when I might be able to return it to her." *Hopefully in one piece.*

"Ah, you got stuck looking after it, huh? Well, I dunno when she's expected to come back, but I'll ask the wife and tell her to give you a call."

"Thanks." A slight movement in the shadows behind Mikey caught my eye and the next moment a dark-haired woman, wearing a black dress and apron, emerged from the shadows. She started to walk quickly past, but Mikey saw her and waved the paper in the air. "Hey, Jill," he called out, "can you take this back to Arnie? It's a to-go order."

The woman hesitated, then nodded. "Sure," she said in a husky voice. She kept her face averted away from me as she plucked the paper from Mikey's hand and walked swiftly back toward the kitchen.

I frowned after her retreating form. Something about her seemed oddly familiar, but for the life of me I couldn't put my finger on it. I glanced over at Mikey and said, "Gee, she's friendly."

Mikey laughed. "Jillian? Yeah, she's not too social. She's new, just started last week." He shook his head. "She's a pretty hard worker. Why, she even came in early the other day and rearranged the entire storeroom downstairs. Gus was pissed at first, but when he saw what a nice job she did he changed his tune. She's less social than usual today 'cause she's got a bad cold. She wasn't even gonna come in, but when I told her we were down two people and if she didn't come in there was a good chance she might get canned, she got her buns in here. Between you and me, I think she needs the money." He leaned in closer and said in a stage whisper, "Boyfriend troubles."

"Ah. A bad breakup?"

"I don't think they're broken up. They just argue a lot. I heard her on the phone with him yesterday, and the conversation wasn't about hearts and flowers. He musta been on her case about something that was misplaced, because she said something like, 'I tore everything apart and I couldn't find it.' She didn't look very happy, I can tell you that." Mikey fiddled with the towel slung over one shoulder. "The burger will take about fifteen minutes. Sure you don't want something to drink while you're waiting?"

My throat did feel a bit parched, so I nodded. "Got any ginger ale?"

"I think so."

Mikey went over to the small refrigerator, rummaged around a bit, then returned with a can of ginger ale and a frosted mug. He filled the mug and pushed it in front of me. I took a sip, then set the mug down and glanced around the diner. "So, is Gus around? I thought he was working tonight."

"He is but he had to go out. He said he had an appointment that he couldn't break." Mikey frowned and glanced at his watch. "Come to think of it, that was over two hours ago. I thought he'd be back by now."

I did some quick mental calculations. Two hours ago would make it right around six o'clock—the time I'd seen the man come out of the woods, right before I'd discovered Martin's body. I took another sip of ginger ale. "But he is coming back?"

"He'd better. I'm supposed to go home at ten. He's got closing duty tonight." He gave me an appraising look. "Did you want to see him?"

"Oh, I just wanted to let him know about his cat. That I took her home." I paused and then added, "I did hear him say something about Grimley Woods earlier today. Maybe that's where he went."

Mikey shrugged. "Maybe. Gus didn't say where this meeting was, or who it was with, and I don't ask. It's better that way." He glanced around, then leaned forward and said in a low tone, "Gus has been real touchy lately, about practically everything. I know he's been having health issues on top of all the money troubles here so I try to ask as few questions as possible. I figure if he wants me to know, he'll tell me."

I raised my mug in a salute. "That's a wise policy."

"You bet it is. I need this job. I can't run the risk of pissing Gus off so that he flies off the handle and fires me. That could happen. Gus is usually pretty calm, but believe it or not, the guy's got a temper, and it doesn't take much to set it off, trust me." He paused, then leaned closer to me. "This isn't for publication, but I heard Martin offer Gus ninety thousand dollars for this place."

My eyes widened. "Ninety thousand! Are you sure?"

Mikey nodded. "Yep. Gus really exploded. Wanted to know where Martin could possibly get that kind of money. Martin told him that he didn't have it yet, but it was coming and he could trust him. That's when Gus yelled at him to get out."

A crowd of college boys came in just then and Mikey wandered over to wait on them. I finished my drink, and a few minutes later a beefy man wearing a white cap and apron who I figured was the chef came out of the kitchen bearing a plastic bag. "Who ordered the burger?" he called out to Mikey. "I haven't got time to stand around here all night, you know. I got orders backed up in the kitchen."

"Okay, Arnie, okay. Keep your shorts on." Mikey stepped forward and the chef plopped the bag into his outstretched hand. "Where's Jill?" Mikey asked.

Arnie threw up his hands. "She took off. Said her cold was getting worse. We really have to speak to Gus. I know he's getting desperate, but he can't hire everyone who comes in with a sob story, at least not until business picks up around here. And we certainly don't need to hire chicks with attitude, no matter how pretty they rearrange the junk in the cellar."

Arnie turned on his heel and stomped back into the kitchen. Mikey handed me the plastic bag. "Sorry about that," he said. "Arnie can act a lot like Gordon Ramsey, sometimes. Honestly, from the way business has been lately, he's got some nerve complaining about being backed up in the kitchen."

I fished a twenty out of my wallet and slid it across the counter. "This should cover everything, with a nice tip left over."

"Hey, thanks, Shell. And I won't forget to ask SueAnn about Eunice."

I carried the bag out to my car. Princess Fuzzypants was stretched out on the backseat, fast asleep, but Purrday was sitting shotgun in the passenger seat. He eyed the plastic bag warily as I set it down on the floor. "You behave, and I'll make sure you get a piece of burger," I told the cat.

"Merow," said Purrday. As I started to set my tote bag down, Purrday's paw snaked out and the bag tumbled to the floor. Several articles spilled out. "Thanks a lot, Purrday," I said. As I bent to collect what had fallen out, Purrday reached down again with his paw and let out another meow. I saw what had captured the cat's attention. It was the faded article and maybe diamond I'd purloined from the jewel box. "Well, well," I said. I reached out to give Purrday a pat on the head. "Thanks, boy. I'd almost forgotten about these." I replaced them in the bag, started the car and headed for home. It was only a few minutes past eight. Gary would still be out with Olivia. I'd have some nice quiet time to eat my burger and do a little internet research.

Eleven

Kahlua greeted us as we walked in the kitchen door with a loud meow and a look that said, *Is some of that burger for me?* I set my dinner on the kitchen table, broke off a small piece of hamburger, and divided it among the three dishes, adding in some tuna for good measure. As the cats slurped contentedly from their bowls, I sat down at the table to enjoy my burger and do a little surfing on my tablet.

The first thing I did was remove the article and the maybe-diamond from my tote and set them on the table beside my tablet. I took a large bite of burger, chewed, and then typed in "how to tell if a stone is an actual diamond" and hit Enter. I clicked on a site entitled "Ways to authenticate a Diamond" and sat for a few minutes, reading. The site listed a few ways, the first of which was to place the stone on top of a printed piece of paper. If you could see any of the print, the stone was likely not a diamond. Gary had left the morning paper folded on the table. I reached out, pulled it in front of me, unfolded it and laid the stone on top of it.

I couldn't see a damn thing through it.

I tried each of the other tests. I breathed on it, and my breath didn't fog up the stone. I held it up to the light, and it reflected white light back. Finally I dug around in my purse and found an old mirror and I rubbed the stone against it. It left a deep scratch on the mirror's surface. I turned the diamond over in my hand. The stone was pretty large, and I wondered just how much it might be worth. I wasn't a gemologist by any means, but I did recall from when Patrick and I had shopped for my ring—which I'd thrown at him when I moved out—the four c's were important: color, cut, clarity, and carat weight.

"Chances are good," I said, holding the stone aloft, "you're the real deal. But we'll let a professional decide." I determined to ask my mother if she could recommend a good, reliable jeweler in the morning. Or, I could just show my mother the stone. If there was anything my mother was an expert on, other than antiques, it was jewels.

That settled, I turned my attention to the partial article. I typed in the date and the title and a few minutes later I was reading the entire excerpt as it had been printed from the *Emporium Gazette*:

Local Man Sentenced to Prison Term

Charles Finley, thirty-one, has been sentenced to twenty years in prison for his part in an attempted robbery. Finley was sentenced to ten years for aggravated fleeing or attempting to elude an officer, and ten years for carrying a concealed firearm, according to a release from the State Attorney's Office. He will serve both sentences concurrently.

Finley approached the victim after she parked her vehicle in her apartment complex. He pointed a gun at her while he took her keys and purse. Fortunately a police cruiser was passing and the suspect fled the scene, only to be caught a few hours later. Finley has been arrested before, mostly on charges of petty theft. He was also a suspect in a jewel robbery a few weeks ago, but was cleared when his alibi checked out.

Finley, who was represented by Doris Sharp of the Wake County Public Defender's Office, declined to comment at his arraignment. His term will begin on Monday. Ms. Sharp also declined to comment.

I leaned back in my chair and closed my eyes. Interesting. What was an article about Charles Finley, a petty thief, doing with what might be a valuable diamond in a secret compartment in a jewel box? The items, I was certain, held some significance for someone, but I doubted they had for Mrs. Johansen. As a matter of fact, I was willing to bet that Mrs. Johansen had no idea those items were in that jewel chest. So if she hadn't put them there, who had?

My thoughts wandered back to the couple I'd encountered. "Don't tell me Granny was a jewel thief," I muttered. "Or maybe someone gave Granny an expensive present." I made a notation on my calendar to ask Eunice more about Mrs. Johansen and the estate sale when I returned her hopefully-repaired and intact jewel chest. I tapped my pen against my chin as another thought occurred to me. The article said that Finley had been a suspect in a jewel robbery. Could it have been the Van Nuys heist? And if so, how did the diamond figure into it? Was it one of the stolen stones? I set down the pen and typed in "Charles Finley—Images" and hit Enter. A few seconds later I was looking at Finley's mug shot. I studied it for a few minutes. He looked just like an ordinary guy you'd meet out on the street—dark hair, dark eyes, thin lips, strong jaw. There was nothing particularly arresting about him, nothing that stood out, and yet the longer I stared at his photo, something niggled at the back of my brain.

I reviewed the timeline in my head. The Van Nuys robbery had occurred on September 9, 2013. Martin had sold the diner to Gus in September of 2013. I didn't know the exact date, but I was betting it was within a few days or a week of the robbery. Coincidence? I recalled the news clipping that had been in the secret compartment along with the stone, the one about Charles Finley being arrested. Did Finley have some connection to Pete Martin?

I typed in "Charles Finley—Van Nuys Robbery," and a few minutes later another article from the *Emporium Gazette* popped up:

Suspect Arrested in Diamond Heist

On Thursday, September 11, a warrant was issued for the arrest of Charles Finley, 31, of Medina in connection with the robbery of the Van Nuys Jewelry Store, 311 Boulevard, Fox Hollow. Unset stones valued at several million dollars that had been commissioned by a local socialite were taken. When questioned, Finley denied having anything to do with stealing the jewels. Finley was also arrested last year on suspicion of robbery of another jewelry store in Raleigh.

As the charges could not be substantiated, the suspect was released. The items have not been recovered. Finley's lawyer, Brad Poltz of Fairfield County, declined to comment on the rumor that an anonymous tip linked Finley to the crime.

The byline on the article was Nicholas Barlow. That name seemed vaguely familiar to me, but I couldn't place why. I plugged his name into the search engine, and links to several pages of information appeared. Barlow apparently was a well-respected reporter who'd worked for a few newspapers. I opened the Wikipedia article on him. The accompanying photo, taken some years ago, showed a good-looking man in his early fifties, with light-colored hair and eyes that crinkled up at the sides. I looked at Barlow's date of birth and determined that he'd be in his mid-sixties now. I scanned the article quickly. Barlow's specialty had been crime, and he'd won numerous awards for his work. The *Emporium Gazette* was his last employer; according to the article, Barlow had retired five years ago. I glanced at the clock. I figured that Rita was probably home by now, so I grabbed my phone and punched in her number. She answered on the second ring. "Hey, Shell. That sure was a great event, wasn't it?"

"It was very successful," I said. "You seemed to be having a good time with Mr. Antoine."

"I know." Rita let out a long sigh. "He's a charmer, and so knowledgeable about antiques. He said that I could bring Wes's stamp collection over to his hotel tomorrow. He'd give it a look before he headed back."

"Uh-oh. And how does Wesley feel about that?"

Rita laughed. "Oh, he's going with me. Between you and me, it's nice to know that my husband can still get jealous."

"I bet," I said. "I heard there was a bit of excitement in Sweet Perks this morning?"

"Excitement? Oh, you must mean that little blowup between Gus and that customer." Rita let out an aggravated sigh. "To be honest, I'd always heard that Gus had a temper, but I never saw him in action. And I hope I never do again," she added.

"I've heard the same. About the other man—you'd never seen him before?"

"No, and quite frankly I hope I never see him again either. Fox Hollow doesn't need troublemakers. It's bad enough the teen population is going off the rails lately."

"I know it's getting late, but there's something I wanted to ask you. By any chance do you recall anything about the Van Nuys robbery?"

Rita let out a low whistle. "Wow, that's a blast from the past. What on earth ever made you think about that?"

"Oh, I heard someone talking about it at the event today," I said. "It sort of piqued my curiosity."

"Knowing you, I can see where it would," Rita said and chuckled. "It was quite the mystery—still is."

"I was reading about it online. Some articles by a Nicholas Barlow."

"Oh, yeah, Nick. He was a nice guy, and a real good reporter. We catered his retirement luncheon at the paper. I remember him saying that his biggest regret was never solving that robbery. He always thought there was something fishy about it." She paused and then added, "He lives over in Chesterfield. You should call him, stop by. I bet he'd love to talk about it."

I chatted with Rita a few minutes more, then hung up and did a quick search for Nicholas Barlow in Chesterfield. Fortunately his number wasn't unlisted. I dialed it, and after about five rings a gravelly voice answered. "Hello? If you're selling something, I'm not buying."

"Mr. Barlow? My name is Shell McMillan. If you've got some time, I'd really like to talk to you about the Van Nuys robbery."

Dead silence, and then: "Shell McMillan? Who are you? A reporter?"

"No, I'm not a reporter. I own Urban Tails Pet Shop over in Fox Hollow."

"Ah, good old Fox Hollow." Another few seconds of silence and then, "So what's a pet shop owner's interest in that cold case?"

"I happen to know that the FBI has gotten a lead on an old case that involves a robbery in Fox Hollow. I think it might be the Van Nuys one."

"The FBI!" I could hear the change in Barlow's tone. Now he definitely sounded interested instead of bored. "Are you sure about that?"

"I'm sure the FBI is here investigating a cold case. Whether or not it's the Van Nuys robbery I can't say for certain, but I think there's an excellent chance it is."

"O-kay. So why call me?"

"Correct me if I'm wrong, but the Van Nuys robbery was your baby, wasn't it? I've just spent over an hour reading all your articles online."

He chuckled. "Yes, I put in quite a bit of work on that case. Never could get anything definitive, though. And I sure as hell couldn't get the FBI's attention on it."

"Well, something has changed their minds," I said. "You might know something that would help in their investigation. I imagine you kept copious notes?"

"Copious doesn't begin to describe 'em," said Barlow. "You still haven't told me what your interest in all this is?"

"I'd very much like to do that, but not over the phone. Would you have some free time tomorrow?"

"Honey, I'm retired. All I've got is free time. You want to come see me, be my guest."

I made an appointment with him for ten thirty tomorrow morning. I'd just put down my cell phone when the door opened and Gary came in. "Hey," he said. He shrugged out of his jacket and hung it on the peg by the door. "How was your evening?"

"Very eventful," I said. "Purrday and I found another dead body."

Gary had been about to toss his keys onto the island. They clattered to the floor as his jaw dropped. *"What!"*

I rose and motioned for him to sit down. "I'll get you a cup of coffee and fill you in."

I scooped up the keys, tossed them on the island, then went to the counter and poured coffee into a large mug. I poured another mug for myself and then returned to the table, where I proceeded to tell Gary all about the night's events. When I finished, he ran his finger along the rim of his mug. "It certainly is puzzling," he remarked. "I agree with you that Gus doesn't seem to be the murdering type, still . . ."

"I know. There are a lot of loose ends. I'm hoping that maybe Nick Barlow can clarify some things. Want to come with me tomorrow? We don't open till twelve, and even if we're delayed, Sundays are slow. Robbie can handle it."

He ran his hand along the back of his neck. "You know I'd love to, Shell, but maybe you'd be better off taking Leila. After all, she's a reporter and will probably know the best way to get information out of Barlow. Besides which, if you're right and Jeremy Jackson is nosing around after that story, I'm sure she'd welcome the opportunity to scoop him."

I set my mug down. "You're right. I'll call her now."

I pulled out my cell phone and dialed Leila's number. The call went to voicemail. I left a message that I might have information about what Jeremy Jackson might be up to and asked her to call me.

Gary got up, poured himself more coffee. "Are you serious about asking your mother about that diamond?"

"I don't want to, but I need to find a reputable jeweler, someone I could trust. I'm sure Mother knows many."

"Sue might too. She deals with jewelry at the shop, doesn't she?"

"That's true. I'll stop by the shop tomorrow after I get back from Barlow's."

Gary cupped his chin in his hand. "What if that turns out to be a real diamond? What if it turns out to be part of the Van Nuys robbery?"

"Good question." I let out a sigh. "I suppose what I should do is tell Josh, but I hate to do that unless I have concrete proof." I shot Gary a thin smile. "I just don't feel like hearing a lecture."

"Josh lecture you? I can't imagine," Gary said with a chuckle. He glanced at the clock on the wall. "Maybe we'd better get some sleep. You've got a full day tomorrow. What time are you dropping the box off at Laverty's?"

"Oh, the box," I cried. "I completely forgot about it. It's in the trunk of my car." I rose from my seat. "I'd better get it. With all that's been going on, I don't feel comfortable leaving it there."

Gary frowned. "I'm not so sure I'm comfortable with it in the house, either. Maybe I'd better keep it in my room tonight. I've got a baseball bat tucked under my bed."

I picked up my keys and started for the door. As I passed the kitchen window, I glanced out, and stopped dead still. I could see the driveway from here, and my car. There was a dark figure bending over the trunk!

Twelve

"Someone's trying to break into my car," I shouted. Without waiting for Gary to answer, I jerked open the door and raced outside. My car was parked at the end of the long driveway and I could see the intruder more clearly now. He—or she—seemed to be medium height, with an oddly shapeless build. The figure shifted to the left and I realized the person was wearing a long coat that hid their figure. The head lifted and I bit back a cry. The person was wearing a stocking cap pulled down low and a scarf wrapped around their lower jaw, making any sort of identification near to impossible. I couldn't tell if the intruder were young or old, male or female, if my life depended on it.

"Hey," I shouted. "Just what do you think you're doing?"

The figure straightened and barreled right at me, hitting me square in the side and sending me sprawling across the grass. They vanished into the thick foliage at the back of my house just as Gary raced up to me. He knelt down, slipped an arm around my shoulders. "Hey, are you all right?"

I nodded. "Just had the wind knocked out of me is all." I pointed toward the rear of the house. "Whoever it was went thataway. I'm sure they're long gone by now."

Gary helped me to my feet and then we went over to look at my car. The trunk and the trunk lock appeared to be undamaged. "At least you stopped him before he could break into your car," said Gary.

"Whoever it was came well-disguised." I described what I'd seen. "It had to be someone who knew I had that box in my trunk."

"Who would have known that? They would have had to have seen you put it there, which I imagine would narrow the field considerably. Someone at the event who saw you put it in the trunk?"

"Could be. My money would be on that couple who wanted it for dear old Granny. One of 'em could have followed me."

Gary opened the trunk and pulled out the box. He opened the flaps and peered inside. "Who'd have ever thought something like this could cause so much trouble." He closed the box and lifted it up. "Maybe we'd better notify the police."

"And tell them what? That my car was almost broken into?" I frowned. "If I did that, then I'd have to tell the whole story about the chest and I don't want to do that, at least not yet."

Gary rolled his eyes. "No, by all means wait until whoever's after it hits you over the head, or worse."

I bit down on my lower lip. "Let's see what Leila and I can find out from Barlow tomorrow. Maybe he'll be able to shed some light on all this. After I speak with him, regardless of what I find out, I promise I'll tell Josh."

Gary shot me a look that plainly said he didn't believe me, but he didn't argue. We carried the jewel chest into the house and Gary took it right upstairs to his room. I wasn't comfortable with it in the house either, but I knew that Gary would keep an eye on it. I checked my phone and saw that Leila had called. She left a message, saying she'd be home and to call her back, and she definitely sounded excited. I called her number and she answered on the second ring. "What do you know about Jeremy Jackson?"

"First off, what I'm going to tell you is mostly supposition. Secondly, you have to promise not to breathe a word of it, not yet. It's definitely not for publication—at least not yet."

"Now you've really got my attention," Leila said.

"Do you promise?"

Leila exhaled a breath. "Yeah, sure. Spill."

Once again, I related the evening's events. When I'd finished, Leila let out a low whistle. "Wow, Shell. You know, you might be onto something. And if you're right, well, that would certainly be one heckuva story." She paused. "And when this is all over, I get the exclusive, right?"

"Right. So you'll come with me to see Barlow tomorrow?"

"Are you kidding? I wouldn't miss it. This is the stuff Pulitzers are made of." Her voice took on a wistful note. "And what I wouldn't give to scoop that idiot Jeremy Jackson."

I told Leila I'd pick her up at ten tomorrow and disconnected. As I put the coffee mugs in the sink, Purrday hopped up on the counter. He butted his head against my arm and looked at me with his one good eye.

"I know, I know," I said to the cat. "I have every intention of telling Josh, but like I told Gary, I'd like to have something more concrete to offer him than just my theories. I'll make a point to talk to him tomorrow, I promise."

Purrday's answer to that was to hop off the counter and pad over to the back door. He looked expectantly at it, his whiskers twitching. A second later I heard a knock. I glanced at the cat. "How do you do that?" I demanded. "That's spooky."

75

"Shell?"

I froze. It was Josh. I looked at Purrday, but the cat was busy washing his tail. I shook my head, went to the back door and opened it. "Hey," I said. "I didn't expect to see you again tonight."

"To be honest, I wasn't expecting to come here," he said. "But Mrs. Potter down the block called the station and reported seeing a dark figure running away from your property. I figured since it was you I'd check it out."

I swallowed. "Mrs. Potter saw him?"

Josh's eyebrow lifted. "Then there was someone here? Why didn't you call me right away?"

"There was really nothing to report," I said. "The person tried to break into the trunk of my car, but I saw him from the window and ran outside. I guess I scared whoever it was away."

Josh frowned. "This isn't the first time something like this has happened. We've had a lot of reports of teenage vandalism lately. Cars seem to be their favorite thing to break into."

"This wasn't a teenager. At least, I don't think it was."

"Did you get a good look at the perp?" Josh asked. He pulled out his notebook and pen, flipped to an empty page.

"For what it's worth, he or she had on a long coat that disguised their figure, and a stocking over their face."

"Hm. You're right, it doesn't sound like a teen." Josh's pen hovered over the page. "Just what did you have in your trunk that someone would want to steal?"

"Meow!"

We both looked over at the counter. Purrday tipped his head to one side and his whiskers twitched. Then he laid his head back on his paws and closed his eye.

"I think he's accusing me of being a bad hostess," I said. "Would you like some tea? There's some French vanilla coffee left. Oh, and I think there might be some hot chocolate in the pantry."

"Hot chocolate would be great." A pause. "With marshmallows?"

"Of course."

He moved across the room, eased himself into one of the kitchen chairs. I put milk in the microwave to warm and got two mugs and a bag of marshmallows out of the cupboard. Josh rubbed at his eyes lightly with his fingers, then dropped his hand to the table. "You haven't answered my question. What did you have in your trunk that someone would go to such lengths to try and steal?"

Darn! Of course Josh wouldn't forget. "In order to answer that, I'd have to tell you everything that happened today. It could take awhile."

He tapped his pen against his notebook. "I've got time, unless I'm keeping you from something important."

"Does beauty sleep count?"

His eyes crinkled. "You don't have to worry about that. So, begin at the beginning. And don't leave anything out."

I started right from the beginning, from the moment I helped get the mannequin of Cher into Leila's Jeep, about Pete Martin and the strange couple's interest in Eunice's jewel box, my visit to Good Eats and subsequent run-in with the masked intruder. I skipped over the part about finding the diamond and article in the box, and about Leila and I deciding to visit Barlow tomorrow. While I was talking, the timer dinged on the microwave. I finished my story as I poured milk over cocoa in the mugs, and added a liberal amount of marshmallows to each cup. I set a mug in front of Josh, then slid into the seat across from him. He picked up the mug, took a sip.

"Um, that's good," he said.

I looked at him. "That's all you have to say? The hot chocolate is good?"

"No." He put the mug down and traced a finger around the inside of the handle. "Let's talk about your discovering Martin's body. You didn't see anyone else around the area?"

I shook my head. "No one, other than that tall man running out of the woods. And before you ask me again, yes, I'm certain that I couldn't identify him. I was too far away." I paused. "Jeremy Jackson seemed to have gotten a good look, though. He described Gus Morton almost to a tee. You know, it was almost as if he were trying to make Gus appear guilty."

Josh's brow quirked. "Why would Jackson do that? He doesn't know Gus Morton from Adam."

I sighed. "True. Sorry. I guess I'm reading too much into it. It's just that Jackson seems to be such an insufferable know-it-all, and well, the idea of Gus actually killing someone seems ludicrous to me."

"Maybe not so ludicrous," said Josh. "According to several people, Gus had a volatile relationship with Martin. They were heard arguing several times, and Gus threatened to shoot Martin more than once."

"Shoot him? Who told you that?" At his look, I threw up both hands. "I know, I know. Sorry."

He took another sip of hot cocoa, put down his cup. "Now, you said that Martin was at the event earlier, correct? Around what time was that?"

"I'd say around three. He offered four hundred dollars for that jewel box. He said that his mother had always wanted one. Later on Marianne told me his mother's been dead for years."

"So Martin wanted to buy this box, and so did that other couple?"

I hesitated. "Yes. And this is the part I think might tie in with the cold case they've got you investigating." At his look I added, "I know how to use Google. It didn't take much to figure out it's the Van Nuys robbery."

Josh raised his hand to rub at his forehead. "You think this jewel box has some connection to the diamond robbery?"

"Not the box per se. What was inside it. I told you the cats had a little accident with it, but I didn't tell you everything."

Josh blew out a breath. "Why does that not surprise me?"

I reached for my tote and whipped out the stone, laid it in front of him. His eyes popped when he saw the diamond. He picked it up, turned it over in his palm. "Wow," he said at last. "It certainly looks real."

Josh placed the diamond in the center of the kitchen table. Little pinpoints of white light reflected off of it as it sat there, winking at us. He cleared his throat. "What made you think this might have been one of the stones from that robbery?"

"Well, for one thing, not many people leave two-carat-plus stones lying around in secret compartments in jewel boxes. And for another"—I whipped out the clipping and laid it in front of him—"this was with it."

Josh was silent as he scanned the article. Then he put the paper back down on the table and picked up his mug again. I stared at him. "You don't seem very excited by all this," I said.

"There's nothing to get excited about . . . yet," he said. "You've shown me something that quite possibly might be a diamond, and a news clipping."

I bit back a groan. This was why I'd been hesitant to tell him about it in the first place. "True," I admitted, "but the fact that someone tried to break into my car after the box makes me think there just might be something to my theory."

"I'm not discounting that," Josh said. "But what we've got here is circumstantial at best. You don't know that whoever owned this jewel box knew Finley was involved in that robbery. Maybe they wanted the clipping for what's on the other side."

I grabbed the clipping, turned it over, and gestured with my hand. "It's an advertisement for cabinet refurbishing. Why would anyone want to put that in a secret compartment along with a diamond?"

Josh shrugged. "Who knows? Anyway, you said Eunice bought the box at an estate sale? Do you remember the name?"

I closed my eyes. "Johnson—no, wait. Johansen. It was Johansen. And they knew that, the man and woman. I remember distinctly they said that they knew the woman as Mrs. Johansen. They didn't know her first name."

"Have you got an envelope?"

I went into the living room, retrieved an envelope from the desk, and went back to the kitchen. Josh had just finished his hot chocolate and put his mug in the sink. He reached for the envelope and dropped the diamond into it. After a minute he folded the clipping and put that in the envelope too.

"I'll have to show this to Special Agent Reamer—he's the FBI liaison. He can have the diamond checked out, ascertain if it is part of that particular shipment or not. He can also dig into this, find out if there's any correlation between this Charles Finley and Johansen, if there's any reason why this clipping would have been in that box." His tone got a bit softer as he added, "You know, Shell, it's possible that Mrs. Johansen got the box the same way Eunice did—at some sort of garage or estate sale. She might never have known about the contents of that compartment. Heck, you wouldn't have known either if the cats hadn't knocked it off the cabinet."

I had to admit he had a point and a good one. I gave myself a mental slap across the forehead for not even thinking of that. "That would probably be a pretty difficult task in that case, huh? Tracing the ownership of this jewel box."

"Maybe, maybe not. That's why I'm getting Reamer involved. The FBI has resources we don't have."

"They could check into a possible connection between Martin and that jewel heist, too. Think about it. The robbery occurred in September ten years ago. Martin left Fox Hollow rather hastily around the same time. Granted, he was trying to avoid being taken for all he had in a messy divorce, but my gut tells me there might be a bit more to it than just that."

Josh's lips twitched. "Your gut, huh? Well, I know from experience how accurate that gut of yours can be, but this time I think it's a little off."

"Meaning you don't think it's possible Martin was somehow involved," I shot back. "You'd rather believe Gus Morton killed him in an angry rage."

"Well, when you look at means, motive and opportunity . . ." Josh started to tick off on his fingers. "Gus had motive—several people heard him arguing with Martin more than once."

"Oh, for goodness sakes." I had to restrain myself from stamping my foot. "That's not a good enough motive. If people killed everyone they argued with more than half of Fox Hollow would be in jail."

To my surprise Josh actually laughed. "True, but from what I understand, the arguments between Gus and Martin were pretty heated." He paused. "And then there's means. Gus does own a gun."

"I've also heard that he's a terrible shot, not like . . ." I paused. I'd been about to say *not like his wife*, but at this point, would it do any good to point fingers at another member of the Morton family? "Not like he's a crack shot," I finished lamely.

"He wouldn't have to be a very good shot to have killed Martin," said Josh. "The coroner's report isn't in yet, but it appears the shot was fired at close range. You'd have to be pretty inept to miss your target." He wiggled another finger in the air. "Lastly, there's opportunity. You saw someone you thought resembled Gus coming out of the woods shortly before you found the body, and Jackson's description of the man who almost ran into him fits Gus."

It certainly does, I thought, and squared my shoulders. "All that is circumstantial, you know. Yet to be proven."

"You're right, which means it's time I started to do my job." He reached out and touched the tip of my nose. "Listen, I've probably told you more than I should, but you've been a big help—really."

"Why, Detective Bloodgood!" I batted my lashes at him. "Was that actual praise I heard from you?"

"Yes, but don't get too used to it. You know how I feel about you getting involved in police business."

I walked him to the door. "Please promise me you'll keep an open mind when it comes to Martin's murder."

"Maybe we should both keep an open mind." He reached out and pulled me to him. "One day soon we're going to get together and have a regular date with no talk of diamond thieves, or murderers, or bodies. I promise."

"That sounds good. I'll hold you to it."

We kissed good night and Josh left. I stood for a minute, my back against the door, thinking. Pete Martin had come back to Fox Hollow with some sort of agenda, I was certain of it. No doubt that was what had gotten him killed. But if said agenda wasn't over the diamonds, then what could it be?

Thirteen

I forgot to set my alarm, so it was after eight thirty when Purrday's insistent nudging finally coaxed me awake. I eased one eye open, saw the time, and threw the covers back, causing the cat to slide all the way down to the foot of the bed. "You should have woken me earlier," I admonished the cat as I pulled on my robe.

Purrday's response was to grunt and roll over on his side.

Fifteen minutes later, showered and dressed in jeans and a coral-striped long-sleeve pullover, I walked into the kitchen, where the enticing aroma of bacon and coffee greeted me. Gary was just pulling the frying pan off of the stove, and he looked over his shoulder at me. "Good morning, sleepyhead," he said. "I was going to give you another five minutes and then start banging pots around."

"Very funny." I went to the refrigerator, found the carton of orange juice and pulled it out. I poured myself a glass and carried it over to the kitchen table. I took a sip, eased myself into a chair and said, "I'm dropping the box off at Ed's and then picking Leila up at ten. As long as traffic is light, we should make it to Barlow's by ten thirty."

"Well, it is Sunday. One thing in your favor." Gary set a delicious-looking omelet on a plate along with three strips of crisp bacon and two slices of buttered rye toast. He walked over and set the plate in front of me. "Coffee?" he asked.

"Please." I picked up my fork, stabbed a piece of omelet, put it in my mouth. The Gouda cheese was melty and delicious. "Um—so good."

"Thank you." He set a steaming mug in front of me and pushed the container of milk forward. "So, what did Josh want last night?"

I paused, egg halfway to my lips. "How did you know Josh was here? You were upstairs already."

"Yes, but my bedroom window faces the street. I saw Josh park his car and walk around to the kitchen."

I took a sip of coffee. "I'm surprised you didn't come down and eavesdrop. Or at the very least, make up an excuse to join us."

"Really, Shell. Give me some credit for manners. I figured the two of you probably wanted alone time." He grinned. "So, what did he want?"

"Mrs. Potter reported seeing a shadowy figure prowling around the property. He decided since it was me he'd check it out personally."

"Ah, good old Mrs. Potter. Our favorite neighborhood gossip." Gary raised his mug. "What did you tell him?"

"The truth," I said. "I ended up telling him everything—about the diamond, the clipping, the whole nine yards."

"Good. And what did he have to say?"

"Not much. He said it was all circumstantial, but he had to tell the FBI agent liaison the whole story. He took the clipping and the diamond." I sighed. "One good thing, at least with the diamond out of the way, I don't have to get my mother involved."

Gary gave an approving nod. "I think it was a smart move on your part to give the diamond up, and the clipping too." His gaze bored into mine. "But you didn't tell Josh everything, did you." The last was more a statement than a question.

"You know me too well," I responded. "I didn't tell him about Barlow, or that Leila and I were going to see him. He'd have just told me to stay out of it."

Gary clucked his tongue. "Tut-tut. I would think Joshy would know you better by now." He took another sip of his coffee. "What time do you have to be at Laverty's?"

"I told him between nine thirty and ten. I hope Ed can fix that jewel box for Eunice," I said. "If he can't, I'm going to have to find someone who can. Where is the box, anyway?"

Gary got up and walked over to the island. He reached into one of the cabinets beneath, pulled out the box and set it on the island. I got up and removed the chest from the box. I frowned. "Is it my imagination or does it look even worse today?" I asked.

"If you ask me, it always looked pretty bad," Gary said. He leaned forward to peer at it more closely. "That piece of wood peeled off somehow. Ed could always remove it and sand over the rough spot. I doubt Eunice would notice, and it wouldn't spoil the rest of the box." His fingers trailed across the wood. "That one hinge looks like it's loose—hello, what's this?"

I watched as Gary stuck his pinky in the small slat between the loose piece of wood and the hinge. A second later he'd wriggled a small piece of yellowed paper free. "Looks like this was jammed in there," he said, and handed it to me. The paper was creased in the middle and the edges were ragged, as if they'd been ripped off. Printed crudely on the paper were the words:

lar
wer

I frowned at it. "This is strange," I said.

"Very," Gary agreed. He peered over my shoulder and tapped at the note with his forefinger. "See how smooth the tear is? It looks as if this paper was deliberately torn in half."

I turned the paper over in my hand. "Maybe it was meant to be some sort of clue."

Gary shook his head. "A clue to what? It doesn't make much sense."

"Does anything connected with this jewel box make sense?" I slid the paper into my tunic pocket, finished my coffee, put the mug in the sink, then pulled on my jacket. "I've got to get going. I'll come by the pet shop after Leila and I see Barlow and fill you in."

"Okay," said Gary. He hefted the jewel box into his arms. "I'll put this in the car for you. And Shell . . . be careful."

I smiled at him. "Aren't I always."

He grimaced. "No comment."

• • •

I got to Ed Laverty's at exactly nine forty-five. He was a slender man with twinkling blue eyes and a shock of curly red-gold hair with a few strands of gray visible on his sideburns. His father had started the hardware store forty years ago and had wanted his only son to follow in his footsteps. Ed had demurred at first and gone off to get a college education, but after spending a few years pursuing accounting in the corporate world, made the decision to come on home and work in the family business. His father was retired now but still came in part-time three days a week to help out so that Ed could pursue his other profession, that of auto mechanic. Ed knew how to rebuild an engine from scratch and he liked doing small auto repairs on the side. Lately he'd added woodworking to his list of accomplishments because, as he put it, he liked to keep busy and his mother had always told him idle hands were the devil's workshop. If that were true, Ed was surely assured a place in heaven. His hands were always busy doing something.

"Hey, Ed. Let me show you the patient." I placed the box on the long table and lifted out the jewel chest. Ed looked at it for a long moment, then ran his hand along the wood. Finally he picked it up and examined it from all sides.

"It's a nice piece of craftsmanship," he said at last. He reached out and touched the loose piece of wood. "It's interesting, the way they made this drawer. Fits neatly against the grain—unless you were looking specifically for it, you'd never even know it was there." He wriggled the end. "There was probably a spring here, some sort of mechanism that opened up the drawer. Did you find a small spring lying around?"

"I didn't see one. Then again, I wasn't looking. I can ask Marianne if she found anything."

He waved his hand. "Doesn't matter. I'm pretty sure I have a few small ones in my tool box that'll do the trick." He paused. "I just assumed you want me to fix the box so that the secret compartment opens up again. You do, right?"

"If you can," I said. "If not, don't worry. Eunice never knew it was there so I suppose it doesn't matter."

"I'll fix it if I can," he answered. "I'm like you that way. I love a challenge." He turned the box over in his hands again, his eyes slitted in concentration, and then he nodded. "Yep, I think I can fix it, all right. How fast do you need this back?"

"I don't have a definite ETA for Eunice, but I would imagine before the end of the week."

He chewed at his lower lip. "I should probably have this done by Wednesday afternoon—sooner if no big jobs come in. I can give you a call when I'm finished, or do you just want me to stop by the shop and drop it off?"

"Better call," I said. He tucked the jewel chest under his arm and I walked him to the back door. "Are you sure I can't pay you?"

"Positive. My mother's convinced doing good deeds for others is what will get me into heaven."

I laughed. "Far be it from me to challenge your mother."

I hurried out to my car. If I didn't hit any lights or heavy traffic I'd make it to Leila's by ten. But I'd just gotten behind the steering wheel when my pocket started to vibrate. I whipped out my phone and saw a text from Leila:

Parker called. I have to cover an emergency town council meeting at eleven. Can you push Barlow off till this afternoon?

I texted her back, *I'll try*, then dialed Barlow's number. When he answered I said, "This is Shell McMillan, Mr. Barlow."

"McMillan, McMillan, oh, yes. The little lady inquiring about Van Nuys."

"Yes. I was wondering if we could meet this afternoon instead? Maybe around two? Something, ah, unexpected came up with my friend."

"No problem," he replied. "Like I said, I'm retired. I've got all the time in the world. It works out better anyway. Gives me more time to get these notes in order. Two o'clock will be fine. Just don't expect coffee and cake," he added with a chuckle.

I hung up, texted Leila the new time, and then debated what I might do next. I reached into my tunic pocket and pulled out the scrap of paper with the snippets of words on it. I stared at it, not knowing where to begin, when my phone vibrated again. I whipped it out and groaned when I saw my mother's name on the screen. My finger hovered over the decline icon, but in the end I swiped the green icon. "Good morning, Mother."

"Good morning, Crishell," my mother said. "I just thought you'd be interested to know that event pulled in nearly two thousand dollars for the shelter."

"Oh, Mother, that's fantastic," I said.

"Yes, it is. What's more, Gerard Antoine offered to do it again, maybe closer to the holidays if we wanted. I'm going to discuss that with Marianne over lunch tomorrow. Would you be interested in joining us?"

"Hm, I'm scheduled to work ten to two tomorrow. I'll see if either Gary or Robbie can cover. If so, yes, I'd love to join you."

"Perfect. I thought we'd go to Cuisine Raffinee in Hartford."

"Cuisine Raffinee?" I knew the place. It was an upscale French eatery. Prices were absent from the right side of the menu, never a good sign for someone on a budget. "Are you sure that isn't a bit . . . much?"

"Of course not, dear. Marianne loves French food. I asked her yesterday. Besides, it's my treat, of course," my mother said. "It's nice of you to be concerned about my finances, but it's tax-deductible, Crishell. I wanted Sue to come too, but she's got some sort of shipment coming in that she has to be here for." She let out a sigh. "Honestly, sometimes I think that she resents some of my ideas. She doesn't realize what a benefit having a high profile can do for a business. The other day, for example, I was trying to explain the difference between Art Deco and Art Nouveau, but she seemed more interested in doing some silly little word game on her tablet."

My eyes popped. Of course. Sue loved all sorts of word puzzles and games. "I'll let you know if I can come later, Mother. I'm in a bit of a hurry now. Goodbye."

I disconnected and called Sue. When she answered she said, "I suppose your mother told you the good news about the fundraiser."

"Yes, she did. Two thousand dollars is wonderful."

"Yes, and supposedly Clarissa made a few contacts who have high-ticket items they plan to bring into Secondhand Sue's to sell." Sue paused and then said, "Is your mother always so . . . high-energy?"

"You have no idea. She's calmed down a lot since coming to Fox Hollow."

"Swell," Sue muttered. "She wanted me to go along with her when she takes Marianne out tomorrow, but I have a shipment of Spode Indian Tree coming in that I want to see to personally. Not that Iris can't handle it, but . . ."

"But you'd like a break from my mother, even if it means giving up a lunch at Cuisine Raffinee?"

"Exactly," Sue said. "I'm glad you understand."

"Believe me, I do. Listen, Sue, you do a lot of those word puzzles. What site would you recommend? I need to look up something, but I don't have the complete word."

"You have part of a word, you mean? Well, I've always found Word Hippo to be good for that."

"Thanks."

"Are you on the trail of another mystery?" Sue asked. "Don't worry, I won't tell my brother."

"To be honest, I'm not certain just what I'm on the trail of. When I figure it out, I'll let you know."

I hung up from Sue and debated where I could go. Gary would still be home. The store opened at twelve on Sunday, and he usually got there around eleven thirty. Robbie always came in early but he was working two to five today. I'd have plenty of time and privacy. I drove to the store, parked my car in the back, and let myself in the back door. I went over to the desk that served as my office area, seated myself and got my tablet out of my tote bag. A few minutes later I was on the Word Hippo site. I typed in: list of words ending in *lar*.

Six pages of words came up. I started to slowly scroll through them. Some were familiar: burglar, binocular. There were lots I'd never heard of: acetabular, acromioclavicular, acicular. I finished the a's and b's and started on the c's. I paused when I got to *cellar*. Seemed to me I'd heard something about a cellar recently. What was it? Oh, right. That was where Martin's ex-wife had caught him and his girlfriend getting cozy.

I started to click on page two when a black box popped up on my screen: Battery Low. I groaned. I'd left my charger at home. Now what? My face brightened as I remembered I'd brought a spare charger to the office for an emergency. After ten minutes of rummaging through the desk, however, I remembered that Robbie had borrowed it the other day. Apparently he'd forgotten to return it. I frowned. Well, I had no other choice. I'd have to go back home.

The house was deserted when I arrived. No sign of Gary anywhere. I set down my tote bag and dialed his cell. "Where are you?" I asked when he answered.

"Having coffee with Olivia at Sweet Perks. Where are you? I thought you and Leila were on your way to Barlow's?"

"We got a bit delayed," I said. "Listen, I'll talk to you later. When Robbie comes in, ask him what he did with the spare charger. It wasn't in the desk in the storeroom."

I hung up before Gary could answer. Well, now I had plenty of time. I started to go upstairs to get my charger from my office desk when the front doorbell rang. "Now what?" I muttered. I peered out the window but the street looked deserted. It was probably some kids selling subscriptions, figuring Sunday morning was a good time to catch people at home. I started back up the stairs but I'd only taken two steps when the bell rang again, more insistently this time. I turned with a groan and hurried downstairs. I opened the front door a crack and peered out.

A man stood on the front porch. He was tall, slightly over six feet, and dressed in a conservative dark blue suit with a white shirt and a blue striped tie. He had chiseled features, probing gray eyes that I thought were actually more silver, and dark curly hair with just a hint of salt and pepper at the temple. I had the feeling I'd seen him somewhere before, but I couldn't place him. He flashed me what I imagined was meant to be a smile. "Crishell McMillan?"

I frowned at the use of my given name and opened the door another half inch, making sure the safety chain was secure. "Actually I go by Shell," I said.

"Fine. Shell McMillan, right?" He reached into his jacket pocket and whipped out a leather case. He flipped it open, held it out.

"I'm Special Agent Trent Reamer. FBI. I believe we need to talk."

Fourteen

I removed the safety chain from the door and swung it wide. Trent Reamer stepped inside. I took a moment to study him and decided that he definitely fit the stereotypic mold of FBI man—he could have stepped right out of an episode of *Criminal Minds*, from the tip of his Brooks Brothers suit jacket to his unsmiling expression. I shut the door and gestured toward the living room. "Won't you have a seat?"

Reamer gave me a brief nod, then crossed the room and settled himself comfortably on the sofa. I hesitated, then walked over to the well-worn wing chair just off to the sofa's left and sat down. There were a few moments of awkward silence, broken as Reamer and I cleared our throats at the same time. "It's nice to meet you," I managed. "Can I offer you anything? Tea, coffee, a hot chocolate, perhaps?"

"Nothing, thanks." The FBI agent stretched his long legs out in front of him. "I'd like to talk to you about the diamond that you gave Detective Bloodgood. I have a few questions."

"You researched the diamond already? Wow, that's amazing." As the agent shot me a sharp look, I added quickly, "I only meant that you work pretty fast. I just gave Josh that diamond last night."

Reamer's lip quirked slightly. "We are supposed to work fast, Ms. McMillan. We're the FBI, after all."

I felt my cheeks start to flame. "Of course," I murmured. "So I guess it was a real diamond? One from the robbery?"

Reamer was spared answering because my doorbell jangled most insistently at that precise moment. I excused myself, got up and went to answer it. Josh stood on the threshold, and he wasn't smiling.

"Where is he?" Without waiting for an answer, Josh pushed past me and went straight into the living room. He walked over to stand in front of Reamer. "I thought you were going to wait for me to pay a call on Shell, ah, I mean Ms. McMillan," he said, not bothering to hide the trace of annoyance in his tone.

Reamer shrugged. "You mentioned you had a pile of paperwork to do. I thought it might save some time if I spoke with her alone."

As Josh continued to glare at the FBI agent, I cleared my throat. "Why don't I make us all some hot chocolate?" I suggested. Without waiting for either of them to answer, I turned on my heel and disappeared into the kitchen. I poured water and cocoa mix into three mugs, stirred them and put them in the microwave. I got out a tray and arranged a plate of tea biscuits on it. The timer dinged and I took out the mugs, squirted a dollop of whipped cream onto each, and then carefully carried it into the living room. I noticed that Josh was now seated next to the FBI agent on the couch, and they were deep in conversation as I entered. They both jumped up, but it was Josh who took the tray from me and set it down on the low coffee table. They waited for me to take my mug, and then they each grabbed one. I noticed that Josh and Trent also grabbed two of the tea biscuits as well. We sipped in silence for a few minutes, and then I set down my mug and looked straight at Trent Reamer.

"You said you had some questions about the diamond," I said.

"Yes, Ms. McMillan." Reamer set down his mug and wiped a crumb from the edge of his lip with his finger. "Detective Bloodgood here tells me you found it hidden inside a jewelry box? At some sort of fundraiser?"

"Yes, for the animal shelter," I responded. "The jewel box was left for appraisal by a patron who couldn't attend." I paused, took a deep breath and then continued, "My cat and another cat were playing, running around, and they knocked it off of the file cabinet. When it fell it jarred loose a secret compartment."

Reamer leaned forward. "I'm sorry. Did you say your cats?"

"My cat and the one I was cat-sitting," I said. "It's a long story. Anyway, the diamond was inside, along with a newspaper clipping. Josh—that is, Detective Bloodgood—had mentioned working with the FBI on a cold case that involved diamonds. When I saw the stone, and that clipping, well, I thought there might be a connection somehow."

Reamer picked up his drink, took a sip, and set the mug back on the coffee table. He fixed me with a penetrating stare. "I suppose congratulations are in order, Ms. McMillan. Your hunch was correct. That diamond was indeed part of the inventory stolen from Van Nuys Jewelers."

I let out a little gasp. "Oh my gosh! You're certain?"

He shot me a look that was somewhere between withering and condescending. I had the feeling that people didn't question what he said very often. "Yes, we are. We were very fortunate in that this particular shipment of diamonds had been previously marked by a laser with a symbol invisible to the naked eye. Not only did the diamond you found match one that was on record, but it also had the symbol etched on it. A definite match."

"Wow." I sat back hard, more than a little stunned, even though I'd half expected it.

"Diamonds are one of the hardest items to recover from thefts like these," the agent went on. "The way the stones are traded makes it very hard to pick out stolen ones. Believe me when I tell you, we lucked out with this diamond. We're usually not so fortunate. Those laser tags can be removed—whatever is cut onto a diamond can be taken off." He reached into his jacket pocket and removed a small notebook and a pen. He flipped the notebook open, then looked over at me. "Do you know the name of the person who brought in the box?"

"Certainly. Eunice Coulter."

"Could you spell that, please?"

I did, as he scribbled in the notebook. "And have you returned the jewel box to her?"

I shook my head. "Not yet. She's still out of town, and from what I understand, she's not expected back until more toward the end of the week."

His head jerked up. "So the box is still in your possession?"

"No. As I said, it was damaged when my cats knocked it over. I gave it to Ed Laverty. He owns the local hardware store, and he dabbles a bit in woodworking. He thought he'd be able to fix it."

"I see." More scribbling. "When did you give him the box?"

"Just a few hours ago." As the agent's brows drew together in a frown, I added, "Would you like to see it? I could call Ed."

He held up his hand. "Not necessary, Ms. McMillan. Right now I'm actually more interested in the estate sale the box was purchased at than the box itself."

"Oh. Well, I can tell you the name was Johansen." I leaned forward. "I'm sure Detective Bloodgood has told you about all the interest that has been generated in that particular box."

Reamer nodded, and once again I noticed that his lips seemed to quirk slightly. "Yes, he did."

"Eunice told one of our volunteers that a woman came up to her shortly after she'd purchased the box and offered her two hundred and fifty dollars for it. That same woman came to our shelter event with another man. I caught them red-handed trying to steal the box. Apparently they were brother and sister. The man said the box was sold by accident, it belonged to their grandmother and they offered a huge sum for it, which I turned down."

"You didn't believe them?"

"Heck no. I didn't believe Peter Martin's story either. He's a former Fox Hollow resident who recently came back to town. He was interested in obtaining that box as well, and offered quite a large sum for it." I paused to let out a breath. "Martin was murdered last night."

Reamer crossed his legs at the ankles. "Yes, I know. I also know it was you who discovered his body. Josh here tells me you've got a certain knack for that."

"It's more like being in the wrong place at the wrong time," I said. "Anyway, I have a feeling there might be a connection between Martin's murder and your cold case."

Reamer's expression remained bland. "And what leads you to think that?"

I leaned forward. "It's a pretty big coincidence, don't you think, that Martin should return to Fox Hollow after a ten-year absence right at the same time a jewel box containing one of the stolen stones just happens to turn up?"

Reamer didn't bat so much as an eyelash. "You're saying you think this was planned?"

"I'm saying I don't believe in coincidences, and that's a whopper."

"I see." Reamer laced his hands in front of him. "Well, one thing I can tell you, Ms McMillan, is that Mr. Martin had quite a few aliases during the time he was away from Fox Hollow."

"Quite a few?"

"Eight, to be exact." He riffled through his notebook, paused at a page. "His last one was Tommy Brancher. He drove a truck for a home supply store in Raleigh." He looked up at me. "However, the man has no criminal record to speak of under Peter Martin or any of the other names. Most likely he was just trying to ensure his ex-wife never got hold of him."

I flopped back in my seat and bit back a sigh. "That makes sense, I guess," I said. "Martin wasn't the only person interested in that jewel box. Someone tried to break into my car looking for it. It couldn't have been Martin. He was already dead." I exhaled a deep breath and went on, "I was at Gus Morton's diner last night. There was a waitress there, a new hire. She was very careful to keep her face away from mine, but I saw enough of her to think she very closely resembled the woman who'd tried to steal the box from the event. I also happened to mention to the bartender that the jewel box was in my care and I'm fairly certain she overheard me. She might have called her partner or it could even have been her who tried to jimmy my trunk. She left the diner early, supposedly sick. I got the feeling she was deliberately avoiding me, but I can't be absolutely certain."

He made a quick notation on his pad. "You wouldn't happen to know this woman's name, by any chance?"

"Mikey called her Jillian. He didn't mention her last name. Gus Morton hired her, I'm sure he could tell you more."

"Ah, yes. Mr. Morton."

A look passed between Josh and Reamer, a look that made me uneasy. "You can't seriously consider Gus," I said. "He certainly wouldn't benefit from the death of Pete Martin. He was going to pay Gus a hefty sum for the diner and Gus would get nothing, now."

"True. Unless, of course, Mr. Morton didn't want to sell the diner in the first place, and then Martin's death would be a welcome relief," said Reamer. "Plus, I understand there are a few witnesses who will swear that just that very afternoon, Gus said he was sick and tired of Martin's interference and he intended to put a stop to it."

I made an exasperated sound deep in my throat. "By killing him? That's rather drastic, don't you think? What about the other people interested in the jewel box, the man and the woman? With Martin out of the way, it would seem to me they'd have a clear field."

Josh held up his hand. "You don't know that there's any connection between Martin and those other two people."

"Just because we don't know of a connection doesn't mean there isn't one." I gave my head a shake. "All I'm saying is, maybe Gus shouldn't be the only person on your radar for this."

"We haven't said if Gus is a suspect or not," Josh returned.

"You don't have to. Thanks to Jeremy Jackson placing him at the scene, it would be ludicrous if you weren't considering him a suspect."

Reamer glanced sharply at Josh. "Jackson placed Gus Morton at the murder scene? You didn't tell me that."

"No? I was pretty certain it was in my report," Josh said stiffly.

"I didn't see any mention of that." Reamer stood up and turned to me. "I think we've taken up enough of your time this morning, Ms. McMillan," he said smoothly. He slid the notebook and pen back into his jacket pocket. "Before we go, though, I was wondering if you wouldn't mind doing one more thing for me." He reached into his other jacket pocket and brought out a small packet. "I'd like you to take a look at some photographs."

Reamer opened the packet and carefully laid out a half dozen photos on the coffee table. I gave them a cursory glance. The photos depicted a man and a woman, dressed very casually, in what looked to be a jewelry store. I noticed both the man and woman kept their faces studiously averted from the camera, almost as if they were aware it was there. One photo had a pretty good profile view of the woman. I couldn't make out her features, but I could tell she was slender, with a strong chin and a thick mane of burgundy hair. I started to shake my head, then stopped. I picked up one of the photos that showed her face clearly and scrutinized it closely. Finally I tapped at the photo with the edge of my nail. "This might sound crazy, but this woman reminds me of the waitress I was telling you about, the one at Good Eats. I didn't see either woman's face clearly, but there's just something about the way they carry themselves, and the way the hair is styled."

Reamer's facial expression didn't change one iota. "Would you say it was the same woman?"

I hesitated, then shook my head. "It's hard to say positively without seeing the face but offhand I'd say no, not the same woman. But perhaps they could be related?"

Reamer didn't answer, but his hand shot out, flicked at the man's image. "What about him?"

I squinted at the photograph, then shook my head again. "I'm sorry. I can't see his face clearly, so I can't say with any degree of certainty that I've seen him anywhere before."

"That's okay." Reamer swept the photos into a pile and replaced them in the brown packet. Then he reached into his other pocket and pulled out another envelope. "One more, Ms. McMillan, if you don't mind." He withdrew a photograph from the envelope and passed it over to me. "Take a good look. Do you recognize him?"

I took the photo and the moment I laid eyes on it I let out a sharp gasp. "Oh my goodness! Yes, this is the man who tried to steal the jewel box in the tent!" I turned to Reamer. "You know who he is?"

Reamer reached out to reclaim the photo. "Absolutely. This is Charles Finley."

"Charles Finley? The man from the clipping? But it can't be." I frowned. "I saw his mug shot on the internet. Finley had a smaller nose, and brown hair."

"The nose got broken in a prison fight. As for the hair, well, he had a dye job. That photograph was taken recently at the correctional facility. Believe me, that is Charles Finley."

I looked at Reamer. "He's the man you believed masterminded the Van Nuys robbery."

"I don't know about masterminding it, but we're still fairly certain he's the one who performed it. Unfortunately our witness couldn't positively identify him and he was able to trump up an alibi and walk." His lips twitched. "In a twist of fate, though, he was arrested and sent to prison on a lesser charge. And then he became a model prisoner and got ten years sliced off his sentence."

"And now he's back in Fox Hollow," I mused. "At the same time Pete Martin shows up. Another stunning coincidence."

Reamer slapped his palms down on his knees and rose. "I think we've taken up enough of your time, Ms. McMillan. I thank you for your cooperation. If we need anything else from you, we'll be in touch."

I walked them to the door. Reamer paused, his hand on the doorknob. "Oh, and I would like to be notified when you return the jewel box to its owner. I'd like to accompany you on that task, if I may."

His tone clearly indicated I had no choice in the matter, so I just nodded. Reamer left first. Josh paused in the doorway and took both my hands in his. "I wanted to tell you all this earlier, but Reamer wanted to be here," he said. "He can be a bit brusque."

I arched a brow. "A bit?"

"Okay, a lot. But he's very good at his job, Shell. It wouldn't surprise me if he does crack this case."

"I hope he does. Right now, though, there's another case that concerns me more."

"Martin's murder."

"Yes." I grabbed his arm. "Tell me you're not seriously considering Gus as a suspect. If he does turn out to be the man Jackson saw in the woods, I'm sure there's an explanation."

Josh cast a quick glance outside at Reamer's retreating back and then he leaned over and whispered in my ear, "There's a lot going on here that I can't tell you, Shell. You'll just have to trust our judgment on this one."

"A lot going on? With what? The murder or the cold case? Or both?"

Josh pulled away from me as Reamer looked back in our direction. "I've got to go," he muttered.

Josh bolted down the steps. I watched both men get into their cars and take off, then shut the door and leaned against it. Purrday and the princess wandered out from the kitchen and hopped up on the sofa. Purrday cocked his head at me, blinked his big blue eye. "Merow."

"I know. It's been a very strange day so far. Strange and disturbing." I leaned over to give him a pat on the head. "The thought of Gus Morton being a cold-blooded killer, well, that's just plain ridiculous! I mean, if I got a gun and shot everyone who irritated me, well, I'd have been in prison long ago."

Purrday butted his head against my elbow, turned around twice, and then settled himself comfortably in the crook of my lap. The princess minced over, settled herself against my other hip. I leaned back against the cushions and closed my eyes. I could see why the witness in the robbery had been unable to positively identify Finley as the man from those photographs. The man who'd performed the robbery must have been well coached as to the location of the security cameras, because he'd made certain his face was never clearly photographed. I agreed with Reamer that the witness had no doubt been nervous and couldn't trust their memory. There was no doubt in my mind, though, that Finley was guilty, particularly in light of the fact he'd been so anxious to acquire the jewel box. I was certain he'd been aware of the precious cargo contained within.

But what about Pete Martin? What had prompted his interest in the box? Had he really believed it was the original Queen Victoria jewel box? Or was his reason for wanting it the same as Finley's?

I was more convinced than ever that Pete Martin had somehow, some way, been involved with that diamond robbery. How to prove that, though, would be another matter indeed. If I could do so, though, I had the distinct feeling that the pool of suspects in Martin's demise would widen considerably.

Fifteen

I picked Leila up at quarter past one and filled her in on my impromptu meeting with Josh and Reamer on the way. When I finished she said, "I've got a bit of a problem wrapping my head around Martin being the brains behind a multimillion-dollar jewel heist. I mean, the man couldn't even run a diner, for God's sake. Then he can't even carry on an illicit affair without getting caught, and he runs off so his wife can't get her hands on the money he got for the diner. Really, does that sound like a criminal mastermind to you?"

"Martin was enough of a mastermind to cover his tracks during his absence so his ex-wife couldn't track him down. Reamer said he had eight aliases."

Leila let out a whistle. "Whoa! Maybe he wasn't as dumb as he looked after all."

I huffed a stray curl out of my eyes. "He was far from dumb. I'd say more sly like a fox. I don't know just how he was involved with that robbery, but I'd bet the farm on it."

"Good thing you don't own one," Leila observed with a smile. "Granted, it does seem suspicious, but maybe it's just as simple as Martin really thinking the jewel box was worth big buckos. Admit it, Shell, you just don't want Gus to be guilty of Martin's murder, that's why you're throwing this other theory out there. But it doesn't hold up."

"Martin was involved with that robbery, and his involvement is what got him killed. I'm almost positive his connection is with Finley, I just have to figure out what it was."

"Good luck with that," Leila said. "As far as I can tell, there's nothing that links those two men together."

"No, but . . . wait!" I snapped my fingers. "Ardis mentioned they were late getting to the event because Gus and another man were having an argument in the sweet shop. At first I thought she was going to describe Pete Martin, but she didn't. Her description fits the man who tried to swipe the box from the tent, and that's Finley."

"Okay, so Gus and Finley argued. What's that got to do with Martin?"

"I'm not entirely sure. Ardis said that Gus told Finley not to threaten him. Maybe Finley was trying to help Martin by pressuring Gus to sell him the diner?"

"But why would Finley do that? Even if he and Martin did know each other, was the relationship close enough for Finley to threaten someone on Martin's behalf?"

"I know, I know, it doesn't make sense, but I find it a little tough to swallow that both Martin and Finley just happened to want to acquire the same jewel box. My gut is telling me both of them knew exactly what was inside."

We were both silent for a few moments and then Leila said, "Okay, so say they planned that diamond heist together. Martin beats it out of town so his wife can't get all his money, Finley gets himself arrested, and what happened to the diamonds?"

"A good question." I digested that for a moment then said, "Wait a second. The woman."

"You mean the female robber?"

"Yes. Reamer asked me if I thought the woman with Finley, aka Jillian, and the woman in the surveillance photos were the same. I said no, but they could be related. What if the female robber is some relation to Jillian, and she's the one who put the diamond and clipping in that jewel box? But if so, why? Was it meant to be a clue of some sort for Finley? And while we're on the subject, where is this woman? How did her jewel box end up at the Johansen estate sale?"

"Maybe I've got the answer to that." Leila reached inside her tote bag, pulled out her phone. "I admit my curiosity was piqued on that subject too, so yesterday I asked Phyllis—that's Parker's new secretary, by the way— about local estate sales. I made some notes on my app."

"Phyllis? What happened to Yvonne?"

"Eloped to Vegas. Left Parker with a day's notice. The way he used to treat her, he deserved it. It was pretty sweet." Leila gave a reminiscent smile. "Phyllis was working part-time already, so Parker just put her in the full-time slot. Anyway, I remembered her saying that her one aunt is an 'estate sale junkie,' so I figured maybe it was worth a shot. Anyway, it seems that a few weeks ago, the sole heir of Mrs. Enid Johansen, her niece Dorothy Clotter, decided to sell some of her aunt's lesser possessions at a giant sale. The inventory papers were mixed up, though, and Mrs. Clotter didn't find out until afterward that some of the stuff she sold had belonged to a woman who used to rent a room in her aunt's house. She was positive that jewel chest belonged to that woman because, according to Phyllis, she said, quote, 'my aunt wouldn't own a piece of junk like that,' unquote."

"That woman must have been the one involved in the robbery. Did Mrs. Clotter know what happened to her, or why she would have left the jewel box with her aunt?"

"Apparently the woman pulled a disappearing act shortly before the aunt took ill. Left all her possessions behind, which didn't amount to very much."

"A disappearing act, huh? I wonder what happened?"

"Well, maybe she tried another theft and got sent to prison like her boyfriend. Anyway, Mrs. Clotter couldn't remember the woman's name, and she couldn't find any lease papers or rent receipts. She thought it was Prudence or Penelope or something like that."

"What about a last name?"

"Couldn't remember that either. She thought it might have started with either an *L* or a *T*, but beyond that nothing."

"Well, maybe Barlow can shed some light on this angle. He's supposed to have done some pretty extensive research."

About ten minutes later we pulled up in front of a small dove-gray cottage with worn shutters and a gabled roof. The shrubbery surrounding the house was overgrown and badly in need of a trim. I parked the car and we got out and walked up the stone walkway and onto the sloping porch. Leila rang the bell, which echoed eerily in the stillness of the quiet neighborhood. A few minutes later the door opened and a short bespectacled man with gray hair that stuck out on the sides peered out at us through the screen door. He had on a baggy red sweatshirt and jeans that looked as if they'd seen far better days. He squinted at us, then pointed a stubby finger at me. "You're Shell McMillan. Or should I say Shell Marlowe. I recognize you from your TV show."

"That's right. This is my friend, Leila Simmons. She's a reporter for the *Youngstown Sentinel*."

Barlow snorted. "Good paper. It's not often I get one pretty gal visiting me, let alone two." He swung the door wide. "Come on in, before nosy Mrs. Twombly across the street gets an eyeful. No doubt she's peering out the upstairs curtain even as we speak," he said with a chuckle.

We stepped over the threshold and Barlow wiggled his fingers, indicating we were to follow him down the narrow hallway. He led us into a dimly lighted room that I took to be a parlor. Barlow turned on a table lamp with a fringed shade and it gave the room a bit more light, although it was still what I considered dim. He motioned toward a well-worn damask sofa and a high-backed chair positioned in front of a fireplace. Leila and I both settled ourselves on the sofa, and I scooted to the edge of my seat as the cushions were pretty worn and I could feel the springs getting ready to jump out and give me a good poke in the you know where. Barlow hovered over us.

"I'm afraid the only thing I have to offer you ladies is some Jack Daniel's. If you recall, Ms. Marlowe—sorry, Ms. McMillan—I did warn you."

"Yes, you did, but we're fine, thanks," I said.

Barlow shrugged, then settled into the chair opposite us. He leaned back and laced his hands across his chest. "So, you mentioned wanting to know about the Van Nuys robbery. The FBI's interested now, I take it? Finally, after all this time?"

"The FBI is definitely interested," I said. "I met the liaison agent, Reamer, earlier today."

"Reamer, huh? I've heard of him." Barlow leaned back in his chair. "That reporter, Jeremy Jackson, called me yesterday."

Leila let out a groan and I leaned forward. "He did! What did he want?"

"He said that he'd heard the FBI was re-investigating that case, and he thought there might be a front-page story in it. He said he'd heard I'd done some investigating and he wanted to pick my brain. I put him off, though. Told him I wasn't sure where my notes were, and I couldn't trust the old gray cells anymore." He tapped at his temple with his forefinger.

"Did he believe you?" Leila asked.

"Maybe, maybe not. It doesn't matter. I'm not telling that pompous windbag a darn thing. Fellows like him are what give reporters a bad name." He glanced up and the corners of his lips tipped upward in a small smile. "I'd much rather share my research with you two. You're much prettier. Besides, that guy needs to be taken down a peg or two. No one's a bigger fan of Jeremy Jackson than Jeremy Jackson."

"On that we agree," remarked Leila.

Barlow chuckled. "I heard a rumor that Jackson's not even his real name. He changed it because he wanted it to sound more glamorous." He leaned back and crossed his long legs in front of him. "But you're not here to garner information on him. You want to talk about the robbery."

"Yes, we do." I leaned forward another half inch and cast a wary eye on the carpet, which also looked as if it had seen better days. "You interviewed the salesgirl who got robbed, correct?"

"Yes, I did. Nola Conroy. That poor girl was a nervous wreck. They made her take a look at Finley in the police lineup, but she was still so shaken by what happened she was second-guessing herself all over the place. One minute she was positive it was him, the next she was changing her mind. A defense attorney would have reduced her to ashes." Barlow shook his head. "She was a pretty little thing, but that whole incident, well, it took ten years off her life. She was never quite the same afterward. She blamed herself—thought that if she hadn't decided to show off and haul out those diamonds, maybe the whole incident could have been avoided." Barlow shook his head. "It wouldn't have. Those two knew all about those diamonds when they went in there, mark my words. If she hadn't offered to get them, they'd have found some other way."

"Then you believed it was an inside job?"

He nodded. "Yes, and one that was very carefully thought out and planned. Van Nuys took great pains to vet all their employees. None of them had any sort of criminal record, not even so much as a traffic ticket. But from my point of view, someone on the inside had to be tipping those robbers off. They knew how to avoid the security cameras. They knew when the store would be practically deserted, and when it was least busy around that area so they could make a clean getaway."

I traced a lazy circle on the arm of my chair. "So Nola was the only witness?"

"There was a couple who saw the man and woman come out of the store, jump into a car and drive away, but they were across the street and didn't get a clear view. The FBI showed them the security camera photos, which were worth squat." Barlow shook his head. "They say there's no such thing as the perfect crime, but believe you me, this robbery comes very close. I know it's a sore point with the FBI, a blot on their record. They would love to have a resolution to this case, and more importantly, they'd love to find those diamonds."

Leila leaned forward. "Do you have any theories as to what might have happened to the diamonds?"

"That's hard to say. They might have been broken down into smaller stones, sold on the black market, in which case no one will ever see them again, but . . . I've always had the feeling that they're stashed somewhere, and I think that's what the FBI believes as well. I'm fairly certain that's why they're prowling around your fair city. They're waiting for Finley to make a move. Finley's probably waiting for them to give up and leave town so the coast is clear for him to make off with the gems. It's a Mexican standoff." He blew out a breath. "As for Nola, she never recovered from the incident, poor thing. She quit her job not long afterward and moved back in with her parents in Charleston. Finally got married a few years ago. Her husband was transferred overseas, so she lives in London now, I believe. The other clerk, Velma McAllister, passed a few months ago from heart failure. She was in the shop that day as well, but she went looking for the store manager and was not around at the time of the robbery."

"So this other clerk and the store manager were both out of the area at the time of the robbery, and left Nola there alone?" I frowned. More and more I was convinced that robbery had been the product of a setup.

Barlow nodded. "The police really grilled both women, but they were exonerated."

"The store manager was a woman?"

"Yes. It's all in my notes. I took copious ones on my talks with both Nola and Velma. There might be something in there you'll find useful. There are also interviews with the officer who'd been assigned to the robbery. I never did manage to get one with the FBI agent. My editor was ordered to can the story before I ever really got it going. I always thought, though, that someday something would happen to change people's minds and that's why I hung on to them." He rose and walked over to a small settee at the other end of the room. He reached behind it and hefted a medium-sized box into his arms, then walked back and placed the box on the coffee table in front of us. "Here they are," he announced.

Leila and I leaned forward for a closer look. The box was jammed to the brim with spiral notebooks. There were easily a dozen, maybe more.

"That's the entire sum total of my research on the Van Nuys case. I didn't have a tape recorder back then, but I was pretty good at speed writing. If there's something you can't make out, just give a yell. Hopefully I'll be able to translate."

"It will probably take us awhile to go through everything," Leila said. "Are you in a hurry to get them back?"

Barlow waved his hand in the air. "Oh, honey, you're welcome to keep 'em. I'm not going to do anything with them anymore. To tell you the truth . . ." He leaned closer and said in a low tone, "I'm moving to Mesa the end of next month to be near my sister and her kids. I'm taking very little with me, and these? They were going to go into the trash compactor. I'll feel better now, knowing that my research is in good hands. And who knows? It might finally amount to something. It would please me to no end if I thought my notes might somehow help crack this case."

"We're hoping that your notes will be helpful too, Mr. Barlow," I assured him. "I have one more question. Was the woman who was Finley's accomplice in the robbery ever identified?"

"Not that I know of. Police thought she might have been Finley's girlfriend, but, as it turned out, the guy was a real ladies' man. Had a string of girlfriends longer than the alphabet. And, of course no one could make a positive ID from those photos."

Leila's jacket pocket started to jangle. She reached in, slid out her phone and glanced at the screen. She shoved the phone back into her pocket and rose. "I'm afraid we have to get going. Thank you so much for your time, Mr. Barlow. We'll be sure to keep you informed."

"Please do." He rose as well and motioned toward the box. "Let me carry this out to your car."

Barlow hefted the box into his arms and started toward the front door. I hung back and touched my friend's arm. "Did something happen?" I asked. "You seem awfully anxious to leave."

"Something happened, all right," she said grimly. "That was my contact down at the police station. The police found a gun in a cistern near the entrance of Grimley Woods this morning."

I felt my stomach start to roil. "Was it the murder weapon?"

"They think so. They're waiting for the ballistics results." She paused. "There's more. Gus Morton has been brought in for more questioning."

"Ouch," I said. "That doesn't sound good."

"It sure doesn't," my friend agreed. "What's more, my source tells me they figure there's a ninety-nine percent chance that Gus could be arrested today." She paused and then added, "And charged with murder."

Sixteen

"If they're getting ready to do that, then that must mean they've found something that links Gus to Martin's murder." I frowned. "I wonder what it could be. Josh didn't indicate they were anywhere close to an arrest when he and Reamer were at the house earlier, not that he would have. Josh is very by the book when it comes to police work."

"Well, my source is usually pretty right on. I've got to get down there and check this out, before Jackson gets wind of it."

I definitely broke more than a few speeding laws as we flew back down the highway to Fox Hollow. Police headquarters was tucked into a skinny two-story brick building located in the downtown section. I flew into the parking lot located behind the building, and thank goodness there was a vacant spot at the far end of the lot, or I might have taken a chance and parked in the area clearly marked "For Police Vehicles Only" near the rear entrance. I thought to cover the box of notebooks with a throw on the backseat. After all, one couldn't be too careful, even in a police parking lot. Then we were out of the car and hurrying up the stone steps that led to the main reception area. A policeman was in one corner, taking a statement from a girl dressed in jeans and a baggy sweatshirt. Aside from them, the waiting area was deserted. I looked over at the wide walnut reception desk and my heart plummeted as I caught sight of a familiar figure. "Uh-oh," I muttered. "There's trouble."

Leila jerked around to face me. "Trouble? You mean Jackson's here?"

"No, worse. Quentin Watson."

The craggy-faced newsman had caught sight of us also. He shuffled toward us, a crooked smile on his face. "Well, well. Shell McMillan. What are you doing here?" His gaze traveled to Leila, and he pointed a finger at her. "Leila Simmons, right? From the *Youngstown Sentinel*?" He gave a dry chuckle. "News travels fast, I see."

"It's true then," I said. "That the weapon used to murder Pete Martin has been found."

Watson reached up to scratch at his forehead. "There's no harm in telling you that they found *a* gun," he said. "It's not necessarily *the* gun. They're waiting on the ballistics report. Josh put a rush on it. I thought I'd stick around, see if I could get a handle on the results." His gaze slid to me. "I bet you could get 'em pretty fast."

"Don't bet on it. Josh doesn't share any details of his police work with me," I said.

Leila pushed forward. "I also heard they brought Gus Morton in for questioning? Is there a possibility they're thinking of arresting him for the murder?"

Watson's eyebrow lifted. "My, my, you certainly want me to share a lot of information with you, a reporter from a rival paper. If I do, what's in it for me?"

Leila lifted her chin. "I have some information I can share. Quid pro quo, right?"

Watson put a finger to his lips. "Okay. You first. What's your information?"

I squeezed Leila's arm. "Do you really want to tell him?" I whispered.

"No, but . . ."

Leila stopped talking as the door to the inner offices opened and Josh came out. He paused as he caught sight of us over by the reception desk, and his brows drew together in a frown. He walked over and gave us a curt nod. "Shell, Leila. What are you doing here?"

"I'm following up on a tip I received," Leila said without any preamble. "I've heard that the police are arresting Gus Morton for the murder of Pete Martin. Care to comment, Josh?"

Josh expression didn't change, but I could tell from the muscle that was flexing in his jaw that he was annoyed. Make that very annoyed. "I don't know where you get your tips from, Leila, but right now we're not prepared to make an arrest." He inclined his head toward Watson and added, "As I've already told Quentin, we've brought Gus Morton in for questioning, and that's all I can say at this time."

"So Gus is a suspect?" Leila persisted.

"Right now I'd say he's a person of interest." He glanced over toward the plate-glass entrance door and his eyebrows drew together. "Oh, swell," he muttered. "Just what I need right now."

I turned and saw Jeremy Jackson striding toward us. He was dressed casually, in a long-sleeved T-shirt, windbreaker and jeans, but he still exuded an air of authority. He flashed his megawatt smile at all of us and leaned his elbow on the counter. Inclining his head toward Josh he said, "Good afternoon, Detective Bloodgood. I hear you're about to make an arrest in your murder case. Care to comment?"

Josh didn't bother to hide his annoyance. "I don't know where you reporters get your information, but you'd better vet your sources more carefully. Listen up, because this is all I've got to say. Yes, we have brought someone in for questioning. At the moment we consider him a person of interest. No, we are not ready at this time to make a formal arrest."

Jackson leaned forward. "I take it there's been no confirmation that the murder weapon belonged to Gus Morton, then?"

Josh placed a hand on his hip, dangerously close to his gun. "What part about we're not ready at this time to make a formal arrest didn't you understand?"

"Okay, I get it." Jackson scribbled something down. "How about that other matter?"

Josh had started to turn away, but now he stopped and faced the reporter. "Other matter?"

"Your other case. Have there been any new developments?"

Josh's expression was bland. "I'm sure I don't know what you mean. Solving the murder of Peter Martin is the Fox Hollow Police Department's top priority at the moment."

Jackson turned and fixed me with a stare. "Is that true, Shell?"

I stared back. "How would I know? The police department isn't in the habit of consulting me on their investigations."

He smiled affably. "Oh, I'm sorry. Then I must have erroneous information. I heard that you received a visit this morning from Detective Bloodgood and the FBI liaison, Trent Reamer, in connection with a certain cold case."

Good Lord, how could he know all that? Was Jackson spying on Josh and Reamer . . . and on me? Before I could summon up any sort of answer, Josh inserted himself between me and Jackson. "The Fox Hollow PD has no comment on any ongoing investigation, cold or otherwise," he said. "Jackson, I understand that you're here auditioning for a job on our town paper, but if I find out that you are harassing the citizens of this town in your quest for news, I'll see you're hauled in for disturbing the peace. Got it?"

Jackson waved his hand in a careless circle. "Oh, I've got it. I certainly didn't mean to harass anyone. Far from it. You're right, I was trying to follow up on a lead, angling to scoop my competition." He slid a glance at Leila, who glared openly at him. "Perhaps I was a bit overzealous. I certainly didn't mean to come on so strong. I intend to get a statement, but if this is a bad time . . ."

"You'll get a statement when there is news to relate," Josh said. He turned and gestured toward Leila and Quentin. "All of you will. Right now, though, there's nothing to tell."

"Are you certain about that, Detective? Or are you just being cagey?" Jackson asked. As Josh continued to glower at him, Jackson held up both hands. "Okay. I can take a hint. For now. But you haven't seen the last of me." He raised two fingers to his forehead in a salute, then turned and walked out the way he'd come in.

"Good riddance," Josh muttered. He ran a hand through his hair and looked at Leila and me. "There's no story here right now. You two can go on home."

I wanted to ask him a bit more about what had transpired at my house this morning, but I knew Josh well enough to see that he was in a mood right now, and questioning him would get me nowhere. He turned and vanished into the back area.

Watson sidled closer to me. "He certainly is something," the older man muttered. "Quite cocky."

I shot him a rueful look. "That's putting it mildly."

Watson looked at Leila. "So, where were we before we were so rudely interrupted. You were about to share some information with me."

"That was before Detective Bloodgood came out and answered the question I was going to ask you," said Leila.

"Ah. Well, if you don't want to share anything, maybe Shell would like to." He fixed his beady gaze on me. "What was all that about you getting a visit from the FBI liaison this morning? Do you know something about this hush-hush case they're supposed to be investigating?"

"I might," I said. "I could share some information with you, if you'd do the same for me."

Quentin seemed to mull that over, then he nodded. "Okay. What have you got?"

I held up my hand. "Oh, no. You first. You reported on the Van Nuys robbery ten years ago, right?" At his nod I continued, "Did anything about your investigation lead you to believe it could have been an inside job?"

"That was everyone's first thought, but the clerks and manager all came up clean."

"Correct me if I'm wrong, but the manager wasn't present at the time of the robbery, isn't that right?"

Watson nodded. "As far as I can recollect, that's right. I thought there was something suspicious about that at first, but like I said, her story checked out."

"Do you remember this manager's name?"

Watson put a finger to his lips. "Not offhand. I'd have to go back and read through my notes, if I could find 'em. Her first name was some sort of gem, I think."

"A gem? Like Ruby or Jade?"

"Maybe. Like I said, I'd have to refresh my memory."

"What about Charles Finley?"

Watson snorted. "A small-time crook. They thought they had him pegged for that robbery, but even I could have told them they were barking up the wrong tree. That little clerk, Nola something or other, testified at his trial, but she wasn't much help. The guy got off."

"But you don't think he had anything to do with it?"

"To be honest, I couldn't say for certain. But nothing new turned up, and we all moved onto other things. The case turned cold, until now, apparently." His lips quirked up at the edges. "Your turn. Has any new evidence been uncovered that would reopen the case?"

I let out a breath while at the same time doing a mental debate on just how much to reveal. At last I said, "The FBI did come to my house this morning. I came into possession of something that might or might not have a bearing on their cold case, and they wanted to question me at length about it."

Quentin's lips thinned. "That's all you have to tell me?"

"That's all I *can* tell you, Quentin, at least for now."

He jammed his hands into his pockets. "Well, it serves me right for trusting you in the first place. I should have known better." He turned and stomped off without a backward glance.

Leila put her hand on my shoulder. "Boy, is he mad at you."

I shrugged. "It's not the first time. Quentin and I usually don't see eye to eye. I might have told him a bit more if his information had been more illuminating."

"Maybe he was holding back," Leila suggested.

"That wouldn't surprise me."

I was just about to suggest to Leila that we go to my house and start digging into Barlow's notebooks when the front door opened again and Inez Morton stepped through. I noticed she had on the same sweat suit as the previous evening. Her hair was uncombed and her face was devoid of makeup. There were dark bags under her eyes. She caught sight of Leila and me standing by the desk and her lips twisted into some travesty of a smile. She hurried over to us, caught me by my hand.

"Did you hear about Gus?" she asked me. "Is that why you're here?"

"We heard he was brought down here. He hasn't been arrested, though, right?"

"Not yet, anyway." She pressed a hand to her forehead. "I'm sorry. I'm starting to feel a bit faint. I haven't eaten yet."

I slipped an arm around Inez's shoulders and guided her over to one of the benches that lined the far wall of the reception area. Leila fished in her tote bag, pulled out a protein bar and handed it to her. "It's not much, but it might help," she said.

Inez unwrapped the bar, took a bite, and sat for a minute, chewing. Leila and I both sat, one on each side of her, waiting. At last Inez glanced over at Leila and smiled. "That hit the spot. Thank you."

"Can you tell us what happened?" I asked.

Inez finished the bar, crumped the paper in her hand. "There isn't much to tell. Gus was reading the paper and I was getting lunch ready when the police came knocking on the door. He asked Gus very politely to come downtown with him, that they had some more questions for him."

"More questions? So they'd already interviewed him?"

She nodded. "We thought that was the end of it but . . . ." She stopped speaking and dropped her head into her hands.

I slipped an arm around her shoulders. "Come on, Inez. It's not as bad as all that."

She raised a tear-stained face to mine. "No, Shell. It's worse." She let out a breath. "When that policeman came by for Gus, he also had a warrant for Gus's gun. But when I went to get it, the box was there, and the gun wasn't. It's gone missing."

Seventeen

"I'm afraid things aren't looking very good for Gus," I said.

It was a little past three o'clock, and I was seated in my parlor. Leila and I had planned to start digging through Barlow's journals, but those plans went down the drain after she received a text from her editor to cover another emergency town council meeting in Youngstown. She had no idea how long it might last, but promised to text me when she was free. I'd returned home to find Gary just arriving—business had been very slow, so he'd left Robbie to close up at five. Now over a late lunch of grilled cheese and tomato sandwiches and sweet tea, I related the day's events to Gary, ending with Inez's admission that Gus's gun was missing.

Gary picked up his glass of sweet tea. "I agree, but don't give up hope yet. At least not until that ballistics report comes in. Maybe the bullet that killed Martin wasn't from Gus's gun."

"Maybe," I said. I picked up my own glass and took a long sip, mindful of Purrday watching me with his one good eye. "Inez said that the last time she saw the gun, it was a few days ago and it was in its box. Of course, it's possible Gus might have moved it since."

Gary picked up his sandwich, eliciting a loud meow from Princess Fuzzypants, who was sprawled at his feet. "What did Gus say about it?"

I shrugged. "Apparently he clammed up on the subject, said he wasn't going to make any kind of a statement about anything until he was formally charged." I smiled faintly. "Inez said that *Law and Order* was always Gus's favorite show. I guess he learned something from it." I sighed. "I just have a hard time picturing Gus as a killer."

Gary leaned back in the chair and stretched out his legs, jarring the princess, who shot him a look and then wriggled over. "Yet he owns a gun," he said.

I bent down, gave Purrday a scratch behind the ears and a tiny bit of cheese. "According to Inez, he's not a very good shot. Inez, however, by her own admission is."

"So you think Inez might have killed Martin?"

"She admitted threatening Martin with Gus's gun when he showed up at their house a few days ago, but he left and that was the end of it. Or so she says."

Gary chuckled and took another bite of his sandwich. "I have to admit, my favorite part of your story was how you got the better of Quentin Watson. Getting him to spill his guts and then telling him squat."

I grinned. "It did work out well, didn't it? I suppose I'll never get another opportunity that good ever again, though. And I didn't learn that much from Quentin. Apparently the Van Nuys robbery wasn't one he particularly remembered. About the most interesting thing he said was that the store manager's name was some sort of gem."

Gary inclined his head toward the stack of notebooks I'd set on the table in front of the fireplace. "I'm betting your friend Nick Barlow has that manager's name in his notes. You didn't need Quentin."

"I thought maybe he might have some juicy detail to relate. Unless he was holding back."

Gary wiggled one eyebrow. "As if Quentin would do such a thing!"

I stuck my tongue out at him and then said, "What I am afraid of is now that I admitted the Van Nuys robbery is why the FBI's in town, he's going to start digging into it himself. His interference, we don't need."

"Especially when he doesn't share."

I grinned. "Exactly."

Gary's phone beeped, signaling he had a text. He pulled his phone out of his pocket and looked at the screen. "Robbie needs help," he said. "He can't find Lou Anne Walker's order."

"Oh, I put it away in the storeroom. It's in a white box on the upper shelf." Lou Anne had ordered several specially made catnip toys for her two Abyssinian cats, as well as some sweaters and a blanket from Kathleen Power, who sold her line of handcrafted pet clothing and accessories at Urban Tails. I half rose from my seat. "Maybe I should go. I know exactly where it is."

He rose and waved me back down. "No, you stay here. Leila will probably be texting you any minute that she'll be over to look at the notebooks. I'm sure I can find it."

Gary left. I let my gaze wander over to the stack of Barlow's notebooks. I so wanted to start digging through them, but Leila had said she'd break both my wrists if I did that and I had every faith that she meant it. I picked up the Sunday paper and decided to concentrate on the local news instead. I'd just turned to the Entertainment section when I heard a loud knock at the door. I got up, walked over and pulled the curtain back a bit so I could see the front porch. I frowned when I recognized the man who stood there. I walked over to the door and yelled through it, "Go away."

"Not a chance," Jeremy Jackson yelled back. "I just want a word with you and your friend Leila."

"Leila's not here. She's covering a town council meeting. Now go away."

"Hey, Shell, I can stand here and shout through the door all day. So unless you want the entire neighborhood to hear me question you about your knowledge of the Van Nuys robbery . . ."

I jerked open the door and gave him the stink-eye. "What do you want?"

His gaze raked me up and down. "I just want to know which case are the two of you angling to solve? The diamond theft or Martin's murder, or—dare I say it—both?"

"And that would be your business how?"

"Let's face it, both are excellent front-page stories. Both are right up my alley, in my area of expertise. I know that your friend desperately wants to get out of that little society reporting niche that Parker has her in, but to be quite honest with you, she's out of her league."

I felt my temper rise. "You have some nerve, you know that."

His lips parted, revealing his impossibly white teeth. "What I have is talent. I can get to the bottom of both these crimes. What I don't need is amateur interference."

I raised my chin. "I'm hardly an amateur," I said with as much hauteur as I could muster.

"Oh, I didn't mean you." Jackson shot me another of his dazzling smiles. "I came here to repeat the offer I made you earlier. Dump your friend and work with me. The two of us as a team would be unstoppable. We'd have these cases solved in no time flat."

I gave my head a brisk shake. "Thanks, but no thanks."

His hand shot out and grabbed mine. "You can't tell me that you have no interest in these cases. Why else would you and Leila have visited Barlow today?"

I jerked my hand free. "You *are* spying on us," I cried. "You have some nerve."

"I'm not spying on you. I'm a reporter, tracking down clues for a story. I went to Barlow but he declined to give me an interview. I went there again today to try and persuade him to change his mind, and much to my surprise, he was already entertaining you two."

"Why did you feel the need to be so sneaky? You could have rung the bell."

"I could have, but Barlow would have dismissed me. I had somewhere else to go anyway. So, how did the interview go? Did you get anything useful out of him?"

There was no way in hell I was telling Jackson about Barlow's notebooks. I shrugged. "Not much. He couldn't remember a lot."

"That's what he told me. At one time he had a slew of notebooks, but he told me he'd misplaced them."

"That's right. He's planning to move to Arizona, did you know that? He thinks he might have thrown them all out. It's not like he's going to do anything with them anymore, anyway."

"I guess not." He paused, his gaze narrowed. "I hear your boyfriend is waiting on the ballistics report to charge Gus Morton with murder."

"Bad news travels fast," I said with a curl of my lip. "I'm sure it won't come to that."

Jackson's brow lofted. "Why not?"

"Because I greatly doubt that Gus's gun is the murder weapon. He might have had his issues with Martin, but I know Gus Morton, and he's not a killer."

"Anne Rule knew Ted Bundy too and she swore the same thing. Look how that turned out."

I was trying to think of a suitable retort when Jackson suddenly reached into his jacket pocket. He pulled out his phone, glanced at the screen, and then slid the phone back into his pocket. "Well, I'll be going," he said. "My offer still stands, though, for us to work together. Think about it."

He glided off my back porch and over to his car, a sporty-looking Mazda, parked right in front of our house. He paused and waved jauntily at me before he slid behind the wheel and pulled away from the curb. As I started to shut the door I noticed a dark sedan that had been parked halfway up the block also pull away and head in the same direction as Jackson. I craned my neck as the car passed, but the driver had on a cap and sunglasses so I couldn't get a good look at his face. By design? I wondered. Who would want to follow Jackson? No sooner had I shut the door than my phone buzzed with an incoming text. I saw that it was from Leila:

Start the notebooks without me. Just got a call. Bullets from Gus's gun match the bullet that killed Martin. Gus being charged with first degree murder.

I texted Leila back: *Where R U? More details?* Then I hit #1 on my speed dial, but I got Josh's voicemail. I figured it wouldn't do any good to leave a message, so I hung up. No sooner had I done that than my phone buzzed with an incoming call. I looked at the Caller ID. It read *Fox Hollow PD*. Thinking that perhaps Josh was calling me from the station, I clicked the answer button and said, "Hello. Josh?"

"No." The voice that floated across the wire sounded old and tired. "It's Gus Morton, Shell. I hope you don't mind, but I didn't know who to call." He cleared his throat loudly. "I've just been formally charged with the murder of Pete Martin. I need to find a good lawyer, and I thought maybe you might know one."

Jeff Ryan was a good customer and a lawyer, but he handled wills and estates, not murder trials. In what I hoped was a soothing tone I said, "One of my customers is an attorney. I don't know if he handles murder cases, but I'll give him a call on your behalf. If he doesn't handle that sort of thing, he can probably refer you to someone who does."

"Thanks, Shell." The relief in Gus's tone was evident. "Could I ask you for another favor? I only get one phone call, and you were the lucky recipient. Inez will be worrying."

"Not to worry. I'll call her before I call the attorney."

"Thanks." He let out a strained chuckle. "I really owe you now."

"Don't be silly. You don't owe me a thing." I paused. "I understand the bullet that killed Martin came from your gun."

Silence, and then, "That's what they say. But I didn't kill him, I swear."

"I believe you, but somehow someone used your gun to do just that."

"I know." He let out a sigh. "I did take the gun with me to work that day. I thought maybe I might use it to scare Martin if he started to get rough with me. To be honest, I was so nervous I just plum forgot it was there."

"Did anyone else know you had the gun with you?"

"Heck, my whole staff knew. The few times I brought it to work 'cause I was going to the pistol range afterward, I always left it in a case under the counter. And I always keep that case locked."

"Did anyone else have the key?"

"I kept it on a chain in the back. I guess anyone could have gotten their hands on it, but who would have wanted to? No one on my staff would do such a thing."

I sighed inwardly. Gus was far too trusting for his own good. "Did you tell this to the police?"

"I started to, but they didn't seem to want to hear it, so I shut up. I said I wasn't doing any more talking without my lawyer."

"That's probably best." I hesitated, and then said, "If I ask you something, Gus, would you tell me the truth?"

"Sure, Shell. I've nothing to hide."

"You were in Grimley Woods around the time Martin was killed, weren't you?"

A slight hesitation, and then Gus spoke so softly I had to strain to catch the words. "Yep. He'd called me earlier, said he wanted to meet. I was going to tell him to leave me alone once and for all or I'd get him arrested on harassment charges. I never got the chance. When I got to the designated spot he was lying there dead. I panicked and took off."

"You didn't see any weapon around? You didn't see your gun?"

"Nope. If I had, I would have picked it up."

"And you saw no one else around?"

"I thought I heard some movement in the bushes nearby, like a rustling. I glanced over real quick, and I thought I saw a dark shape take off."

"A dark shape? Could you tell if it were male or female?"

"No, sorry. If I had to guess, I'd say female, because it looked slight of build, but to tell you the truth, I was pretty rattled. I just hightailed it out of there fast as I could."

"In your haste to leave, do you remember almost hitting another car?"

"Why, no," Gus said. He sounded genuinely puzzled. "I was upset, but I'm pretty positive no one was around when I took off. Then again, I didn't know you saw me, so maybe I could be mistaken." He cleared his throat again. "They're signaling me my time is up. You'll take care of the lawyer? And Inez?"

I assured Gus that I would and hung up. I dialed Jeff Ryan's number and got a voicemail message. I left my name and number, said it was urgent, then hung up and dialed Inez. "I know this is all upsetting, Inez, but try and stay calm. I've a call in for an attorney for Gus."

"Oh, thank you, Shell. Our attorney would have no idea about a criminal proceeding. As for staying calm, well, that's easier said than done. Someone is framing my Gus, and with his own gun! Oh, I wish I had known what that stupid fool planned to do! I'd have talked him right out of it." Inez wrung her hands in front of her. "I'm just afraid that now the police have Gus in their sights, they won't look anywhere else."

"I know it looks bad but try to stay positive. Josh is in charge and he doesn't think Gus is a killer."

"Josh might be in charge, but he's got to answer to someone. And if the evidence points to Gus they won't care if Josh thinks Gus is capable of murder or not."

I didn't voice my opinion aloud to Inez, but I had the same feeling. "Inez, I wonder if I could ask you something. Was anyone else besides Pete Martin badgering Gus about selling the diner?"

Inez cleared her throat. "As a matter of fact, there was another man. He called here twice looking for Gus. He said that he was a friend of Martin's, and that Gus would do well to consider his offer." She sniffed. "The second time he called I told him I could speak for my husband, and exactly what both he and Martin could do with their offers."

"Did he leave a name?"

"Not that I recall." Inez drew in a breath. "I'd better call Gus's sister. If she hears this from anyone but me I'll never hear the end of it."

I hung up and my cell jangled again. This time it was Jeff Ryan. I apologized for bothering him and told him the reason for my call; he was immediately sympathetic and offered to go to the jail before I could even suggest it.

"I've had some dealings with Gus Morton," Jeff said, "and he's about as far from being a murderer as they get. I'm not a trial attorney but I can speak with him and assess the situation. If need be, I know a few really good attorneys I can call." He paused. "They'll be expensive, though."

I knew money was tight for Gus, but I figured that if he ended up in jail money probably wouldn't be that much of an issue. "See what you can do. I'll have his wife meet you there."

I phoned Inez back and after ten minutes of profusely thanking me, she ended the call to fix her face and hurry down to the station. I dialed Leila next but it also went into voicemail. I left a message telling her she should either text or call me the minute she got home, and then I went over and opened the box of Barlow's notebooks. I selected two fat notebooks from the top of the pile, walked over to the kitchen table and set them down with a loud *plop!* I stood looking down at them for a minute, my hands on my hips. "Maybe this job deserves a pot of nice strong coffee," I murmured. Purrday lofted onto the table, butted his head against my arm and mewled in agreement.

I put some coffee on the stove and went back to the table. I selected the top notebook and turned it over in my hands. The journal cover depicted a large flower with a hummingbird hovering over it. Hardly the type of book I'd have figured a hard-bitten newsman like Barlow to be using—it was probably the only one in the stationery store that day. I settled down in one of the chairs, picked up the book and flipped to the first page.

Barlow hadn't been exaggerating. His handwriting was cramped, small and hard to read. I stumbled through the first dozen or so pages, relaxing a bit as I got the hang of his handwriting. The first part of the notebook I'd selected consisted of his interview with one of the policemen who'd been called to the scene. From what I read, there was nothing particularly outstanding about that interview, just standard. The second interview was with Nola Conroy, the woman who'd been threatened at gunpoint. I read her interview with interest. Nola described her initial impression of the robbers as vagrants, which changed when they expressed an interest in purchasing a diamond. Her descriptions of them were vague. She didn't seem to remember much about them other than the woman was very thin with red hair, and the man was dark-haired. Barlow's notes indicated her manner was "shaken" and "highly nervous," understandable reactions for someone threatened at gunpoint.

I noticed the coffee was ready, so I got up and poured myself a large mug. I added cream and two sugars and then returned to the table. I picked up the notebook and turned to the third interview. Barlow had written this name in bold, black letters, underscored:

Opal Griffin

I paused. Why did that name seem familiar? My brow furrowed as I thought, and then I let out a little cry.

Of course. Opal was a gemstone. This had to be his interview with the Van Nuys manager!

And just as I reached that epiphany, I heard a soft footfall behind me. The next thing I knew, a hand came down on my shoulder, hard!

I dropped the notebook and screamed.

Eighteen

"Golly, Shell, take it easy."

I whirled around and saw Gary, fighting to suppress a grin. I reached out and swatted at his arm. "Why do you persist on sneaking up on me like that," I growled.

He raised both hands in a gesture of surrender. "Hey, sorry. I didn't mean to startle you."

"I know," I said. I bent down to retrieve the fallen notebook and added, "Jeremy Jackson was here earlier. He wanted to recruit me to help him solve the Van Nuys robbery. He apparently followed Leila and me to Barlow's. He urged me to dump Leila and take up with him."

Gary's eyebrow rose. "Did he now? I hope you told him to get lost."

"I did, but I get the sense he's not the type that gives up easily. He told me to think about it." I paused. "They've charged Gus with Martin's murder."

"Too bad. So I take it his gun was the murder weapon?"

I nodded and then snapped my fingers. "Now that I think of it, Jackson got a text and beat it pretty quickly. I bet it was about Gus." I held up the notebook. "More than ever, I think there's a connection between Martin's murder and this robbery. I'm hoping Barlow's notes will give me some sort of clue."

Gary poured himself a mug of coffee and then sat down opposite me. "Well, since Leila isn't here, want some help?"

"I thought you'd never ask." I pointed to the stack of journals. "I was just about to read Barlow's account of his interview with the absentee store manager."

"That sounds as if it would be interesting," said Gary. He leaned back in his chair. "Why not read it aloud? Two heads might be better than one."

"Okay," I said. I leaned back in the chair and started to read.

> Today I interviewed Ms. Opal Griffin, the manager of the Van Nuys Jewelry Store. Ms. Griffin was not in the store at the time of the robbery. She said that she had a personal errand to run that she didn't think would take as much time as it did. By the time she returned to the store, the police had been summoned and the diamonds were long gone. Nola Conroy was quite distraught and had to be sedated, and Velma

McAllister, who'd been in the storeroom looking for her and missed the entire episode, was beside herself.

Ms. Griffin did mention that her roommate had often tried to recommend her boyfriend, whom she referred to as Chuck, for a part-time job. Ms. Griffin said that she'd been hesitant to hire Chuck because she'd heard her roommate mention his prior arrest record on several occasions. Ms. Griffin remarked that considering the nature of the goods sold in the store—high-priced jewelry—she had to be careful whom she hired. She maintained, however, that she never spoke of the shipment of diamonds to her roommate, so there was no way that her boyfriend could have learned about it.

One thing that struck me as odd, though. When I asked her if she'd spoken to anyone else about the diamonds, she hesitated before shaking her head no, and also did not look me straight in the eye, all of which leads me to believe that she did tell someone.

I questioned some of the other employees as to Ms. Griffin's personal life. Apparently she kept pretty close-mouthed about it, but Velma McAllister told me that Opal did tell her one day about a man in her life. She referred to him only by initials—PJ. Never a first or a last name. Ms. McAllister stated that she thought there might have been a reason for her being so secretive—she had a suspicion the man was married. She did say that she doubted he had a criminal record, as Opal had never struck her as the type to get involved with a man of such a low caliber, in her opinion.

I stopped reading and tapped the edge of the spiral notebook against my chin. Gary looked at me. "What's the matter? Have you thought of something?"

"Actually, yes. A married man who went by the initials PJ? That's setting off an alarm bell in my head. Now, what is it?" I flipped back through the notebook and stopped when I came to Nola Conroy's interview. I scanned the written words, then lifted my gaze to meet Gary's. "Here it is," I said. "Nola Conroy said that she overheard the woman robber say to the man that 'PJ had done his part.' PJ—the same name that Opal Griffin used in referring to her boyfriend."

Gary pursed his lips. "It could be a coincidence."

"It could be," I said. "Or maybe not."

I set the notebook aside and reached for my phone. I punched in Rita Sakowski's contact information. She answered on the third ring. "Hey, Shell. What's up?"

"I'm sorry to bother you at work, Rita. I know Sunday afternoons can get pretty hairy at Sweet Perks."

"Well, fortunately, you caught me in a lull," Rita said with a laugh. "So what can I do for you?"

"Did you hear the news about Gus?"

"Yes, Mamie Gummer called. Isn't it horrible! I just can't wrap my head around Gus being a murderer, although there's no doubt in my mind that if he did do it, Peter Martin deserved it," she said with feeling.

I figured it was best to gloss over the subject of Gus for now. "Actually, Rita, I called to ask a question. It's about Peter Martin. Inez is the one who originally mentioned it, but this isn't the right time to bother her. I thought maybe you might know the answer."

"I'll try. Shoot."

"Inez mentioned the ex-wife catching Martin and his girlfriend in a compromising position in the cellar, which prompted her filing for divorce."

"Oh, that's true all right," Rita said, and I could almost see her head bobbing up and down. "It was quite the scandal back then."

"I don't suppose you remember the name of Martin's girlfriend?"

Rita was silent for so long I thought we'd gotten disconnected, and then she let out a long sigh. "Sorry, Shell. It seems like it should be on the tip of my tongue, but I just can't think of it."

"Could it be an unusual name, like a gemstone, maybe?" I prompted.

"Maybe," Rita said. "Like I said, it's one of those things that's just on the fringe of your mind, but I just can't grasp it. Inez would know, for sure."

"One more thing. Did Peter Martin go by any sort of nickname?"

"None that a lady would repeat," Rita said sweetly. "Oops, gotta go. Some customers are coming in. If I remember that woman's name, I'll give you a call."

I hung up and slid a glance over at Gary. He'd pulled my laptop computer in front of him and was typing away. "What are you doing?" I asked.

"A little investigative work." He turned the computer screen toward me. "I put in Opal Griffin to see what would come up. There are twenty scattered around the United States."

For the next fifteen minutes Gary and I went through the list. We eliminated ten of the names from the West Coast, and four by the age of the listing. That left six names in the tristate vicinity. "It's just a hunch," Gary said. "Maybe nothing will come of it. Then again . . ."

"Merow," said Purrday from his spot underneath my chair.

We split the names and whipped out our cell phones. I dialed my first number and Opal Griffin answered almost immediately. I made up an excuse that I was connected to a design house and we were doing a survey of jewelry stores, and did she ever work in one?

"God, no," she responded. "I'm an estate planner. I haven't got the patience to be a clerk, or heaven forbid a waitress. Who did you say this survey was for, anyway?"

I thanked her for her time and hung up, then tried the next number. It came back with a recorded message that the number had been disconnected and was no longer in service. The third woman was hard of hearing and I had to shout every word. I disconnected and looked over at Gary, who'd just ended his call. "Any luck?"

He shook his head. "One housewife, one retired schoolteacher, and this last Opal Griffin is a secretary in the Hartford Board of Education. Looks like our Opal Griffin either has an unlisted number or she goes under another name."

"Swell. A dead end." I stretched my arms wide and sighed. "Well, it was worth a try. Maybe there will be something else in the rest of Barlow's journals."

I started to pull another one out of the pile when my phone buzzed with an incoming call. I saw "Mother" on the screen and shook my head. "I'd better take this," I said to Gary. I swiped the accept icon and said, "Hello, Mother."

"Crishell, dear. I was wondering if you had Marianne's number handy. I can't seem to locate it."

"I might have it in my contacts list. Are you trying to set up another fundraiser?"

"No, it's something else. One of my good contacts has a friend who runs a shelter in Willbur that is not a 'no kill' facility. She has about fifteen beautiful purebred kittens that will be euthanized by the end of the week unless she can convince a no-kill shelter to take them. My contact told his woman about the Fox Hollow shelter and the fundraiser. She called the shelter number but no one answered, and she's in a bind. She needs to find out today if Marianne might have room for the kittens and if so, she needs to make arrangements for transfer tomorrow. I said I'd contact Marianne, but I can't find her number." My mother paused. "I don't want to disappoint this contact. He has quite a few excellent pieces of Asian art that I'm trying to get him to sign over to Secondhand Sue's. Up till now he's been hesitant, but doing this for him might tip the scales in my favor."

"Well, if I can't find it I'm pretty sure Leila or Olivia might have it. Can you give me this woman's name and number and I'll pass it on?"

"Wait, I put it in my notepad. Let me find it." I could hear the tap-tap of my mother's nails against the screen. "Ah, here it is. Funny thing, my contact said she used to work in Fox Hollow, years ago. Her name is Opal. Opal Griffin Black."

I forced myself to suppress the involuntary squeal that rose to my lips. I took down the number, told my mother I'd take care of it, and disconnected. Gary came over to me and laid his hand on my arm. "Take two deep breaths," he advised. "You look like you're about to jump right out of your skin."

"I think we've finally caught a break!" I told him about my mother's request. "What are the chances two Opal Griffins used to live and work in Fox Hollow? It's got to be the same woman. Her last name being Black now also explains why we didn't find her in our search."

"Well, it certainly sounds promising," Gary agreed. "But I wouldn't do the happy dance just yet. We've been disappointed on sure things before."

"True. So let's find out." I waved my phone in the air. "Here goes nothing."

I dialed the number my mother had given me and Opal Black answered after about four rings. She had a nice voice, soft and well-modulated, which took on a more excited tone once I identified myself and the reason for my call. "Oh, thank you for calling me back," she said. "You have no idea what I've gone through these last few days, trying to get these kittens homes. They're all purebred, six are Siamese, two are Himalayan and the rest are Persian. All the no-kill shelters I contacted unfortunately were full up and had no space. Finally a colleague recommended the Fox Hollow shelter. They were fairly certain it's a no-kill."

"I believe it is as well. I'll be speaking to the director later on but I know that they are always interested in saving kittens' lives. I'm sure that she'll be glad to make arrangements."

"Wonderful. I hate to sound pushy, but how soon do you think they could come down?"

"As I said, I'll need to speak with the shelter director but I'm sure it won't be a problem. Barring any complications, how does tomorrow afternoon sound?"

Opal Black let out a giant sigh. "Like heaven."

She promised to text me directions to the shelter and I told her I'd call back to make definite arrangements. Convincing Marianne was next on my agenda. She sounded hesitant until I mentioned the fact that the kittens were all purebred.

"Pedigreed kittens always get adopted quickly," she said. "And, of course, with our reputation, how can I refuse. But if she needs them picked up tomorrow . . . well, that presents a bit of a problem for me. I'm down two volunteers and I have meetings for funds that I can't get out of."

"No problem," I said. "I'll be glad to pick up the kittens. I'm sure I can get someone to help me."

"If you could do that, Shell, that would be great. You can even use the shelter van."

I hung up and turned toward Gary, my eyes bright. "All set. I'll go get the kitties, and get to interview Ms. Opal Griffin Black as a nice bonus."

Gary crossed his arms over his chest. "What time are you planning on doing this? It's my turn to open the store and your night to close."

"Hm, I'm not sure. I'll have to call Opal back. She wanted the kittens picked up early, so I'm sure that I'll be done by three to work my shift."

"Okay, but I won't be able to accompany you, unless Robbie wants to work an extra shift, which I doubt. He was telling me earlier he needs all his time off to study for exams." Robbie was studying veterinary medicine at Connecticut University. He leveled me with a gaze. "I don't want you going alone."

"No worries. I'm sure I could get either Leila or Olivia to come with me. If all else fails, I'm sure I could get Jeremy Jackson," I added teasingly.

Gary frowned. "Not funny."

I called Opal Black back and told her that the Fox Hollow shelter was more than willing to accommodate her kittens. I asked her what time would work best for her and she suggested nine thirty. No sooner had I hung up from her than there was a knock at the back door. Gary opened it, and Leila rushed in. She took one look at my face and exclaimed, "Okay, Shell. Why do you look like the cat who just ate the canary? No offense, kids," she added with a hasty look at my cats. All three were lined up in front of their food bowls, casting disparaging looks Leila's way.

"Don't mind them," said Gary. He started to open the cabinet where I kept the cat food. "It's their suppertime. They'd look at anyone that way."

I steepled my fingers beneath my chin and looked at Leila. "What do they call it when events intersect just so?"

Leila eased a hip against the kitchen island. "Fate?"

"Well, Fate sure has been working overtime today. Thanks to my mother, of all people, I think we've caught a break."

While Gary fed the cats, I brought Leila up to speed. When I finished she said, "I hope all this pans out. I just can't wait to stick it to Jeremy Jackson. I can't believe he had the nerve to come here to try to convince you to dump me and work with him."

"Well, rest assured he will never succeed in that regard," I said. I grinned at Leila. "So what do you say? Want to accompany me to the shelter tomorrow morning?"

"Are you kidding! Try and keep me away!" Leila said, and then her tone turned more serious. "What if this Opal Griffin Black and the Opal Griffin from Barlow's notebook do turn out to be the same woman? Taking it a step further, what if she ends up being Martin's connection to the diamond heist?"

"Then I'd say it would be time to contact Josh and that Agent Reamer," put in Gary. He'd finished filling the food bowls, and as the cats contentedly crunched away, put away the bag containing the dry food. "You don't want a confrontation with these people. It's best left to law enforcement to handle."

"Maybe Reamer already knows," I mused. "The FBI has suspected Finley for quite a while. It wouldn't surprise me if they had him under surveillance."

"That's a possibility, but you don't know that for sure." Leila crossed over to the table, sat down in the chair next to mine. "I was so interested in your news, I almost forgot I've got some of my own to share. I made a stop at the police station before I came here."

"You did!" I leaned forward, and Gary leaned both elbows on the kitchen island. "What happened?"

Leila laced her hands behind her neck. "It was pandemonium down there. Your boyfriend Josh has everyone keeping mum. If I had a nickel for all the 'no comments' I heard I could probably retire to Hawaii. Anyway, I did manage to corner Denny Miller. He reluctantly admitted they got an anonymous tip to nose around the cisterns near the entrance to Grimley Woods."

"Was the tipper male or female?"

"They don't know. Apparently the caller used one of those devices that make your voice sound like Artoo-Detoo."

"Figures. Dare I ask if Jeremy Jackson was anywhere around? I told you he took off like a bat out of hell after getting a text."

My friend cut me an eye roll. "Oh, of course he was there. Apparently he was on the scene at Grimley as well. Denny said that Jackson was right there when they found the gun."

I scrunched up my lips. "He always seems to be around for the key events, doesn't he?"

"Like a bad penny." She picked up a paper napkin from the table and started to fiddle with the edges. "I guess it's true. He does seem to have a radar for ferreting out news."

"Ferreting it out, or making it happen?"

Leila stared at me. "What do you mean?"

"What I mean is, I'm wondering just how far Jackson might go to get a story. He told Josh that Gus's van nearly ran him over that night, but when I asked Gus he didn't remember nearly crashing into a car."

"Well, Gus was understandably upset. Maybe he just didn't see Jackson's car. That would tie in with Jackson's statement about the van nearly hitting him. I don't like Jackson, but I can't see him lying about something as important as that."

"Maybe. But I just don't trust that guy. He asks entirely too many questions and he's always popping up when you least expect him." Leila stifled a snicker. "I heard his nickname over at the *Post and Courier* is Columbo Junior." I rapped my knuckles on the table. "Enough about him. Any news on Gus?"

Leila nodded. "I saw him briefly. He was just coming out of the interview room. Inez was with him, and she looked like she was going to burst into tears at any second. I saw Jeff Ryan with them. I don't know if he's going to represent Gus, but Gus definitely needs someone good in his corner." She paused. "I also saw Bud Frisbee hanging around. Whether or not he was there to see Gus as well I have no idea."

I frowned. Bud Frisbee was fresh out of law school and had recently joined the public defender's office. If Gus couldn't manage to get a decent lawyer, he might have to settle for Bud, which could turn out to be a disaster. I sincerely hoped that after tomorrow, some of the pieces of this puzzle would start to fall into place. I was afraid that otherwise, poor Gus might find himself looking at some serious jail time, guilty or not.

Nineteen

It was a little after nine thirty on Monday morning when Leila and I pulled the shelter van up in front of a two-story boxy building. We got out and walked up the wide path and up the short flight of steps. Over the front door was a wooden sign that read *Willbur Pet Shelter* that was decorated with cartoonish figures of dogs and cats. I saw a bell off to one side of the door and pressed it. We heard it echo hollowly through the building, and a few minutes later the door was opened by a young girl wearing a red shirt that had *Willbur Pet Shelter* stitched over its pocket. "You must be the folks from Fox Hollow," she said. "I'm Connie, one of the volunteers. Mrs. Black's in the back."

We followed Connie down a narrow hallway. A large Ragdoll cat emerged from a side room and looked at us. I bent down to pet the cat. "Well, hello there."

"That's Amelia," Connie said. "She was our first rescue, so she's kind of our mascot."

I gave Amelia a scratch under her chin and then we continued down the hall. Connie led us to the very end, to a door on the left, and gave a sharp rap on the wood before opening it. She stepped to one side, and Leila and I stepped over the threshold.

The room looked more like a parlor than an office, with two comfy-looking chairs and a small love seat upholstered in burgundy and green plaid arranged in a circle off to one side. There was a desk in the center of the room, and a woman sat behind it. As we entered, she rose with a smile and held out her hand.

"Shell McMillan? I'm Opal Black."

I extended my hand and took a minute to study her. I judged her to be in her early fifties or maybe a tad older, although she didn't look it. Her skin was clear and unlined, and she was very attractive. Golden blonde hair skimmed her shoulders, and she had well-defined facial features. Hazel-green eyes framed by a thick fringe of lashes that didn't need the help of mascara bored into mine. I imagined that ten or fifteen years ago she must have been quite a beauty. She also had a pretty steely grip, and I flexed my fingers as she released my hand. "Nice to meet you. Nice place you have here."

"Thanks. And thank you for coming. This means a lot to me." She glanced over at the doorway, where Connie hovered. "I'm going to take them back to the cattery." She looked over her shoulder at me. "If you'd follow me, please."

Leila and I followed Opal back into the entry area. This time we turned left under an arch and emerged into a large two-tiered room with an upper balcony perched above the lower floor. Each level was lined with cages, and all of them looked to be full.

"We're an open admission shelter," Opal said. "We accept all animals regardless of age, breed, and so on. Unfortunately, this means we are required to euthanize based on the duration of stay in order to have enough space to accept all animals. The kittens in question will reach their limit in a few days and I have to tell you, I was shocked when we couldn't get them all adopted. We rescued them from an elderly woman who'd been hoarding them. Originally we had over forty purebred kittens. These fifteen are the last. I can't tell you how thankful I am you agreed to take them. I've no doubt they'll all find good homes. If I'd had a bit more time . . ." Her shoulders lifted in a shrug. "It wasn't meant to be, I suppose."

We stopped at the first enclosure. Two senior women were gathered around a long table, grooming a Siamese and a Persian kitten. The kittens were squirming around, batting their paws at each other and at the women. They looked healthy and happy.

"They're getting them ready for transport," said Opal. "Do you have carriers?"

Leila and I looked at each other. "I'm not sure," I said. "I didn't notice any in the van."

Opal waved her hand. "No matter. Connie," she called. Connie appeared almost instantly. "Get some of those spare carriers out of the storeroom for the kittens."

Connie gave a brisk nod and hurried away, and I turned to Opal. "You seem to be a natural at this."

Opal smiled. "What can I say? I love animals, always have." She cocked her head to one side, studying me. "You look awfully familiar. Have we met before?"

"You've probably seen her on TV," piped up Leila. "Shell used to be on a syndicated spy show."

"Of course!" Opal snapped her fingers. "*Spy Anyone*, right? I watched that every Thursday night, right after *Gray's Anatomy*. I just loved the chemistry between you and the guy who played your husband, Gary

Presser, right?" She tapped at her chin. "Your name was different. Shell Marlowe, right?"

"Right. After the show was canceled I went back to my real name."

Connie reappeared in the doorway. "The carriers are stuck behind some of those large boxes of feed. I could use a hand getting them out," she said.

"I'll help," Leila said. She turned to me and murmured, "She seems to be a fan. You might find out more one-on-one."

I silently agreed. Leila and Connie left and Opal turned to me. "What made you relocate to Connecticut, if you don't mind my asking. You're such a talented actress, I'm surprised you didn't get another series."

"I'd had enough of Hollywood," I admitted. "I was ready for a change. My aunt passed away and left me her house and her business. I run the Urban Tails Pet Shop in Fox Hollow."

"Oh, so that's why you left show business," said Opal. "I thought it might have been because you broke up with your fiancée." She looked a little embarrassed as she added, "I'm sorry. I know I shouldn't, but I do read those gossip rags."

"Well, there's some truth behind that story," I said. "I won't lie, my breakup with Patrick played a part in my decision to leave LA."

Opal bobbed her head up and down in agreement. "Funny how men sometimes figure into those equations, isn't it?" Her voice took on an almost dreamy quality as she continued, "I had quite a career change myself. I guess you could say it came about on account of a man."

I wanted to ask more but was afraid she'd think I was overly nosy. I hoped she'd elaborate more on her own, but instead she lapsed into silence. We continued walking through the cattery. Opal showed me the rest of the kittens. One Himalayan in particular caught my eye. He was tiny, cream and brown, and his big blue eyes watched everything that went on around him.

"That's Harvey," Opal said with a smile. "He's the runt of the bunch, but he's also the friendliest. I hope he gets a good home. Truthfully, I thought about adopting him myself, but I don't think Byron, my Labrador, would approve."

"You might be surprised. Dogs generally like cats. It's usually the cats who take umbrage with dogs."

"I have noticed that," Opal agreed. "I'm a cat person myself, but my late husband loved dogs. Do you have any pets yourself, Shell?"

"Three cats. Kahlua, a Siamese that was a gift from my mother. Then there's Purrday, a white Persian who belonged to my late aunt. The newest member of our family is a gorgeous red Maine coon that Purrday found caught in the bushes behind the pet shop. We named her Princess Fuzzypants."

"They sound divine, especially the Maine coon," said Opal. "I assume you tried to find her owner?"

"Of course. The vet said she wasn't microchipped so I put out some flyers, but no one claimed her. Well, one person tried to but it was a false claim. She was just trying to get the cat thinking she could sell her for big bucks."

Opal's lips thinned. "Amazing what some people will do."

"Isn't it? Anyway, now I hope that no one steps forward to claim her, because the princess is part of our family. Purrday would be devastated if she had to leave."

"Yes, the attachment can be great. I had a beautiful cat when I was a teenager. She was a dilute calico I'd named her Mrs. Potts after the teapot in *Beauty and the Beast*." She smiled at the memory. "She was such a good cat. I really loved her. I cried for days when she passed."

"Animals do leave an imprint on one's life." I figured now was as good a time as any to take the plunge. "I understand you're originally from Fox Hollow?"

She nodded. "Yes. I left there about ten years ago, but it seems like a lifetime."

"I can relate," I said with a nod. "Did you work with animals there as well?"

Opal paused. "No," she said at last. "Far from it. I managed a jewelry store. It's not there anymore—they went out of business shortly after I quit."

"Went out of business? Did the store fall on hard times?"

"You could say that." Opal hesitated, then added, "You'd have no way of knowing this. There was a major robbery at the store. Two people, a man and a woman, came in and robbed the store at gunpoint of several million dollars' worth of diamonds."

I gave a sharp intake of breath and let my hand flutter nervously over my heart. "Oh my goodness. No, I hadn't heard."

"It was a real disaster for the store. Those diamonds had been commissioned by a local society matron. She made a big stink afterward and sued. It drove them out of business, which was a shame. They were an excellent store up until that incident."

I gave a shudder. "That must have been horrible for you, experiencing a robbery like that. Gunpoint, you said?"

"It would have been, but fortunately I didn't experience it. I was running an errand for my boyfriend at the time. I took an awful chance, because I was supposed to be in the store, but . . . well, who knew all that was going to happen?" She shook her head. "The one I felt most sorry for was the salesgirl on duty at the time. She always blamed herself, said if she hadn't gotten cocky and wanted to show off the diamonds, it would never have happened. The FBI man, though, he said it wouldn't have mattered, that the robbers knew what they were doing. The FBI grilled all of us. I'm positive they thought those robbers were tipped off by someone who worked in the store."

"Oh. What they call an inside job, you mean?"

Opal nodded. "That just wasn't possible. The upper management of Van Nuys was fanatical about vetting their employees. By the time they finished digging into my background they knew everything about me, even when I cut my first tooth. When they say the FBI sees all and knows all, they aren't kidding. Anyway, they cleared me and I stayed on for a while after the robbery, but the stigma of it stayed with me. I had no ties. My family was gone, my boyfriend had up and left me, so I decided to leave and make a fresh start somewhere else. I ended up here in Willbur."

"That's a shame you had to go through all that," I said. "I imagine your boyfriend not sticking by you made a tough time tougher."

"You can say that again," Opal said, and this time I caught a note of bitterness in her tone. "Pete wasn't the stick-with-you type, although at the time I didn't know that. I was pretty much a fool for love, like that old song goes. Although in the end, I was actually grateful to him." Her lips twisted into a crooked smile. "If he hadn't asked me to run that errand for him I'd probably have been the one held at gunpoint and tied up."

"Possibly. Is that what broke the two of you up?"

"Not really. We were, ah, sharing an intimate moment when his wife interrupted." She held up her hand, traffic cop style. "Before you say anything, yes, I should have known better, but I fell for that old line of 'my wife doesn't understand me' and 'I'm getting a divorce so we can get married.' He was having a bit of trouble with his business at the time. He owned a diner and it wasn't doing too well." She gave me a dismissive wave.

"His wife caught us in a compromising situation and threatened to take him for all he had. I have to hand it to him, he wasted no time. Dumped me, sold the diner and got the heck out of Dodge."

I could feel a tingle inch up my spine, and my palms were sweaty with moisture as I leaned forward and remarked, "This is an amazing coincidence. I recently ran into a man who was originally from Fox Hollow. He came to an event we had last weekend. I didn't know him personally, but one of our volunteers told me that he owned a diner, which he sold. She also said he left town in a hurry, presumably to avoid a messy divorce." I paused. "His name was Peter Martin."

Opal's eyes snapped wide and she inhaled sharply. "Oh my goodness," she murmured. "What—what did this man look like?" I gave a brief description, and she put her hand over her heart. "My goodness, I can hardly believe it. After all this time, PJ finally came back?"

I felt a sudden rush of satisfaction flow through me. "PJ?"

She blushed. "It was a nickname. He hated to be called Pete or Peter, because that's what his wife called him. He was very fond of peanut butter and jelly sandwiches, so I called him PJ." She smiled then and her eyes took on a faraway look. I had the feeling she was remembering happier times. Finally she turned to me. "I wonder what's made him come back after all this time. Not to look me up, I'm sure."

"I guess we'll never know. I'm sorry to have to tell you this, but he's dead. He was murdered in Grimley Woods Saturday night."

"Murdered!" Opal's face paled. "Are you sure?"

"I'm afraid so. As a matter of fact, I'm the one who found his body."

"Oh my God." She started to sway, and I caught her by the arm.

"Are you all right?" I asked her.

She brushed her hand across her eyes. "I'm fine. It's just, even after all this time . . ." She took a step, swayed again. "I'm so sorry. I just need to sit for a minute."

There were two stools over on the other side of the cattery. I led Opal over to them, and she slid onto one. There was a water cooler nearby, so I went and got her a cup of water. She downed it in one gulp and crushed the cup in her hand. "I'm so sorry," she said. "Even though I haven't seen him in years, it's still a shock. Certain feelings never quite go away, I suppose."

I remembered just how it had made me feel when I'd recently received an unexpected gift from my ex-fiancé. "No, they don't," I agreed. "Even though we wish they would."

Opal, apparently, was now in the mood to talk. "I really did love him," she said. "He was so gentle and caring. He was married, and I knew it was wrong, but he kept telling me that his marriage was a mistake, that as soon as he straightened out his finances things would be different. And fool that I was, I believed him."

I remembered my own experience with Patrick. I'd believed all his promises of happy ever after too, until my world came crashing down around me. "It happens."

Her jaw set. "His wife had a PI following us, and the guy tipped her off to our rendezvous. She surprised us down in the cellar. I took off, and that was the last I ever heard from him. He never even called me to tell me he'd sold the diner. I had to hear it from a mutual friend, a girl who worked at PJ's. Phoebe. Oddly, we bonded over our boyfriend troubles." Opal rolled her eyes. "Hers was a real rake. He was always having close brushes with the law."

"That's a shame. Did Pete—PJ—know Phoebe's boyfriend?"

"Chuck? Oh, yes. As a matter of fact, he knew Pete first. He did a few odd jobs at the diner. That's how Phoebe met him, I think. She always was a sucker for a lost cause. That and puzzles."

"Puzzles?"

"Yeah, puzzles of all kinds. Crosswords, the kind you put together, word games. She loved 'em all. She liked to make puzzles up, too, and the harder the better. Anyway, she called me right after he left, told me he'd taken off. She said that she hadn't heard from Chuck either. She sounded disgusted. I remembered thinking she sounded fed up, and it was high time. Anyway, Phoebe said she couldn't stay around here anymore either. She was thinking of taking a long trip somewhere. Asked if I wanted to go with her, but by that time I'd already quit my job at Van Nuys and gone back to live with my parents. I told her no, that I needed to figure out what to do with my life.

"A friend of mine said she could get me a job at a department store here in Willbur, so I decided to move here. One Saturday she invited me to a church dance, and it was there I met John Black. He was older than me, a veterinarian, and very into animal rescue. I took a course at the university and he hired me as a vet assistant, and we got married a year later. We started up this shelter together five years ago." Her eyes misted over. "He died last spring, cancer. I treasure the eight years we had together. And I still carry on with this shelter. He would want me to."

She slid off the stool, brushed at her wet eyes with the back of her hand. "I'm so sorry, Shell. I didn't mean to bore you with the story of my life. I'm sure you have better things to do. It's just when you said PJ had been murdered, all those memories, good and bad, came flooding back."

"I didn't know Pete Martin, but I heard that he wasn't very well liked," I said. I leaned in a bit closer to her and said, "To be perfectly honest, a friend of mine is under suspicion for his murder. Gus Morton. He's the person that Pete sold the diner to when he left. He'd come back to town a few weeks ago and was pestering Gus to sell Good Eats back to him."

Opal's brows drew together. "PJ wanted the diner back? That's strange."

"Offhand, could you think of anyone who might want to see him dead?"

"Good question." Opal was silent for a few moments. Finally she said, "Possibly his ex-wife. I understand she was really steamed when he left." Her frown deepened. "Maybe his partner?" she ventured.

My ears perked up. "His partner?"

Opal bobbed her head up and down. "PJ had a silent partner in the diner. He told me once that was the only way he could afford to buy it. This partner wanted to be really silent, too. Insisted his name be kept off of everything, including the deed of sale. He told PJ that his ex-wife had kept him from seeing his son, so he was going to make sure she never learned of his investment. Said he was sure if she did, she'd try to get her cut and he wasn't having any of it—he wanted to have something to leave his kid."

An elusive memory niggled at the corners of my brain. "That's very interesting. I don't suppose that Pete ever mentioned this partner's name to you?"

"If he did I don't recall. The only other person who might know besides him would be Phoebe. She did the business's books, and PJ used to confide in her."

"And you don't remember her last name?"

"No, I'm sorry. Oh, wait—she used to rent a room from a crotchety old woman. Now *her* name I do recall. She had the same last name as my best friend from grade school. Johansen. I think her first name was Enid. You should look her up. Maybe she could help."

Twenty

It didn't take long for the kittens to be loaded into the shelter van. Opal thanked me again, not only for taking the kittens but for lending her a friendly ear. I gave her my card with the shop number and wrote my cell number on the back. She took it and promised to get in touch if she remembered anything else that might be useful. In turn, I also promised to put up posters advertising kittens available for adoption in Urban Tails.

Leila waited until I'd pulled out of the shelter driveway and then turned to me, her eyes bright. "Okay, she told you something useful, I can tell. Spill."

I repeated what Opal had told me. When I finished, Leila leaned back with a triumphant grin. "I knew it was a good idea to leave the two of you alone. Now that's what I call a satisfactory morning's work," she said. "It sounds as if we've established a link between Martin and the diamond robbery. And should this Phoebe's mysterious boyfriend Chuck turn out to be Charles Finley, there's yet another."

"True," I agreed. I looked at Leila. "You said that Phyllis in your office spoke with Mrs. Johansen's niece?"

Leila's brow furrowed. "Yep. Clotter, I think the name was. Why?"

"Can you ask Phyllis for her number? I'd like to talk to her. I know she said she couldn't remember anything about that tenant, but maybe we can jog her memory."

"Okay," said Leila. She whipped out her tablet and started typing.

"Opal mentioned Phoebe had an affinity for puzzles," I went on. "That could explain the clipping and note in the jewel box, along with the diamond. They'd been meant as a message for either Peter Martin or Finley, perhaps a clue as to the location of the other diamonds? Opal mentioned Phoebe was fed up, so maybe she just grabbed her share and took off."

"And left the rest for the others?" Leila asked. "If that's so, it says something about Phoebe's character. She had to be more honorable than the other two if she left their share for them to find." She jotted something else down in her notes and then said, "I find it awfully convenient that Martin had Opal run an errand at the time of the robbery. If the robbers were Finley and Phoebe, Opal surely would have been able to identify them."

"What this all adds up to, at least to me, is that Charles Finley is a far better candidate for the murder of Pete Martin than Gus Morton," I said.

"Yeah, maybe they argued over how to split up the diamond stash. Maybe Finley tried to cheat Martin out of what he felt was his rightful share."

"Well, one thing I'm certain of," I said. "Without his cut of those diamonds, Martin wouldn't have been able to pay Gus ninety cents for that diner, let alone ninety thousand." I accelerated the van to pass a slow-moving dump truck. When I'd moved back into the middle lane I said, "The other thing that puzzles me is Jillian's role in all this. Did she get acquainted with Finley through Phoebe? Gus said the dark shape he saw at the scene of Martin's murder could have been a female."

"Okay. So we don't rule out either Jillian or this Phoebe as the killer either."

When we got to the shelter, Marianne and two of her volunteers were waiting for us. I'd texted them before we left that we were on our way. One of the volunteers, Margery Wilson, declared she was going to file an application to adopt Harvey. "I've heard such good things about this breed," she gushed, "and Harvey's just so stinking cute!"

"Himalayans are very similar to Persians," I said. I had a customer who ordered special food for his Himalayan, because they were prone to obesity. I'd picked up quite a few tidbits from him. "For example, did you know there are two types of Himalayans, the traditional or the doll-faced, and the peke-faced."

"No, I did not," Margery replied. "What's the difference?"

"Well, the peke-faced has the more extreme squashed-looking facial features. Both types have very large round eyes with the nose leather directly between the eyes. Harvey here looks to be a doll-faced Himalayan."

"I love his coat," gushed Margery. "He's such a pretty color."

I leaned over to pet Harvey where he was snuggled in Margery's arms. "Looks like a lilac-point. He's got a white, bright body color and his points are a diluted brighter blue. The others are chocolate and cream."

Leila hurried over to me. "I've got to get going. My editor wants me to cover a rally over in Ford. Keep me posted, okay?"

I promised to do so and then went to the shelter office to find Marianne. She smiled when she saw me. "Those kittens are stinking cute," she said. "And they'll go fast. I'm glad we rescued them." She glanced down at some papers on her desk and then back at me. "Eunice is due back

Friday. What's the story with the jewel box?"

Oy, I'd completely forgotten about it. "Ed said he'd give me a call when it's done. He thought by Wednesday."

"I hope he can fix it," Marianne said.

"Don't worry. If he can't I'll find someone who can and pay for it, since it was my catnip-inspired cats who caused the damage."

Marianne smiled. "That's nice of you, Shell. Let's hope it doesn't come to that."

"Eunice didn't happen to leave any contact information about that box with you, by any chance?" I asked.

Marianne frowned. "What do you mean?"

"Well, she got the box at an estate sale. I just wondered if there were any receipts or proof of ownership that she might have brought with her when she left the box, you know, to prove it was hers."

Marianne tapped her pencil against the desk. "You know, I never thought to ask her for anything. I just figured, you know, it was Eunice and I knew her so that was good enough. I suppose in retrospect I should have done that with all the items left for appraisal, regardless."

"Eunice is coming back Friday?"

"According to her sister, yes. She said Eunice would stop by here sometime in the morning to pick up the jewel box."

I glanced at my watch. "Well, I've got to get over to Urban Tails. I'll let you know when Ed calls me about the jewel box." I started to leave, and then paused. "Did Eunice's sister leave a number, by any chance?"

"She didn't give it to me, but it's on the caller ID on my phone."

"Could I have it? I'd like to give her a call. I remember that Eunice mentioned her sister was interested in getting some nyjer seeds for her parakeet, and we just got a shipment in."

Marianne pulled out her phone, jotted down the number and handed the paper to me. "Here you go."

"Thanks." I slid the paper into my pocket. With any degree of luck, maybe Eunice's sister had accompanied her to the estate sale, and maybe she might be able to fill in some of the blanks.

• • •

It was quiet at the pet shop, so I pulled Gary into the back room and related the morning's events in detail. He listened intently, not saying a word. When I'd finished he leaned back in his chair, his hands laced behind his neck, and stared down at the floor for several minutes. Finally he looked at me. "I think you should tell Josh all this," he said. "Or that FBI agent."

I made a face. "Reamer? Mr. Personality?"

"Now, now, you're forgetting how things used to be on our show," Gary said. "Fibbies aren't supposed to be personable. They're supposed to be protective and efficient. Besides, you know what I mean. This information could help Gus's case, and it might even be useful to the FBI in their search for the missing diamonds."

"Maybe you're right," I said grudgingly.

Gary rose, walked over and patted my shoulder. "I know I am. Now, since my shift has ended, I'm on my way home to shower and change. I told Olivia I'd pick her up at five. We're going to have dinner in Emporium and then there's a dance exhibition at the Rialto she wanted to see."

I knew Gary enjoyed dance. He was an excellent dancer. He'd competed on a dance competition show the year before our show ended and had come in second. "Enjoy," I said.

After Gary left I dialed Josh's number, and it went to his voicemail. I left him a message that I had some information that might be useful to both cases, and for him to call me as soon as possible. Then I went back out front, since I was working solo for the rest of the day. On Mondays we closed at six, and business began to pick up shortly after three thirty. I was busy right up until closing time. As I flipped the sign on the door from *Open* to *Closed*, my stomach let out a loud growl, reminding me that I hadn't eaten since lunchtime, when I'd scarfed down two power bars I had in my purse. I thought of the burger I'd gotten at Gus's diner the other night. It had been juicy, cooked just the way I liked it. I could go for one right now, and as an added bonus maybe someone would be working there who could shed some light on Jillian the waitress. I just needed to make a quick stop home, then feed the cats and myself and hopefully my curiosity.

• • •

Twenty minutes later I pulled into the Good Eats parking lot and went inside. A large group of men in sweatshirts crowded around the counter, but I saw an empty stool all the way over at the other end. I made my way over and had barely sat down when a familiar voice asked, "Well, well, Shell McMillan! What can I get you?"

I looked up at Ted Trainor and smiled. "Hey, Ted. I thought you quit?"

He chuckled. "I did, but as it turned out that food chain is more of a slave cave than anything else. They like you to work overtime, but they only want to pay straight time, not time and a half. Then, when I heard about Gus"—he spread his hands—"I went to Inez and offered my services. She talked to Gus and he told her I could come back."

"Oh, that's great," I said. "I know he was bummed when you left."

Ted hung his head. "Yeah, Inez said as much. The grass always looks greener, you know? Anyway . . ." He let out a long breath. "I guess you heard Gus had his bail hearing today."

"Today? Wow, they didn't waste much time, did they?" I studied Ted's face for a minute and then sighed. "He didn't make bail, did he?"

"Nope. The judge set it at two hundred thousand. The ADA really thinks she's got a slam-dunk case. She argued Gus was a flight risk, and I guess the judge bought it."

"Poor Gus. I imagine he couldn't make the bail?"

"Nope, although I understand his sister was going to try and see if she could swing a loan on her house." He fiddled with a napkin on the counter. "I imagine that's another reason he decided to hire me back. He needs someone who can run the place until he's cleared of this nonsensical murder charge. Anyone with a drop of sense who knows Gus knows that guy isn't a killer. A yeller, yes. Can he pound a counter hard with his fist to make a point? Yes. But shoot someone in cold blood? Not on your life."

"I agree." I glanced over at the cluster of men. "I see business hasn't slacked off any. If anything it's improved."

"Who, them?" Ted jerked his thumb in their direction. "That's the KC bowling league. They always have a pregame appetizer here." He slung his towel over one shoulder. "Now, what can I get you?"

"I was in here Saturday and had a burger and fries. It was so good I thought it deserved a repeat performance."

"The cook will be glad to hear that." He whipped out a pad and pen, scribbled my order down. "Anything to drink?"

"Just a club soda with a lime twist."

"You got it."

As Ted filled a glass with club soda, I leaned forward. "Do you by any chance know what happened to the waitress who was here Saturday? Jillian?"

Ted looked up from slicing the lime. "That new hire? I sure do. She called in today and quit."

I drew in my breath. "Quit? Really? I thought she was just hired."

He shrugged. "Maybe it was for the best. From what I understand she was a strange duck. She only put in one full day, and she spent most of it down in the cellar, rearranging everything. One strange bird." He looked at me. "Why'd you ask about her?"

I thought fast. "I saw her here briefly on Saturday. I heard her talk about adopting a Himalayan cat, and I happen to know the shelter got a few in. I thought I'd let her know. I don't suppose you have any contact info for her?"

Ted snorted. "She wanted to adopt a cat? That's a good one. From what I hear, I doubt she'd be a good parent to a cat or any other animal, for that matter. But give me a few and I'll see if I can find her file in Gus's office," Ted offered. He placed a napkin on the counter in front of me, set the glass of club soda with lime on it, then picked up the order pad and pushed through the swinging door that led to the kitchen. I picked up my glass, took a sip, and then turned so that I had a good view of the diner's interior. Most of the tables were deserted, except for a few of the rear tables. One man was seated there in a black turtleneck, drinking a coke. I took another sip of my drink and turned as I heard someone slide onto the stool beside me. My face fell as I recognized the newcomer.

"What's a nice girl like you doing in a place like this?" Jeremy Jackson asked, his eyes twinkling.

I looked the handsome newsman up and down. Once again, he was impeccably dressed in tan slacks and a long-sleeved brown and tan shirt, open at the collar. A thin gold chain glinted around his neck. "I might say the same about you."

He grinned. "I'm a relentless newsman. You'll always find me where you least expect to."

I narrowed my gaze at him. "It seems that wherever I go, you're never far behind. It's almost as if you're keeping me under surveillance."

Jackson smiled but didn't answer. He plucked a napkin from a stack at the edge of the counter and fiddled with its edge. "A shame about Gus Morton not making bail. I hear his sister couldn't swing a loan."

"Yes, it is," I said evenly. "But I'm sure it will all work out in the end. Gus is innocent."

"You sound pretty sure. From what I hear the evidence against him is pretty damning."

"Evidence that's mostly circumstantial."

"Circumstantial evidence can be the worst kind," Jackson said. He lifted his hand, started to tick off on his fingers. "One, he was at the scene of the crime. Two, his gun was found in a cistern not far from where the body was discovered. Three, the bullet from his gun matches the one taken out of Martin's body. Four, only Gus's fingerprints were on the gun . . . should I continue?"

"Is there more?"

"Isn't that enough?"

I held up my own hand. "One, there might have been a good reason for him to be in the woods, if he was indeed there. As for two, three and four, someone could have stolen his gun, killed Martin with it, and they could have worn gloves, which would account for only Gus's fingerprints being on it."

Jackson held up his other hand. "Gus already admitted to being in the woods to meet with Martin. He swears, though, that Martin was already dead when he found him. He also admits to taking the gun out of the box at his house and bringing it here."

"And he also said that he didn't take the gun with him when he went to meet Martin, and I for one believe him," I shot back.

"Believe him all you like, it doesn't make him innocent."

"Doesn't make him guilty either," I said. "What happened to keeping an open mind?"

"I pride myself on doing just that. But when the evidence is this overwhelming . . ." Jackson shrugged. "Gus is guilty, Shell. You'll see."

"Maybe you're the one who'll see."

Jackson clucked his tongue. "Don't tell me I was wrong about you. I thought you were a pretty good sleuth. Maybe it was for the best you didn't accept my offer. Seems to me you've picked up some bad habits, hanging around with that reporter friend of yours. You should tell her she should stick to her garden shows and leave the crime reporting to the pros."

I arched a brow at him. "Like you?"

He grinned. "Maybe. You have a good evening now. Enjoy spinning your wheels with your friend."

Jackson gave me a brief wave and ambled out the door. I looked after his retreating form and mentally counted to ten. He really was an insufferable individual. He made me more determined than ever not only to clear Gus but to find out what the heck ever happened to those diamonds. Once I did that, I'd make sure Leila got the exclusive scoop.

That would ensure her getting the crime reporter spot on the *Herald* and not Jackson. If anyone was ever in need of being taken down a peg, it was him.

I glanced toward the rear of the diner and saw the man in the black turtleneck toss a bill on the table and head out the door after Jackson. I felt a tap on my shoulder, and I turned around and saw Ted, a Good Eats business card in his hand. He extended it to me. "There wasn't much in her file," he said. "Just her name and phone number. Hope that helps."

I looked at the card, turned it over. *Jillian Henshaw. 555-2231.* I tucked it into my jacket pocket. "Thanks, Ted. It does."

"Glad I could help. Your burger will be out in a few," he said and then leaned in closer to me. "Was that Jeremy Jackson I saw talking to you?"

"None other than."

Ted shook his head and then said in a low tone, "That guy's a real bear on tracking down stories. I've got a friend who works the news desk at PLK, the radio station? He said that Jackson's like the Mounties—never gives up until he gets his man. Said he'll do anything for a story, too. Did you know he was the one who found Gus's gun at the crime scene?"

I almost dropped my glass of club soda. "Say what?"

Ted nodded. "Jackson was out at Grimley Woods even before the police. They were getting annoyed at him, but he's the one who spotted the muzzle of the gun in the cistern and called them over."

I frowned. I thought about the anonymous call the police had received, tipping them off about the gun. Was it possible Jackson was trying to deliberately implicate Gus in Martin's murder so he could get a big scoop? Unlike Leila, I thought the newsman perfectly capable of framing someone to further his own career.

Whereas minutes before I'd been ravenous, my appetite now seemed to have taken a nosedive.

Twenty-one

All three cats were there to greet me as I walked in the door. I bent over and gave each of them a scratch behind one ear. Purrday looked expectantly at the plastic bag I had clutched in one hand. "Oho, so you're really not glad to see me," I said. "You just smelled this burger and fries, didn't you?"

Purrday made a noise that could best be described as a snort, which I took to mean, "Who, me?" I waggled my finger at him and then touched it to the tip of his nose. "Yes, you. Your powers of super-smell are working overtime."

All three cats shot me a look and Purrday murped something under his breath. Kahlua padded over to her fleece bed and arranged herself comfortably. Purrday and the princess continued to sit and stare at me.

I chuckled. "Fine. You can all have a small piece of burger."

Both cats meowed loudly. I got a plate and a glass out of the cupboard and set them on the kitchen island. I found a pitcher filled with sweet tea that Gary had made yesterday and filled a tall glass with it, then got the burger out of its foam container and put it on the plate. I picked up the plate and glass and took them over to the kitchen table, pulled out a chair and sat down. The cats, on their haunches by the island, watched every move I made. I took a large bite of the burger and gave an appreciative nod when it tasted just as good as the one I'd had on my previous outing. I lifted up the edge of the bun and broke off three small pieces of hamburger, then crossed over and deposited one in each cat's dish. Purrday and the princess immediately plopped down and started eating. Kahlua raised her head, sniffed, and had just sauntered over to her dish when a loud knock sounded on the back door. I took a quick peek through the curtains and then snapped back the lock and opened the door wide. Josh stepped through into the kitchen. His eyes looked bleary and there were dark shadows under them. He leaned over and gave me a quick peck on the cheek.

I smiled up at him. "Is this a social call or are you here about my message?"

He frowned. "Your message?"

"The one I left on your cell earlier."

He shook his head. "Sorry, Shell. Between Martin's murder and Reamer on my case with the diamonds I haven't had a spare minute. I haven't listened to my phone all day." He looked me right in the eye. "I imagine you've already heard the news?"

"About Gus? You bet. What was that ADA thinking, calling him a flight risk? And that bail amount is ridiculous." I folded my arms across my chest. "I'm sorry, but I just can't buy the idea of him being the number-one suspect."

Josh let out a sigh. "I can't either, Shell, but the evidence—"

"Is circumstantial and you know it," I shot back. "Gus said that he took the gun to the diner. He thought he might use it to throw a scare into Martin, but in the end he didn't take it out. He left it there where anyone might have taken it. And as for only his fingerprints being on it, didn't you ever hear of gloves?"

Josh's eyes narrowed. "Just how do you know about the gun, and about only Gus's fingerprints being on it? That's not public knowledge. We didn't release that to the press. Not even Quentin Watson knows."

"Yeah, well, ace reporter Jeremy Jackson apparently sees all and knows all. Really, do you think it's just a coincidence he keeps popping up at these crime scenes?"

Josh's face flushed with annoyance. "Oh, so it was Jackson who told you this? When did you see him?"

"Over at Good Eats." I gestured toward the kitchen table and the plate with my barely touched burger on it. "I stopped by to pick up dinner, and he was there. From the way he talked, Gus has already been tried and convicted."

Josh blew out a breath and jammed his hands into his pockets. "Great. Just great."

I let the silence hang between us for a moment and then said, "Ted Trainor's back working there. He told me that he's got a friend over at PLK who said Jackson is the one who found the murder weapon."

Josh let his gaze flick over me. "That's partially true. Jackson didn't actively search for the weapon. He happened to be standing by the cistern and he looked down and saw the muzzle of the gun sticking up, so he shouted to the officers."

"How convenient," I said with a curl of my lip. "You guys get an anonymous call about that gun, and wham! Jackson's on the scene. He even just happens to be standing by the very cistern where the gun was dropped. And let's not forget his very convenient description of a man who looks remarkably like Gus hightailing it away from the scene of the crime. Why, it's almost as if he's leading you by the nose in the direction he wants you to take—the one that gives him the scoop of the century."

Josh pulled his hands out of his pockets, swiped them on his pants. "What are you getting at, Shell? You think Jackson is trying to set Gus up for a murder rap just to get a front-page story?" He clucked his tongue. "That's ridiculous."

"I'm not so sure. Nick Barlow intimated Jackson would sell his own mother for a front-page story, and Ted's friend pretty much substantiated that claim."

Josh's eyes narrowed. "Who's Nick Barlow?"

Uh-oh. I'd made a slip, but it was too late to cover it up now. "He's the reporter who covered the Van Nuys diamond heist ten years ago." As Josh continued to stare at me, I stammered, "Leila and I went to see him."

Josh balled one hand into a fist, slapped it against his thigh. "I knew it. You've been investigating."

"We-el, yes. Sorta kinda." I gestured toward the table. "Let's sit down. This could take a while. Would you like some iced tea?" I paused. "Or something stronger?"

Finally, his lips twitched upward. "Tempting, but I suppose since I'm on duty, iced tea will have to do."

I poured Josh a tall glass of iced tea and refilled mine, then I sat down in the chair across from him. "I think Martin and Finley were in on that diamond heist together. Finley and his girlfriend committed the robbery, and Martin made certain no one was around who could identify them."

"Why do you say that?"

"Because of Martin's girlfriend, Opal," I answered promptly. "She was the manager of Van Nuys Jewelers. She told me the reason she wasn't at the store at the time of the robbery was because she had to run an errand for her boyfriend, who happened to be Pete Martin. No doubt it was something he made up to get her out of the store so she wouldn't be there when Finley and his girlfriend stole the diamonds. She would have been able to identify them." I paused. "And then there's Jillian Henshaw."

Josh swiped at his chin. "Who?"

"She's the woman who tried to steal Eunice's jewel box with Finley, the waitress at Good Eats. I think she's connected to another woman who also worked there. Opal told me about a girl named Phoebe. She couldn't remember her last name. Phoebe had a boyfriend named Chuck, who I think is Charles Finley."

Dead silence. Then Josh cleared his throat. "I see. And you think this Phoebe could be the female robber?"

I nodded. "Yes. I'm thinking that Phoebe was put in charge of stashing away the diamonds until they could all get together to split them up. I think that after Finley's arrest and Martin's abrupt departure, she decided to skip out with her share before she got caught. But she had a sense of honor, so she left one of the diamonds and clues to the whereabouts of the others in that jewel box for the other two to find when they finally returned to Fox Hollow."

Josh nibbled at his lower lip. "Not much of a clue, a clipping about Finley's arrest and an advertisement for cabinet refurbishing."

I swallowed. "There was something else. Donna happened to notice it when I showed her the chest." I got my tote, fished inside for the scrap of paper and handed it to Josh. He studied it a few minutes, then handed it back to me. "That seems like even less of a clue than the clipping," he said. "Two words cut in half?"

"I know it doesn't seem like much," I admitted. "I'm sure if we had the entire note it might make a lot more sense."

Josh scratched at his head. "Maybe. Or it could be that note refers to something that has absolutely nothing to do with the robbery."

I frowned. "I realize you don't think much of my investigative efforts," I said stiffly, "but at least promise me you'll have Reamer look into a connection between this Jillian Henshaw and Charles Finley. I think this Phoebe might be the common denominator between them."

Josh hesitated, then reached out and caught my hand. "Shell, I'm not trying to give you a hard time about this. I'm just trying to keep you safe."

I sighed. "I know. I'm sorry if I sounded, well . . . abrupt? I guess I'm just a bit frustrated."

He grinned. "I'm sorry too. This should all be over soon, though, and we can go back to our normal lives—have a normal date."

"All except poor Gus," I murmured. "He'll be stuck in prison for a crime I'm sure Finley committed."

Josh put his hands on my shoulders and gazed deeply into my eyes. "Can we agree to disagree on this? For now?"

"I guess," I mumbled.

His eyes searched my face. "And you promise to stay out of this? Leave the investigating to us?" When I hesitated, he went on, "We've been down this road before, Shell. I'll be the first to admit you've got a knack for putting clues together, but you've also got one for getting into some pretty tight situations. You have to promise me you'll stay out of this one."

"Okay, fine."

His eyes narrowed. "Say that again and put your hands out where I can see them."

I waved both hands in front of his face. "Fine."

Josh's pocket buzzed, and he whipped out his phone. He looked at the screen, then slid the phone back into his pocket. "I've got to go. I promise I'll pass on your theory to Reamer and let you know the outcome. Okay?"

I shot him a resigned look. "Okay."

We kissed and then Josh took off. I closed the door after him and leaned against it, not entirely satisfied with the way our conversation had turned out. I chuckled inwardly, thankful that Josh hadn't wanted me to take my shoes and socks off as well, then I wouldn't have been able to cross my toes when I was making him that promise.

I sat down at the kitchen table and drummed on it with my fingertips, mentally reviewing all that I'd figured out. I was ninety-nine percent certain Martin and Finley had been partners in that diamond robbery. Martin returned to Fox Hollow around the same time as Finley and the two of them converged on Gus, trying to get him to sell them the diner. I paused, frowning. That bothered me. I might understand why Martin would want it, but why would Finley?

Before I could ponder further, my phone buzzed. I picked it up and saw Ed Laverty's number, so I swiped the answer button. "Hey, Ed. What's up? Please tell me you were able to fix the box."

"Oh, I fixed it. Looks as good as new, and the secret compartment's back in place." He paused. "I found something, though, that I think you need to see. Can you come down to my shop right now?"

I could tell from his tone that he was excited about something. I pushed back my chair and reached for my jacket. "I can be there in ten," I told him. I shrugged into my jacket, grabbed my tote and jerked the back door open just as Gary started to open it. "Hey, hey," he said. "Where's the fire?"

I stared at him. "What are you doing home so early?" I asked. "I thought you were taking Olivia to dinner and the dance exhibition?"

"That was the plan," Gary said. "We were just finishing up dessert when she got a call from the nursing home about her aunt Grace. Apparently she fell again, and Olivia wanted to go out there to see her. I offered to drive her but she said she wasn't sure how long she'd be. I didn't feel like going to the exhibition by myself, so I came home." He looked me up and down. "And just where are you off to? Got a hot lead?"

"As a matter of fact, yes. Ed Laverty called. He fixed the jewel box, but he said that he found something I needed to see."

Gary reached out and plucked the car keys from my hand. "Well, then. What are we waiting for? Let's go."

• • •

We pulled up in front of Ed's shop exactly ten minutes later. Ed was at the door, waiting for me. "Boy, when you say ten minutes, you really mean it, don't you?" he said with a grin. He looked over at Gary. "Hi, Gary."

"Hey," Gary said. We stepped inside the shop and I turned to Ed. "Thank you for fixing that box, Ed. I really appreciate it."

"No problem. The box is in the workshop." He started toward the rear of the shop and Gary and I followed. There were tools everywhere, on the floor and covering the low-slung bench and table at the far corner of the room. I saw a familiar object on the table and let out a little gasp.

"Oh my, it looks great." I walked over to the table and peered down at the jewel box. No one would ever have known it had been damaged. If possible, the box looked even better than it had before. I ran my hand along its side. "You did a fantastic job."

Ed shuffled his feet. I could tell by the expression on his face he was pleased at the compliment. "It wasn't all that hard. The compartment just needed some adjusting, and I sanded the whole thing down so there were no jagged edges and it looked even." He picked up the box and ran his hand along the side. "See this piece with the knot in it? Well, when you press against it like so . . ." He jabbed his finger on the wood, and the drawer shot out. "It activates the mechanism."

I leaned in for a closer look. "Looking at it you'd never be able to tell it was damaged at all," I marveled. "I can't thank you enough, Ed. You really helped me out of a bind. Now, what was it you wanted to show me?"

"Just this," said Ed. He tipped the box to one side and pointed inside the drawer. I held my breath and waited.

Twenty-two

Ed tipped the box to one side and pointed inside the drawer. "See right there? The lining ripped a bit when I was trying to fix the drawer. When I went to sew it, I found this jammed inside." He reached into his shirt pocket and pulled out a small key, which he dropped into my palm. "It was wedged in pretty tight. I don't think it got in there by accident."

I turned it over in my hand. "It looks like a safe deposit box key," I said at last.

Ed bobbed his head up and down. "That, or it could also fit a custom-made box." His lips curved slightly and his eyes took on a faraway cast, as if he were reliving a pleasant memory. "Sam Weatherly used to design custom boxes, similar to the ones they use in banks. Some locked, some didn't." He reached out and tapped the key in my hand. "This looks like one of Sam's keys, although I can't be certain."

I closed my fist around the key. "Sam Weatherly. If I recall correctly, he did woodworking too, right?"

"Oh yeah! He was a genius. He could carve anything out of wood. He was an excellent refinisher too." I could see Ed's face getting more animated as he warmed to his subject. "I think Sam was my inspiration for taking up woodworking. I remember going into his store after school and examining all the wonderful things he did." Ed walked over to a small dresser in the far corner and ran his hand along it. "See this piece? It was my mother's. Sam refinished it. He even put a special drawer into it for her. The drawer locks under a panel, and when closed it appears to be only a strip of decorative molding." He ran his hand along the side of the dresser and suddenly a drawer shot out. "Pretty good, huh? Almost like that secret compartment. I think that's why I was able to fix it. Sam was good about explaining how he fixed things. I used to like to go to his shop and listen to him talk, watch him work. I was really sad when he sold his business."

"He retired, right?" Gary asked.

"It was more like a forced retirement. He didn't confide in many people, but he liked my father. He told him that he made some serious business errors, and it was costing him now. Told my dad that it never paid to keep silent, and if he ever went into business with someone be sure to get his name on everything. He was sick, too, but no one knew how sick until he passed."

149

Something pinged at the back of my brain. I wanted to quiz Ed a bit further, but I could see that talking about Sam upset him. I laid my hand on his arm. "I'm so sorry, Ed. I didn't know."

Ed brushed at his eyes, and I caught a hint of moisture in them. "He was a good man. It always puzzled me why his wife just up and left him. About the only vice he had was hanging out at Good Eats." He chuckled. "He claimed he liked the burgers, but I think he liked Martin too. He was one of the few people who did." He chuckled. "My dad asked him once why he didn't give the other eating places in town some of his business, and he told him that since he'd redone some of the cabinets in Good Eats's cellar, Martin had given him an unlimited tab. As he put it, 'ya can't beat free.'"

"True enough." I slid the key into my jacket pocket and picked up the jewel box. "I'll take this back to Marianne at the shelter and she'll make sure Eunice gets it back. I can't thank you enough, Ed. It looks beautiful." I reached inside my tote bag, pulled out my wallet. "Let me give you something for your hard work."

He made a dismissive gesture with his hand. "Nah, you don't owe me a dime. Tell you what, the next time Purrday and his friends have an accident with something in need of repair, you can just bring it right to me."

I grinned at him. "Count on it."

"Do you have a box we can put the jewel chest in?" Gary asked.

"Sure." Ed moved to the other end of the workroom, opened a cabinet, and pulled out a large cardboard box. "This should do."

Gary put the jewel chest inside the box and then hefted it into his arms. "Thanks so much, Ed," he said.

Back outside, Gary put the box in the backseat of my convertible, then looked at me. "What now? Do you feel safe bringing this back to the house?"

I glanced at my watch. It was a little after seven. "Maybe Marianne is still at the shelter. I think they're open tonight till eight. If she is, we can give her the box and she can lock it up in her office."

"Sounds like a plan."

Fortunately Marianne was there. Her eyes lit up when she saw the box. "What a wonderful job Ed did," she exclaimed. "Why, you can't tell that it was broken at all."

"He wouldn't take any money," I said, "but I promised to keep him in mind if I heard of anything else that needed repair."

"There are a few cat trees that could use a good repair job. I wonder if Ed would be interested in doing something like that?"

"No harm in asking," I said.

"It's good that you brought it to me tonight," said Marianne. "Eunice's sister Chloris left me a message that Eunice's return has been delayed, and she asked Chloris to pick up the box tomorrow. I was putting off calling her, but now that I have the box back I can."

That reminded me that I hadn't yet made my own phone call to Eunice's sister. "If you want, I can do it," I offered. "I still haven't told her about the birdseed."

Marianne shot me a grateful smile. "If you wouldn't mind, Shell, I'd appreciate it. Chloris can be a bit of a gabber."

Once we were outside again, Gary looked at me. "What was that about birdseed?"

"I just told Marianne that to get Chloris's number," I said. "Now at least I don't have to make anything up. I just want to find out if Chloris by any chance went to that sale with Eunice. If so, she might remember some information."

"What sort of information?"

"Specifically, information about the owner of the jewel box. The woman who rented a room from Mrs. Johansen."

Gary pursed his lips. "Sounds like a long shot to me, but one never knows."

We got back in the car and drove back home. Once in the kitchen, I plopped down at the table and dug out the number Marianne had given me and dialed it. The call went to voicemail, so I left a message saying I had news about the jewel chest and could Chloris call me back as soon as she got this? No sooner had I hung up than my phone buzzed with an incoming call. The caller ID told me it was Chloris.

"So sorry," she said when I answered. "I get so many telemarketers that when I don't recognize the name or number I let it go to voicemail. So, what happened with that jewel chest? Eunice was wondering how much Antoine would appraise it for."

"Well, from what I understand it's not the original that belonged to Queen Victoria," I said.

Chloris laughed. "We didn't think so. Neither did that woman's niece at the sale, or I'm sure she'd never have let us take it for five bucks. What did he appraise it for, do you know?" she asked curiously.

"I believe it was either fifty or sixty dollars, but I'm not entirely certain," I said. "Marianne has all the paperwork."

"Oh." Chloris sounded disappointed. "Well, it's still a bargain. Eunice wanted to give it to our niece Beverly as a birthday gift, but we were holding off just in case it just happened to be the real deal."

"About that estate sale," I cut in. "You went with Eunice, right?"

"Yes. We often go to estate sales or antiquing together. Our tastes are pretty much the same."

"You spoke with Mrs. Johansen's niece, then?"

"Yes. She struck me as a rather abrupt woman. All business, no chitchat. Her name was Clotter, I believe. Dorothy Clotter."

"You wouldn't by any chance have any contact information for her, would you? I'd like to give her a call, see if she's planning any other sales."

"Probably not," said Chloris. "She sold most of the stuff at the one we attended."

"But not everything," I persisted. "So she might have another sale."

"True. I didn't think of that. She did mention there was some more stuff that she didn't have room to put out at that one, so she just might." Chloris clucked her tongue. "I'm not sure I have the info, though. I think Eunice has it."

Disappointment arrowed through me. "Are you sure?"

"Well now, I might have her name and address written down somewhere. I was, after all, the one who found the notice in the paper, so maybe I did jot it down. Just give me a minute and I'll go in my den and look."

I held my breath while Chloris disappeared. A few minutes later she was back on the line. "Well, what do you know? I did write it on my pad." She gave me her number.

"Thanks, Chloris. Give Eunice my regards."

I disconnected before Chloris could respond and turned to Gary. I gave him a thumbs-up. "Success. She had the number." I dialed it and a few minutes later a well-modulated voice answered. "Hello?"

I depressed the speaker button so Gary could hear. "Dorothy Clotter? My name is Shell McMillan. I got your number from Eunice Coulter."

"I'm sorry, I don't know a Eunice Coulter," said Dorothy. I could hear the suspicion in her tone so I added quickly, "She purchased a jewel chest at an estate sale you held recently?"

"Oh, my mother's things. Yes, I do remember that transaction. The jewel chest wasn't my mother's. I told that to Mrs. Coulter. It belonged to her tenant who just up and took off one day without paying the month's rent. I told her that I felt perfectly justified in selling the few things she left behind."

"Yes, Mrs. Coulter did mention that," I said. "I was just wondering if by any chance you might recall the tenant's name."

"Why would you want that?" Dorothy asked. "Say, you're not a lawyer representing that gal, are you? Because let me tell you, I was perfectly justified in selling off her things. After all, she just up and left, without so much as a word to anyone. A real disappearing act!"

"I'm not a lawyer," I interrupted her. "I own a pet shop in Fox Hollow."

"A pet shop?" I could hear suspicion dripping in her tone. "Why would a pet shop owner be interested in finding out information about that tenant? There's something you're not telling me!"

Gary took the phone away from me. In a voice about two octaves lower than his own he said, "Mrs. Clotter? This is Special Agent Reamer. I'm with the FBI."

Dorothy gasped. "The FBI?"

"Yes. Ms. McMillan has been kind enough to aid us in our investigation. We suspect that your mother's former tenant might have been involved in something illegal, and we're trying to track her down. Whatever information you might have will be helpful."

"I always knew there was something off about that girl," Dorothy Clotter cried. "I never liked her. She handed my aunt some sob story when she rented the room about being deserted by her boyfriend and having nowhere to go, and my aunt bought it hook, line and sinker."

"As I said, we'll take whatever information you can give us," said Gary. "And I trust that you will keep this absolutely confidential. You can't breathe a word of this to anyone . . . not your husband, children, best friend . . . anyone. Now, do you know that woman's name?"

"As it happens, I did find one of her old rent receipts just yesterday when I was going through some files my aunt kept. If you can hang on a minute, I'll get it."

"I'll wait." Gary hit the mute button. "I bet she knew the name all along. She was just afraid of legal repercussions. That's why I decided to impersonate Reamer. I figured it might put a scare into her, and I think it worked."

I held up my crossed fingers. Dorothy Clotter came back on the line, and Gary unmuted the phone. "Agent Reamer," she said, "I have the receipt in front of me. She signed it Phoebe Henshaw."

"Henshaw!" I cried, and then clapped a hand over my mouth.

The same last name as the waitress from Good Eats, Jillian. Was there a connection?

Twenty-three

After another admonition to Dorothy Clotter not to say a word to anyone, Gary hung up and handed the phone back to me. "You almost blew it," he chided. "Fortunately Dorothy didn't hear your little outburst."

"Sorry. I couldn't help it. Phoebe has the same last name as Jillian from Good Eats."

"The waitress you think was part of the couple who came after the jewel box? That is interesting," Gary said. He rubbed at his chin. "What's that connection? Maybe they're sisters?"

I brandished my phone. "We can both do searches. First one to find something doesn't have to open the store for a week."

"But has to close every night?"

"Well, we can't stick Robbie with closing every night. He's got school."

"That's no prize," said Gary. "How about this? First one to find something gets breakfast in bed for a week. If I win, you'll have to buy mine every morning. And FYI, I'll be wanting something more substantial than just doughnuts and coffee."

I wrinkled my nose. My fingers were already flying over the phone keypad. "Deal."

I'd typed in "Phoebe Henshaw, Winfield," and got nothing. I tried some other combinations too. I got several hits for Phoebe Henshaw but none seemed to be the right age. I was debating what else to enter when Gary let out a shout. "I think I've got it," he said triumphantly.

My face fell. "You got something? What did you put in? I wasn't getting anything."

"Neither was I, but then I got to thinking. What might make someone just up and leave?"

"You mean other than not wanting to serve jail time?"

"Yes, that. I put in 'Phoebe Henshaw accident.'" He stuck his phone under my nose. "Read that," he directed. I made a face, clicked on the article and read:

Niece of Councilman Henshaw severely injured in auto accident

Phoebe Lattimer, 32, of Fox Hollow, was severely injured when a tractor trailer hit her convertible on

Sunday morning. Ms. Lattimer is the niece of former
Buck County Councilman Harper Henshaw. She is
currently in County General Hospital. Her condition is
listed as critical.

I skimmed through the rest of the article, which gave a brief
description of how the accident happened and mentioned that the driver,
whose injuries weren't serious, was arraigned on manslaughter charges. I
looked at Gary. "So her name wasn't Henshaw. It was Lattimer. She used
her uncle's name."

"She was trying to hide, all right," Gary said.

"Maybe," I said. "It seems to me if she really wanted to hide she'd have
chosen a name other than her uncle's."

"Maybe she wasn't thinking clearly, or maybe she wasn't too creative,"
suggested Gary. "Let's see what else we can find." He typed in "Phoebe
Lattimer—Obituary," and a few minutes later we were reading the notice
that had appeared in the *Post and Courier* eight weeks ago.

Phoebe Lattimer, 42, passed away today in the
Mount St. Carmel Nursing Home. Ms. Lattimer
sustained severe injuries in an auto accident ten years
ago from which she never recovered. Ms. Lattimer is the
niece of former councilman Harper Henshaw. A private
funeral will be held Sunday at Lady of Mount. St.
Carmel Church.

There was no mention of any surviving relatives. I typed in "Harper
Henshaw" and found an obituary for him. He was survived by his wife,
Dora, and three daughters, one of whom was named Jillian.

I pointed to her name and said to Gary, "That's interesting. Could
Harper Henshaw's daughter and the mysterious waitress Jillian be the same
person?"

"Obviously these people lack imagination. They can't even think up
good phony names."

"Or they think people won't make the connection. After all, Harper
Henshaw was out of politics for years." I stared at the screen, suddenly
snapped my fingers. "Wait a minute." I pulled the paper Donna had found
in the box out of the zipper compartment of my tote. I stared at the words:

lar and *wer*.

Gary peered over my shoulder. "What's that? Some sort of word game?"

"You could say that."

I was fairly certain the first word was *cellar*, and I had an idea about the second. I picked up my phone and called up Word Hippo. When the site opened, I typed *wer* in. Seven pages came up, and right at the top of page two one word in particular caught my eye: *drawer*. I picked up the paper and looked at it again. I rummaged in my tote, found a scrap of paper and a pen, and I wrote:

Cellar

Drawer

Gary peered over my shoulder. He frowned at what I had written. "What does that mean?" he asked.

I reached for my phone again. "If my hunch is right, quite a lot." My fingers flew over the keypad as I punched in a number. A few minutes later Opal Griffin Black answered. "Oh, Shell," she said. "You must be psychic. I was just going to give you a call. How did you make out with the kitties?"

I gave her a quick rundown. She was happy to learn that Harvey already had a home. "I figured he'd go fast," she admitted. "He was such a cute little thing." She paused. "I'm sorry that I couldn't remember anything else that might help your friend. How is he doing?"

"Not good. He's still in jail." I hesitated and then continued, "Opal, there was something I meant to ask you but it slipped my mind the other day. The errand that Pete Martin sent you on the day the jewelry store was robbed—what was it, exactly?"

There was a moment of hesitation and then she said, "You're going to think it's really silly. I did too, at the time." She paused and then said, "He wanted me to pick up a key."

I felt my pulse start to race. "A house key?"

"No. It was for some sort of custom-made box. I had to go all the way across town to pick it up." She let out a sigh. "It turned out to be a fruitless quest. When I got there, I found out that the key had already been picked up."

"Martin picked it up himself?"

"No." Opal sighed. "Phoebe had gotten it earlier that day. When I told Pete he seemed surprised."

I'll bet he was, I thought. "I don't suppose you remember the man's name, or the name of the store?"

"Sure I do. The guy's name was Sam Weatherly. Weatherly's Woodworking."

Gary opened his mouth to say something, but I gave him a sharp poke in the ribs. He clutched his side and made a face at me as Opal continued talking. "The store was right on the main drag. It probably isn't there anymore, or if it is, it's most likely under new management. I heard Weatherly retired years ago."

"He's really retired. He's dead," Gary grumbled. I clapped a hand over his mouth. "One other question, Opal. Did Phoebe ever mention a relative named Jillian?"

"Jillian? Not that I recall. She had a cousin, GiGi, she was very fond of. She spoke of her a lot." Opal clucked her tongue. "I remember her saying that she and GiGi were both rebels, and Gigi's family in particular would be shocked at some of the things she'd done. I gathered the family was pretty conservative. I think her cousin's father was involved with politics in some way, but I'm not entirely certain."

"Okay, well, thanks for your help, Opal."

"Anytime, Shell. Keep me posted. I'm curious as to how all this turns out."

I hung up, removed my hand from Gary's mouth. He swiped at it with the back of his hand. "What did you do that for?" he demanded.

"To keep you from blabbing." I got up, started to pace. "I've got a theory," I said. "Granted, it's got a lot of holes, and there are still unanswered questions, but I think I've got it figured out."

Gary leaned back. "Okay, let's hear it."

"There's just one thing I have to check first." I whipped out my phone. "I need to see Sam Weatherly's obituary."

"His obituary? What for?"

"You'll see. If I'm right . . ." I pulled up the obituary, read it quickly. I passed my phone to Gary with a broad smile. "I was right! Okay, now listen to this . . ."

Gary listened to me in silence as I outlined my theory. When I finished I said, "I think I've pretty much got the basics down pat, what do you think?"

Gary nodded slowly. "It sounds logical," he said. "But as you said, it's just a theory. It's all conjecture on your part. And without solid proof, Reamer will never listen."

"I know," I said. I tugged at a blonde curl. "That's where I'm stumped. Something's got to be done before Finley and Jillian make their move, which should be very soon."

Gary rose, stretched his arms wide. "Well, I'm going to take a shower. Then tomorrow I think the two of us should go and see Josh. Maybe he'll have some ideas on how to present your theory to Reamer."

Gary disappeared up the stairs and I leaned over the table and plopped my chin in my hands. The key to this whole thing was staring me right in the face, I just knew it. What was I missing?

Purrday came over to me, butted his head against my ankles. When I looked down at him I saw he had something between his paws. I bent to retrieve it, and saw that it was the Good Eats business card Ted had given me. It must have fallen out of my tote.

I tapped the card against my chin. "Merow," Purrday said insistently. He swatted at my ankles with his paw.

I looked at the cat and suddenly a lightbulb went off in my head. "You're right, Purrday," I said. "Maybe the diner itself is the missing link I'm looking for. That's something I totally put out of my mind. Both Finley and Martin were anxious to buy the diner from Gus. Why? There's got to be a reason, and the only one I can think of is . . ."

The diamonds. Were they hidden in the diner? If the note was right, they could be hidden in a drawer in the cellar.

I jumped up so fast I startled the cat, who backed up. "Sorry, boy," I said. I could hear the water running upstairs in the shower. I didn't want to wait for Gary. I had to find out now. I grabbed a pad and a pen and scribbled a hasty note:

Following a hunch. Be back soon.
Shell

I propped the note on the counter and gave Purrday a pat on the head before I left. "If I'm not back in an hour, send the calvary, okay?"

Purrday let out a sharp merow as if he understood. And he probably did.

Twenty minutes later I parked my convertible across the street from Good Eats. I cut the lights and sat there in the dark, thinking. There weren't very many cars in the parking lot, and I recognized Ted's Jeep Wrangler.

"Okay," I said. "It's now or never."

I pocketed my car keys, but instead of heading for the diner's entrance, I circled around the building. Calling up my flashlight app, I played the light against the stone structure. I saw a small opening with a flight of stone steps leading downward. This had to be the outside cellar entrance.

I glanced swiftly around, and then slowly descended the steps. When I reached the bottom I stared at the door in front of me. If it were locked, I had no idea what I'd do. Saying a silent prayer, I grasped the knob and turned it.

Luck was with me. The door was unlocked. It swung inward on rusty hinges.

I stepped inside the dark interior and swung my light around. I noticed a light switch just a few inches away. I reached out and flipped it. Dim light flooded the interior, and I paused to take stock of my surroundings.

The cellar had the musty smell one would associate with such a place, but all the shelves and counters were clean and neat, a sharp contrast. No doubt this was where Jillian had spent most of her time cleaning, and I had to admit, she'd done a thorough job. Then again, I was fairly certain making the place neat and tidy hadn't been her only motivation.

I noticed several large boxes pushed off to the side and figured that was where she'd stored everything that had previously been cluttering up the counters. I walked around slowly, examining each and every cabinet and counter. Finally I came to stand in front of a low-slung cabinet with glass doors that held a good amount of fancy liquors. There was decorative molding around the sides of the cabinet, and I remembered Ed's demonstration with the dresser in his shop. I leaned over and pressed my hand against the molding on the left side. Nothing. I did the same to the one on the right. Again, nothing.

"Okay, not you. But you're here somewhere, I know it."

My gaze swept the room again, and I noticed a stone fireplace over in the far corner. I walked over to the fireplace and examined it closely. In a mystery story I'd read as a young girl, I remembered detective sisters finding jewelry hidden in a secret cache in a stone fireplace. I ran my fingers over the smooth stones on the hearth. I paused. Was I imagining it, or had one of the stones shifted slightly beneath my touch? I pressed on the stone again, then jumped back as a drawer suddenly shot out from beneath it. I stuck my hand inside and my questing fingers touched a hunk of metal. A few seconds later I was holding a medium-sized black box in my hands. I took it over to the counter and carefully set it down.

I pulled the key Ed had given me out of my pocket and fitted it into the lock. I turned it and heard a soft click. Holding my breath, I raised the lid. Inside lay a chamois pouch. I picked it up and untied the drawstring. Even in the pale overhead cellar light I could see the diamonds twinkling brightly. There had to be at least a dozen, maybe more, jammed into the little pouch. I felt like doing a jig.

"I was right," I crowed. I was sorry that Gary wasn't here to see this. I pulled out my phone and was just about to hit Josh's number on speed dial when a voice from behind me said, "I wouldn't do that if I were you, Ms. McMillan."

My head snapped around and I saw Finley emerge from a door all the way over on the other side of the room. I caught a flash of blue steel and my breath stopped in my throat.

He had a gun in his hand, and it was leveled right at my heart.

Twenty-four

It took every ounce of my acting ability to remain outwardly calm. I slid my phone back into my jacket pocket and rocked back on my heels. I looked him square in the eyes as he approached me. He pointed toward the pouch I held in my hand. "I'll take that, if you don't mind," he said.

"Actually, I do," I said. I tightened my grip on the pouch. "This is what you've been looking for, isn't it? And it's the reason you killed Pete Martin. He wanted them all for himself, didn't he?"

Finley's brows drew together. "You've got your facts wrong, missy. I didn't kill Pete Martin. Gus Morton did."

"That's not true." I thrust my jaw forward. "Pete Martin was your partner. The two of you planned that robbery together. Or should I say the three of you. You, Martin and Phoebe."

"Once again, your facts are wrong." Finley waved the gun in the air. "Phoebe was good friends with Martin's gal Opal. Opal worked for Van Nuys and she told Phoebe all about the big shipment of diamonds." He puffed his chest out. "Phoebe and I, we planned the whole job out. Both of us had it tough growing up, and we were ready to have a taste of the good life for a change. We figured that with all that money, we could get away to a nice tropical island, start over fresh. The only fly in the ointment was Opal. We knew she'd be able to identify us."

"So you approached Martin to ask him to find a way to get her out of the store?"

"Actually it was the other way around. Martin is the one who approached us. He was always snooping around. He happened to overhear me and Phoebe making our plans." He shook his head. "I'd been unjustly accused a few years prior of manslaughter when I lived out West under another name. I had no way of proving my innocence, but I managed to get away and change my looks and my name and start a new life. Somehow Pete found out about it, and he threatened to expose me if I didn't cut him in."

"So he convinced Weatherly to make a box to hide the diamonds in, and then he asked Opal to pick up the key so she'd be out of the store when you and Phoebe came to rob it."

Finley's lips twisted into a sneer. "Very good. I see someone's been giving this a lot of thought. You're right, we didn't want to have to worry

162

about Opal identifying us, and Phoebe didn't want her harmed. We all intended to lie low for a while and then meet up and split the diamonds later, once all the hoopla died down. We had to be careful because we knew the feds would be watching everywhere for those diamonds. Phoebe and I knew it could be a long time, years even, but Martin got impatient. He wanted to get his share of the diamonds early."

"So he could leave his wife."

"Right again. He couldn't wait to leave that shrew. She'd put a bad taste in his mouth for women."

"So he never had any intention of marrying Opal."

Finley shook his head. "Heck no. Phoebe sensed that, and she didn't trust him. We'd put her in charge of hiding the diamonds. She didn't tell either one of us where she'd put them, but she'd chuckle about it so often I was convinced it had to be somewhere right under our noses."

"And then you got arrested," I said, "and your plans had to be changed."

His face darkened and his hand came down hard on the counter. "Yep. I got careless and I paid for it. I was arrested and went to prison. Phoebe said that once she got rid of the diamonds and had her hands on some cold hard cash, she'd make sure I got a lawyer and an appeal. Martin tried to strong-arm her into telling him where the diamonds were hidden. That's when she quit and took off."

"And that must have been when Martin's wife caught him and Opal down here in the cellar."

"That fool," Finley spat. "He had to have one last fling with Opal, and sure enough his wife was having him watched. She caught the two of 'em down here, right there as a matter of fact." He pointed to the shelf where the box sat. "Caught 'em on that very shelf. Gus Morton had been after Pete to sell him the place. Pete decided he'd better take him up on it and take a powder before his wife got everything he had. He sold the diner and insisted Morton pay him cash. Then he got the hell out of Dodge."

"And left the diamonds?"

Finley shrugged. "He didn't have much choice then. Neither of us knew where Phoebe'd stashed them, or why she hadn't contacted us. It wasn't until much later that we found out why."

"She was in the auto accident."

Finley's eyes misted over. "Yep. She laid in that coma for years, and she was mute after she woke up, until right at the end. She stayed conscious long enough to tell her cousin what happened. The day she was in the accident, she'd planned on taking off with her share. I'd just been arrested, and she didn't want Pete on her case. She was on her way to get them when that tractor trailer crashed into her. Before that, though, she'd written out clues and left them in her jewelry box. She wanted me to find the rest of the diamonds, cut Pete out and meet her in Costa Rica." He smiled faintly. "Phoebe always did like to make everything about a puzzle. She gave her cousin a half slip of paper before she died. Said the other half was the key to finding the diamonds, and it was in her jewel box. Only problem was, by the time Jillian figured it all out, that darn woman sold the box at the estate sale."

"And the two of you went looking for it. That's when I caught you in the tent," I said. "But how did Martin figure into it?"

"Well, by this time Martin had reinvented himself, and he figured it was time now for him to return to Fox Hollow and get those diamonds. He knew darn well I was in prison, but he wasn't sure if Phoebe had ever made off with them or not until Jillian made the mistake of contacting him. You see, Phoebe told Jillian she'd stashed the diamonds in the diner but she never told her exactly where. Jillian thought that Pete and I should join forces and offer to buy Good Eats back from Gus. She'd found out Gus was having medical and financial troubles and figured it'd be an easy sell. Well, guess what! She was wrong. Gus didn't want any part of it. So we had to find another way."

"And your way was to kill Martin and frame Gus?"

Once again, Finley shot me a puzzled look. "No. My way was to try and steal that jewel box back from you. Jillian called me, told me she heard you say you had the box for safekeeping in your car."

"So it was you who tried to break into my trunk."

He nodded. "Yep. I saw you put it in your trunk at that event and followed you. When you and your guy pal came out guns blazing, I figured I'd better make a quick getaway." His hand came up, swiped at the beads of sweat on his forehead. "Jill and I have been sneaking in here, searching on our own. I decided, though, that tonight was it. The feds are getting too close for comfort for me. I planned on ripping apart every square foot of this cellar until I found those diamonds, but, thanks to you, that won't be necessary now." He made an exaggerated bow and tapped at the box with his forefinger. "I really appreciate your doing all the legwork. With Martin gone, it's all mine now."

I swallowed. Somehow I had to keep him talking, stall for time until I could figure out how to get away from him. "You mean yours and Jillian's."

He laughed. "No. All mine. I plan on blowing this joint just as soon as you hand over the gems. I've got a one-way ticket to South America and a phony passport in my car. Once I'm safely in another country, I'll hire a plastic surgeon to change my appearance and live out the rest of my life in luxury. I hate to leave Jill behind, but it's every man for himself and she's becoming somewhat of a liability."

"A liability? What do you mean?"

"I mean she's been having an attack of conscience. She's been thinking of getting in touch with the FBI, making a clean breast of everything and taking her chances. Said that she didn't want to live out the rest of her life in fear, looking over her shoulder all the time. I told her that I'd think about it, but it doesn't matter much if she goes to the FBI or not. As I said, I'll be long gone." He waved the gun at me and held out his other hand. "Now, if you don't mind, Ms. McMillan, I'll take those off your hands."

I wet my lips and looked at Finley. "Martin had a silent partner in this diner by the name of Sam Weatherly. He'd invested a lot of money and he lost it all when Martin took off. Martin probably also promised him a share of the diamonds so he'd make that box, but never intended to go through with it."

When Finley didn't respond, I continued. "Weatherly kept journals, which, no doubt, went to his son when he passed. I'm thinking that the son read those journals and decided to come here, to Fox Hollow, to get his share of the diamonds and to make Martin pay for what he did to his father." I whipped my head to stare directly at Finley. "You're that son."

Finley's jaw dropped as he realized what I was getting at. "Hell, no. You're nuts. Your theory about Weatherly's son might be right, but you've got the wrong guy."

I stared at him. Something in the tone of his voice made me think he was telling the truth. "Then you didn't kill Martin?"

Finley nodded. "I told you I didn't. I'm guilty of grand theft, but murder? Like I said, they've got Pete's killer." He waved the gun. "Now be a good girl and hand me those diamonds!"

I shook my head. "Sorry. I can't do that."

"Then I'll take them." Finley advanced toward me, and as he did so, I caught a movement in the shadows off to my left. I sucked in my breath as I saw Jeremy Jackson come up behind Finley, and in the next instant, he had the man in a hammerlock. Finley gave a little moan and slumped to the floor.

I stared at the newsman. "This is one time I'm actually glad you were following me. You were, weren't you?"

Jackson smiled. "Now, now, didn't your friend Leila tell you a good newshound never reveals his secrets?" He glanced at the chamois bag I held tightly in one hand and raised an eyebrow. "Are those . . ."

"The diamonds. Yes." I bobbed my head up and down. "I never thought I'd be glad to see—"

I stopped speaking as my eyes fell on the jacket he wore. The buttons caught my eye—wood, with a sailboat etched on them. There was a thread at the bottom of the jacket where the last button should have been.

The button I still had in my jacket pocket, the one I'd picked up near Pete Martin's body.

The button his killer, Jeremy Jackson, had dropped.

Twenty-five

Jackson raised his arm and trained the gun he held directly at my chest. "Tsk tsk," he said. "Someone's remembered something they'd have been better off forgetting."

My hand closed around the button in my pocket next to my phone and I fought desperately against the wave of nausea that rose in the back of my throat. "You weren't just passing through Grimley Woods Saturday night, were you? You followed Pete Martin there."

Jackson kept the gun trained on me as he took a step closer. His hand reached out toward the bag I held. "At last," he murmured. "Justice is served. I've waited a long time for this—far too long to get what my father should have."

I fought back a gasp as the realization hit me. "Oh my gosh. *You're* Weatherly's son."

Jackson made a little bow. "I take it all back. You are a pretty good detective, Shell. You had it all figured out. The only detail you were mistaken about was the identity of Weatherly's son."

I licked at my lips. "You killed Martin, didn't you? And you used Gus's gun to frame him."

He nodded. "I suppose there's no harm in admitting it to you, since you'll never tell anyone what you know. Yes, I did kill Martin. I was at the diner and I overheard Gus make plans to meet him in the woods. I saw Gus put the gun under the counter. I waited until everyone was busy and then I slipped behind the counter and forced the lock on the case and took the gun." He shook his head. "It was a piece of cake. They're all a pretty trusting group. Anyway, I left and got to their meeting place early and hid. Gus didn't believe Martin would come through with the ninety thousand. Smart thinking on Gus's part, really. Gus stormed off and then I confronted Martin. I told him who I was, and that I'd found out about the diamonds from some entries in my father's old journals I'd gotten after he died. I said that since he was responsible for my father's having to work his whole life, he owed me a portion of his share. And do you know what that fool did? He laughed at me. I told him no one laughs at Jeremy Jackson."

Jackson raised his thumb and forefinger in an imitation of a gun and mimed pulling the trigger. "He didn't laugh after that. Then I heard you and those cats of yours coming and I hid. I knew once Gus's gun was found, he'd be suspect numero uno. I also figured once he was convicted his wife would be glad to unload the diner and I could take my time and hunt for the diamonds. From the entries in my father's journals, I figured they were probably hidden in one of those secret drawers he loved to build. The only question was where." He gestured around the room. "As you can see, there are quite a few cabinets."

"But you still had Finley to deal with."

He waved his hand as if swatting off a fly. "Finley's a grandstander. I figured it would be only a matter of time before he and his little girlfriend made a mistake and landed themselves back in prison, and I'd be home free." He gestured toward the chamois pouch. "Finley had the right idea though. With these babies, I can escape to South America, start a whole new life for myself. No one here appreciates my journalistic talents anyway."

"That's not what I heard. Why do you want to ruin your life like this? You're the front-runner for the job on the *Sentinel*."

"Hah," he spat. "Who wants to work on a tiny rag like that anyway? I only pretended to be interested so I could be free to snoop around here. I've interviewed at the *New York Times* and the *LA Journal*, but did they want me? No! Now I don't care." He moved closer to me. "I am sorry about you, though, Shell. You should have taken me up on my offer to work with me. Now, I'm afraid, you're just a liability, along with Finley. Now, hand them over." He wiggled his fingers toward the chamois bag.

I tightened my grip on the pouch and lifted my chin. "What do you intend to do with me?" I asked.

Jackson smiled, but the smile didn't reach his eyes. "Obviously I can't let you go. You know too much."

I gasped. "So you're just going to shoot me? Leave my body here in the basement?"

"Oh, I've got something special planned for you. You're going to be my insurance ticket out of here. I doubt anyone else has figured out my connection to the diamonds, but on the off chance they aren't as dumb as I think they are, I've got you as my bargaining chip. Trade your safety for my freedom."

I twisted my head so I could look him straight in the eye. "But my safety isn't guaranteed, is it?"

Jackson made a tsking sound deep in his throat. "Well . . . no. You're a loose end. A very loose end. I can't take any chances on leaving you alive to sic the authorities on me. But don't worry. Your end will be swift. You and Finley here are going to have a little driving accident. Your car will take a tumble off Briar's Cliff. The resulting explosion should leave your bodies so badly burned no one will be able to discern the actual cause of death. But even if that clever cop boyfriend of yours figures it out, I'll be far removed from all this." He grinned wickedly and waved the gun in the air. "This is Jillian's gun. I'll leave it in the car. If it's not too badly burned, it'll be traced back to her."

I backed up a step. "Your plan will never work. Gary knows I'm here," I said. "I left him a note."

Jackson raised an eyebrow. "All the more reason for us to hurry. Now, hand over the diamonds."

I shook my head. "Sorry, I can't do that."

"Oh, but you will," he growled.

Suddenly we heard a loud meow and the next second a red blur hurled itself at Jackson, spitting and clawing. Jackson threw both hands up in the air. "What the—get this cat offa me."

Apparently the princess had decided to accompany me. She must have snuck out of the house and hidden in my backseat, then followed me inside—and I was sure glad she had. I was afraid that Jackson might end up hurting the cat so I called out, "Down, Princess Fuzzypants. Come here."

The princess leapt off of Jackson and trotted over to me. Jackson was on the floor. He appeared a bit dazed but he still held fast to the gun. I knew it would only be seconds before he recovered, so I picked up the princess and then raised the hand holding the pouch in the air. "You want 'em? Then you're gonna have to look for 'em." With that, I flung the pouch right in his face. The diamonds glittered in the pale overhead light as they scattered all over the floor. With Jackson momentarily distracted, I lunged for the light switch. I flipped it and the cellar was plunged into darkness.

Jackson let out a yell. I set the princess down and we inched our way slowly along the back wall, away from him. "I'll get you for this," he shouted. "You won't get away from me."

I remained silent, thankful that I had worn thick-soled sneakers. I padded silently forward, hugging the wall. If my calculations were correct, the door leading outside should only be a few feet away from me.

To my left, I heard Jackson grunt. I imagined that he probably was on his hands and knees, feeling for the diamonds. Apparently he didn't have a flashlight or a phone with a flashlight app on him. Score one for me.

My questing fingers found the knob of the door and I jerked it open. Immediately soft moonlight illuminated a portion of the room. I chanced a look over my shoulder and saw Jackson struggle to his feet. I saw something shine in his left hand and knew that he'd found some of the diamonds. Right now, though, I couldn't worry about that. I had to get away and get help.

I scrambled up the steps and reached the top, the princess beside me. I heard movement behind me and figured that Finley wasn't too far behind. My car was off to the right, but the wooded area to my left was closer. I took off at a run in that direction. I tripped over a tree root, caught myself, hung on to the trunk and rounded another tree. I looked over my shoulder just in time to see Jackson's head emerge from the cellar entrance.

No doubt he was in shape, but I was too. Maybe I could fool him and circle around, or maybe climb a tree. I hadn't done that in years, so I was keeping that as a last resort. My hand went instinctively to my pocket. I'd left Gary a note, true, but I hadn't said just where I was going. Would he figure it out? I needed to get to a safe place so I could dial 911. As I hurried through the brush, I heard a loud grunt, followed by equally loud swearing. Maybe Jackson had fallen over a tree root too. The princess and I ran faster, putting more and more distance between us.

My cell vibrated in my pocket. Thank God both Finley and Jackson had been too fixated on the chamois bag with the diamonds to think about taking my phone away. Without pausing in my sprinting, I whipped it out and looked at the screen in the dimming light. Gary. I clicked the phone on. "Sorry, can't talk," I gasped. "We're running away from Martin's killer."

I heard Gary's sharp intake of breath on the other end. "Shell, where in hell are you?" he growled. "I got your note, or rather Purrday did. It was on the floor. He kept pawing at my pants until I looked at it."

Behind me I heard the sound of brush cracking and branches moving. If I talked to Gary, Jackson would surely hear me. "Can't talk," I mumbled. "I'll text."

I heard Gary's muffled voice call out, "Wait—did you say *we?*" before I disconnected. I moved deeper into the brush and curled myself behind a large elm. I pulled the princess onto my lap, hoping that the tree's large trunk would be enough to shield us and the glow from my phone from Jackson. I tapped out a quick text to both Gary and Josh:

Jeremy Jackson is the killer. I found the diamonds hidden in the diner cellar. I'm in the woods and the princess is with me. We're trying to hide from him. Hurry!!!!!!!

I hit send, then pocketed the phone and moved deeper into the brush. I heard more thrashing behind me and decided that maybe the best course of action would be to climb one of the trees. It would be hard to shoot at me through the leaves, and maybe Jackson didn't know how to climb. I could only hope. I looked at the princess. "Ever climb a tree, Princess?"

The cat cocked her head. "Merow."

"Good. Here we go." I selected the tallest one and jumped at a low branch. Catching it with my arms, I used my sneakered feet to shimmy up the trunk, and the princess was right behind me. When we reached the top I positioned myself. The foliage was so thick I could barely see through to the ground below.

I crouched there, waiting for what seemed centuries. I couldn't detect any movement. Had he given up and gone back to grab the diamonds? Minutes ticked by. I was just about to shimmy down when I spotted a pencil-thin beam of light moving slowly through the woods. Had Jackson somehow found a flashlight? Just my luck.

As if he could read my mind, Jackson called out, "I had a flashlight in my van, Shell. I'm going to find you and your cat, so you might as well surrender."

I took a few shallow breaths. He was moving the flashlight in a circular motion, but not as yet shining it up into the trees. If only Gary or Josh would arrive! The light inched closer to the tree I was in, and I held my breath, scarcely daring to move. I pulled the princess's furry body close against me, and then . . . .

The beam of the flashlight pinned us in its glare just as the wail of sirens broke the stillness of the night. The sound was faint at first but then grew louder. Below me Jackson paused, obviously torn over what to do. Apparently his desire for survival was greater than his need to capture me. With a muffled oath, he turned around and ran back toward the building.

The princess and I scrambled back down the tree, lit up my phone's flashlight app again, and ran as fast as I could back toward Good Eats. As I approached I saw two squad cars parked near the back entrance. Two uniformed officers were holding a squirming Jackson. I let out a sigh of relief and quickened my steps. As I approached I heard him arguing loudly with the officers. "I tell you, I was only taking a walk through the woods. I've done nothing wrong. Unhand me at once."

I burst forward. "That's not true," I gasped. I pointed at Jackson. "He killed Pete Martin and framed Gus for it. Finley is down in the cellar. He's the one behind that jewel heist ten years ago. I found the pouch with the diamonds. What's not in his pockets is probably still scattered over the cellar floor."

"That's news to me," protested Jeremy Jackson. "I'm a reporter and I demand you unhand me at once. I need to get this story out to my newspaper ASAP."

"I think the only story you'll be getting out is the one you'll be telling your lawyer," said one of the officers. "You have the right to remain silent . . ."

"Shell!"

I turned and saw Gary running toward me. He rushed over to me and grabbed me by the shoulders. "Are you all right? I called Josh and then got here as fast as I could."

I nodded. "I sent you both that text," I said.

Gary's face was pale. "I should have known you wouldn't stay put. That note you left, that didn't really tell me anything."

I let out a sigh. "I told Purrday to call in the calvary," I said. "I swear, that cat understands every word I say." I grinned. "Plus, I bet Purrday sensed the princess followed me. He was trying to save us both."

"I'm tempted to believe you," said Gary.

"Gee, thanks," I said. I turned my head slightly and saw a car slide to a screeching halt. Josh emerged and hurried toward us. He took me immediately into his arms. "Shell, are you all right?" he asked.

I snuggled against him. "Fine, now that you're here. Finley and the diamonds are down in the cellar. He and Jillian were searching for them, but it was Jeremy Jackson who killed Pete Martin."

Josh put a finger to my lips. "I know about Finley and the diamonds. Jillian came to the station earlier and made a full confession." His gaze slid toward Jackson. "I knew there was something off about that guy," he muttered.

"He's Weatherly's son. Weatherly was the silent partner in the diner. He confessed the whole thing—oh, wait."

I whipped out my phone and handed it to Josh. "I almost forgot. When Finley surprised me, I switched on the recording app when I put the phone in my pocket. I thought it might come in handy. His entire confession should be on there."

Josh hit the button to replay. A few minutes later we heard Jeremy Jackson's smug voice detailing how he'd killed Martin. I looked at Josh.

"That should clear Gus, right?"

"Damn straight." Josh looked at me. "You know, Shell, you can be the most exasperating female I've ever met. Right now I don't know whether to shake you silly or kiss you senseless."

Josh didn't have to worry. I made the decision for him. I grabbed him around the neck and kissed him . . . hard.

Twenty-six

"More tea, Shell?"

Gary glanced at me over his shoulder as he lifted the whistling teakettle off the stove. I was seated at my kitchen table, my feet propped up on a chair, bundled in a warm sweatshirt and jeans. I watched as Gary sorted through an assortment of tea bags, selected one, and dropped it into a giant mug. "Sure. What kind is that?"

"Oolong and lemon balm. It's very soothing." He finished pouring the water into the mug and handed it to me. "Drink it slowly."

"Yes, Dr. Presser."

I took a sip of the tea, then set the mug down and stretched my arms wide. "Where is Josh? I do remember him promising to come by and fill me in on the particulars of what happened with Jackson."

"Oh, he'll be here soon." I glanced up and saw Leila standing in the doorway. She walked over to the table, leaned over and gave me a hug. "How are you feeling?"

"Pretty good now," I answered. "I have to admit, though, this was my closest call yet."

Leila came over and perched on the edge of the sofa. "Well, Jeremy Jackson, or should I say J. J. Weatherly, is in custody."

"J.J.?" I said.

"James John Weatherly. He changed it to Jeremy Jackson because he thought it sounded better. Anyway, once he found out you'd recorded his confession, he didn't even argue." Leila turned her hand inward and pointed at herself. "And thanks to you giving me an exclusive, we scooped every other paper! Parker was so thrilled he's giving me a trial run on the crime beat! I start tomorrow!"

"Oh, Leila, that's wonderful," I cried. "At least something good came out of all this."

The doorbell rang, and Gary went to answer it. He returned a few minutes later with not only Josh but Reamer in tow. I shot them both a sheepish grin. "All's well that ends well?" I ventured.

Josh pulled out the chair next to mine, sat down and took my hand in his. "In this case, at least," he said, trying to look stern but failing.

Reamer stood just behind Josh. "We had Jackson under surveillance for a while. We knew that he was Weatherly's son, and we wondered if his sudden presence in Fox Hollow was all due to that job on the newspaper. We knew he'd been to the prison inquiring about Finley, but we weren't certain if he was working on a story or if there might be some other motivation. We were aware Finley was acquainted with Weatherly through Martin, and that Weatherly had been Martin's partner in the diner."

"You knew a lot. Then again, you are the FBI." I tipped my head at Reamer, who grinned. Then I turned my gaze on Josh. "I imagine that was the part you couldn't tell me about."

Reamer cleared his throat. "You took some chance, Ms. McMillan, going to the diner by yourself."

"I had an idea that was where Phoebe had hidden the diamonds," I said. "Finley scared the daylights out of me, though. I wasn't expecting him to show up. I was actually relieved when Jackson showed up, until I saw the missing button on Jackson's jacket. It matched the one I found near Pete's body, and that's when I knew the truth." I ran a hand through my hair. "I never even pegged Jackson as a killer until then. I thought he was capable of framing Gus for murder to get a story, but doing the actual deed . . . not so much." I turned my attention back to Reamer. "What about Finley and Jillian?"

The FBI man cleared his throat. "We found Finley unconscious downstairs and two big diamonds in his pocket. He's looking at a long stretch in prison for that jewel robbery. Jillian will get off very lightly, thanks to her coming forward. She really did have a conscience." Reamer worried at his lower lip, and I had the fleeting impression he was trying hard not to smile. "I can see why Bloodgood was concerned about you. You are headstrong and stubborn, Ms. McMillan. But you also have very good instincts. You had it all figured out, except for the part about Jackson being Weatherly's son, that is."

I raised my eyebrow at the FBI man. "Tell me the truth. You knew all along Gus was innocent, didn't you?"

His lips curved upward ever so slightly. "We figured there was some reason he was being set up, and we figured he was probably safer in police custody."

The doorbell rang again, and Gary went to answer it. He returned a few minutes later, followed by Gus and Inez. Inez had Cleopawtra clasped in her arms. "We won't stay long," Gus said. He walked over and extended his hand to me. "I just wanted to say thank you for everything you did."

"You're welcome," I said as I shook his proffered hand. "But no one really believed you were guilty, Gus."

Gus laughed. "You could have fooled me. Anyway, if you hadn't been so persistent we might never have known the truth."

"Persistent being the operative word," Josh said.

Reamer regarded me, finger to his lips. "I don't suppose you'd like to consider a career with the FBI, Ms. McMillan? Aside from your penchant for putting yourself in danger, you do have excellent deductive skills."

I flushed. "Thanks, but I'll pass. I'd much rather run my pet shop with Gary."

"And solve the occasional murder," Gary put in.

"Well, the FBI thanks you for your aid in this matter, Ms. McMillan," Reamer said. He turned to Josh. "I'll see you back at the station. She's all yours, Bloodgood." As the agent turned away, I saw him mouth silently to Josh, "Good luck."

Gary walked Reamer to the door. The bell rang again, and Gary reappeared a few minutes later with my mother in tow. She crossed the room, swept me up off the couch and clasped me in her arms. "Crishell! Thank goodness you're all right."

"I'm fine, Mother," I mumbled into her shoulder. "You can let go of me now."

My mother removed her hands from around my shoulders and cocked her head at me. "You're my daughter, after all. I had to make certain you were all right." She patted my shoulder. "And when you're feeling better, we have to talk, dear. I've just had another idea for a fundraiser that will be even better than Appraise for Strays."

"Oh?" I looked at my mother suspiciously. "What sort of fundraiser?"

"A murder mystery dinner. Doesn't that sound divine! Who knows, maybe Patrick's schedule will lighten up and he can come out here and help."

I swallowed, remembering the note I'd recently gotten from my ex-fiancé. "Oh, yeah. That would be swell," I said. I couldn't stop the sarcasm from creeping into my tone as I added, "Maybe you can get him to direct."

"Hm, that's not a bad idea." My mother glanced at her watch. "Goodness, I've got to get going. I've got some antiquities coming into the shop and I have to instruct Sue on how best to display them."

My mother gave me a peck on the cheek and swept out. Gary chuckled. "I give that partnership three more months, tops, or there just may be another murder in Fox Hollow."

I turned to Gus and Inez and said, "You know, if Purrday, the princess and Cleopawtra hadn't knocked over that jewel box, maybe those crooks would have gotten away with the diamonds. If the princess hadn't decided to stow away in my car, I might not have escaped from Jackson. And if Purrday hadn't called Gary's attention to my fallen note, neither of us might be here now. So I guess the cats are the real heroes of this case."

"As usual," Gary said with a laugh.

Purrday lifted his head and let out a loud merow. Then he raced over and jumped into my lap. He snuggled close to me and his tongue snaked out, licked at my chin.

"If anyone ever doubts that cats can understand humans," I said, "just send them to me and I'll be happy to set them straight."

Purrday looked at me with his one good eye. Then he squeezed it shut and blinked twice.

About the Author

While Toni LoTempio does not commit—or solve—murders in real life, she has no trouble doing it on paper. Her lifelong love of mysteries began early on when she was introduced to her first Nancy Drew mystery at age ten—*The Secret in the Old Attic*. She and her cat pen the Urban Tails Pet Shop Mysteries, the Nick and Nora mystery series, and the Cat Rescue series. Catch up with them at Rocco's blog, catsbooksmorecats.blogspot.com, or her website, tclotempio.net.

Milton Keynes UK
Ingram Content Group UK Ltd.
UKHW031047120324
439302UK00006B/523